TRUE KIN

TRUE KIN

Ric Jahna

 THE OHIO STATE UNIVERSITY PRESS • COLUMBUS

Library of Congress Cataloging-in-Publication Data
Jahna, Ric, 1971–
True kin / Ric Jahna.
    p. cm.
ISBN 978–0–8142–5167–6 (pbk. : alk. paper)
I. Title.
PS3610.A37T78 2008
813.'6—dc22
                    2007052450

This book is available in the following editions:
Paper (ISBN 978–0–8142–5167–6)
CD-ROM (ISBN 978–0–8142–9165–8)

Cover design by Fulcrum Design Corps.
Text design by Juliet Williams
Type set in Bitstream Aldine
Printed by BookMobile™

♾ The paper used in this publication meets the minimum requirements of the American National Standard for Information Sciences—Permanence of Paper for Printed Library Materials. ANSI Z39.48–1992.

9 8 7 6 5 4 3 2 1

CONTENTS

ACKNOWLEDGMENTS

I have been blessed with a large and loving family, whose unfailing support has sustained me throughout this project. My love and gratitude go to the Jahnas, Whittles, Bonnays, Bridges, Ferrells, and Schlueters.

I am indebted to the many instructors who offered their time and insights during my long and ongoing apprenticeship. Special thanks go to Larry Sutton, Rita Ciresi, Sterling Watson, Robert Houston, and Aurelie Sheehan.

I'm also lucky to associate myself among a community of gifted writers and artists. They include Sally Binard, D. Seth Horton, Erin "Ace" Kilian, Daniyal Mueenuddin, John Mull, Ari Olmos, Miranda Presley, Justin St. Germain, and Carol Test. Thank you all for your friendship and encouragement.

My extreme gratitude goes to The Ohio State University Press and the OSU MFA program.

INDEPENDENCE DAY, 1983

THAT DAY WE SET UP for a cookout down by the lake, underneath the huge oak tree, just below the orange grove and the empty house where, until the previous spring, I had lived with the rest of my family. Dad would finally rent out the house at the end of that summer, to the old snowbird couple from Pennsylvania. This was Ridgedale, Florida, and I was eleven, sitting in the warm shallows of the lake and hoping that the defiant bump in my swim shorts would subside before someone called me up to help with one thing or another.

I had been thinking about the secret club that I was in. We met in the tree house of Eric Davidson, my next-door neighbor in town. We held special meetings and made big plans, but mostly I hung out there because of the weather-tattered copy of *Penthouse* that Eric had stolen from his older brother and that he kept hidden under a stack of *Boys' Life* and *Sports Illustrated*.

I stared down the beach, past the dock, to the place where my sister, Claire, and the Pritchett boy had been. I squinted and watched where the cattails quivered in the rising heat and the shoreline curved to the right, where they had paused an instant, two tiny figures linked at the arms, before vanishing in the sunlight. I dug two mussels out of the sand and squeezed them together hard with both hands. My forearms shook with the strain until the larger mussel cracked, and I pried open the shell and peeled away the soft contents. A swarm of minnows gathered over my lap and tore away at the pinkish flesh.

"You'll attract a moccasin like that, Ronnie." My cousin, Littlepaul—always on guard for lurking dangers—stood above me, wearing his faded-orange life jacket, over-tightened and too small now, which made his tiny head thrust forward like a sickly turtle. "That right there's how I almost got moccasin-bit once," he said. "Feedin' the minnows like that. Looked down and there he was, right by my foot. Near about got hold of my toe before I seen him and ran." Littlepaul squirmed in place. "That's the last thing you want to see by your foot," he said. "'Cept maybe for an alligator." His face turned bluish as he spoke.

"Can you breathe okay in that life jacket?" I said. "Maybe you ought to loosen it up. Just a little, I mean."

Littlepaul swatted at a horsefly, which circled his head and finally landed on his temple. He smacked the side of his face, missing the horsefly. It circled once more and was gone. "What did you say?" he said. His skinny arms continued to flail about.

"It's already left," I said. "I said I think you ought to loosen up that life jacket before you go swimming. You look like you're liable to faint."

Littlepaul stopped swatting. "If I do decide to go swimming, I don't need this." He squeezed the jacket, glared at me, indignant. "I'm older than you are. Reckon I can swim for myself 'cept my Mama made me wear this on account of Uncle Jubal and them're coming down later. You remember what he did last time."

I did remember. Uncle Jubal had carried his youngest son, Emmit, about six at the time, piggyback down to the lake. Jubal swam well into the deep water with Emmit still clinging to him, only to pry the boy away, turn him loose into the water alone. Emmit had started to panic, but Uncle Jubal just said, "Swim or sink, son," offering no other help. In the end, the boy had swum, enough to save himself at least, bobbing and choking toward his father, who kept backstroking a few feet ahead of him until they reached the shallows.

"It's not that I cain't swim, though" Littlepaul said. "My Mama just made me wear it, that's all."

We were born just six days apart, Littlepaul and I, but he was already two years behind me in school and frail even among his own classmates. As an infant, he had developed a high fever, almost died, didn't, but was later prone to painful ear infections and occasional gazing spells that we would later find out were a certain type of seizure. Also, Littlepaul had what my mother called an ugly streak. He could turn mean and hateful in an instant, and he liked to bite, or maybe he just knew he was good at it, at finding a way of slipping his teeth into you if a disagreement went too far. So, when he said that he could swim, I—knowing full well he could not—let it go at that. It was easier that way.

I looked behind me, up the hill, where under the oak Mom and Aunt Louise were spreading sheets over the picnic tables and taking food from the ice coolers. They worked steadily. Mom, in her green, skirted bathing suit and white baseball cap with her ponytail sticking through the back, seemed so small next to Aunt Louise. Mom was still pretty then, a lean strong woman who could throw a baseball as well as any of my uncles.

Music blared from the radio where Dad and Uncle Paul stood at the end of the shade, seeming strange in their shorts and old tee shirts with the sleeves cut out. Their legs and shoulders, unaccustomed to the sun, were milky-pale compared to the red of their arms and faces. They were partners now, ever since my grandfather died and left the orange groves to Dad and Aunt Louise. They drank cans of beer and fanned the grill with their caps. I breathed in the pleasant smell of lighter fluid and burning charcoal and thought about the coming food.

I turned back around. The smooth surface of the lake shone white in the sun, and the music seemed to spread out all around me. Far across the lake, two horses grazed in a pasture. Beyond them were the woods, and beyond that the highway to town. I turned again toward the sunlight and the curved shoreline and watched for Claire and Pritchett. I wondered if anyone else had seen them leave.

THE SOUND WAS FAINT at first but grew louder as it approached, the high-pitched cry of Uncle Jubal's Kawasaki, rising out of the orange trees at the top of the hill. Jubal Taylor was a Vietnam veteran, a loud and unsettling man, who fascinated us children by sometimes bringing along his wonderfully exotic knife collection to family gatherings. We would huddle around and listen quietly, watching him unroll the red velvet carrying case, the contents varying, if only slightly, on each visit.

We looked for our favorite pieces, each with stories filled with war and jungles, Charlies and Gooks, or sometimes women. Then there were the older stories, ones about his own boyhood. The knives that went with them were old and weathered, given to him by his father or his grandfather. We would sit, hushed, watching at a respectful distance, even the impulsive Littlepaul, until Uncle Jubal's big red hands slipped one out of its elastic band, sometimes a butterfly or even a switchblade—they were the best—opening, suddenly, in a flash of brilliance, the clean steel blade in front of our eyes.

He was at the top of the hill now, a pause as he shifted gears, and the motorcycle came into view in a cloud of orange dust where the clay road met the trail that led down to the lake. Uncle Jubal lived with his wife, Aunt Cheryl, and five children in their trailer near the opposite corner of the lake, where there were no orange groves then, just big pines, scrub oaks, palmetto thickets.

I stood and watched him steer the motorcycle with one hand, using the other to hold tight to Emmit, who sat propped up in front of him. They made their way down the trail, past the house and toward us. The Taylors' gray pickup turned the corner and followed. Rhonda, J.T., and Jack sat balanced along the walls of the truck's bed, bouncing as it drove too quickly down the hill after Uncle Jubal, who was now passing the oak tree with a wave of his hand. The pickup slowed and pulled alongside Uncle Paul's van. Littlejubal, Uncle Jubal's oldest, drove the pickup. His mother, Aunt Cheryl, sat on the passenger's side. Before the truck could stop, J.T. and Jack and their ugly cur named Gator jumped to the ground and began chasing Uncle Jubal and Emmit, who coasted down the hill at a noisy idle.

Littlepaul clutched his life jacket and frowned. "Here come our cousins, I reckon," he said.

Cousins. I started to speak but changed my mind. I had explained it many times, how Uncle Jubal was brother to Littlepaul's father, who was relation to me only by marriage to Aunt Louise. This meant that the Taylors weren't my true kin, not in blood. But I always seemed to lose Littlepaul halfway through, and he would shake his head, annoyed, refusing to believe that cousin to him could mean anything less than cousin to me. It made me angry sometimes because he wouldn't try to understand and also, I now believe, because I knew he was right.

I watched the boys run behind the motorcycle. Littlejubal, looking almost like a grown man, caught up to his brothers. They were all bare-chested and wearing cutoffs except Jack, the youngest after Emmit, who wore full blue jeans that were too long for him. The legs flopped over his feet and tripped him up every few strides. Gator ran along with them, barking with excitement and nipping at their ankles. At school, I had already begun to avoid them, to take pains to set myself apart from them, remind anyone who asked that the Taylors weren't my cousins, not really. Here, though, at the lake, it was different. At the lake everything was more straightforward, immediate. If you acted up or talked back, you might get a whipping in broad daylight, held tightly by the arm by your mom or dad and whipped in a circle with a belt or a flyswatter or whatever was handy. Here, away from the town and all of the new rules that I still didn't understand, I could love the Taylors without shame.

The motorcycle was loud, smoking, and headed right toward us. Littlepaul retreated into the shallows, but I tried my best to hold still. I watched Uncle Jubal coming closer. His hair hung over one side of his sunburned face. A cigarette dangled from his mouth, and a mean smile rose beneath his bushy auburn beard. Emmit smiled too. He had thin white hair, almost pink, and his little face was drawn up and gray, giving him the appearance of a tiny old man. He held Uncle Jubal's can of beer tight to his chest. I felt fragile watching them come like that, like I should retreat the way Littlepaul did, but I knew also that it was important that I not retreat, that I hold my ground.

I'm sure that I flinched, probably even closed my eyes, but I didn't move from my spot as Uncle Jubal stopped at the last moment. He lifted Emmit and dropped him off at the edge of the lake. Then the motorcycle was turned away from me, the back tire spinning in the mud and sending a stinging spray of sand and muck. I wiped a clump from the corner of my mouth and spat out some of the glassy grains. Uncle Jubal shut off the motorcycle. The air around us was smoky and smelled of gasoline. He walked down to us and took the beer from Emmit's hands, looked at me, and laughed. "Boy," he said. "Looks like you need you a bath."

Gator ran up to Uncle Jubal, jumping and barking. The boys, yelling with anticipation now, hit the water full speed, tripping in the shallows and disappearing in violent splashes. They came up with their long hair flat against their heads and began wrestling the way they always did, which sent Littlepaul out of the water and, truth be told, always made me a little anxious too. The Taylors were different from me, even before I moved to town, tougher and more reckless. Whatever we played, a game of football or a dirt-bomb war, they always seemed to bring a natural abandon that I would have to work very hard to match. They cursed with ease, like men. Sometimes they would have cigarettes or a can of beer sneaked from their refrigerator. They urinated freely into the open air, sending great streams of gold from their uncircumcised members that reminded me then of miniature elephant trunks.

Up the hill, Aunt Cheryl eased herself out of the truck, one hand braced against her back and her swollen belly jutting ahead of her. Rhonda, about twelve then, followed behind her mother as they joined the other women. Mom made a loud happy squeal as she reached out toward Aunt Cheryl's middle. Aunt Louise, sipping a can of RC cola, dwarfed both of them. She wore her pink sun hat and a blue print cotton dress that hung from her giant body like a circus tent. She didn't talk to the other women but stared down at Uncle Jubal and at us. Dad and Uncle Paul ignored everyone as they poked at the grill, probably talking about orange trees, citrus canker, about the best way to protect a crop from a hard freeze.

I glimpsed movement near the wooden dock to my left and turned to see Claire and the Pritchett boy sitting on the bottom step, their faces flushed red and both breathing like they had run all the way back. They smiled and pretended to be calm, like they had been sitting there all along. I adjusted my shorts and watched them as I waded into the water with the others. Claire was thirteen. Her soft blond hair moved slightly in the breeze, and she looked hard at me like, *Don't you dare say one word.*

MEMORY FUNCTIONS in strange ways, preserving some things in detail while others seem destined to dissipate, wither away, or mutate into something altogether different. My ex-wife says that my brain is far-sighted, that I remember clearly from a distance but tend to blur events close at hand. Sometimes I think she's right. I forget many things. Appointments, telephone numbers, names of new people: they slip from my mind like fleeting specters. Each time that I manage to locate my car keys is its own small miracle.

That cookout was the last at the lake house before the Yankee couple moved in, the first of several sets of strangers to invade the place that I still thought of as my home, that, as much as anyplace else, I still think of as my home. It was the day that Littlepaul learned how to swim, a Fourth of July when the city sponsored no community fireworks. It was before Mom started getting headaches, the day when Claire and Pritchett walked off together, and it was the summer of *Penthouse* and the throes of an early puberty.

"He's got a whole mess of fireworks," Littlepaul said. We were eating now, sitting at a round table that was once a spool for electric wiring. Littlepaul was talking about what Uncle Jubal had supposedly shown him in the cab of his pickup. "Ladyfingers, Black Cats, bottle rockets." He dipped a potato chip into his baked beans. "He says one of his friends brought 'em down from South Carolina. I just hope my Mama lets me shoot some off."

I looked over to Jack for confirmation. He nodded sleepily. His high thick bangs had dried like a brown helmet on his head. "That's true," Jack said. "He's got some M-80s too."

The sun had dropped lower in the sky, big and orange and silent, but the air was still hot. I scraped the rest of my potato salad into the trash. Jack and I began moving back toward the lake. As he walked, the legs of his blue jeans made soft whining sounds. Littlepaul got up to follow, but Aunt Louise saw him.

"Paul Junior," she said and swallowed. She had just finished a handful of Fritos and was licking the salt off her fingers. She stood with her free hand on one of those immense hips, watching Littlepaul fasten his life jacket. "Don't make me blister your behind for you, son. I don't want to see you go near that water till your food settles. Hear?"

"Mama!" He was on the brink of tears. "I finished a long time ago, and I didn't eat but one hotdog."

Jack and I waited, watched Aunt Louise take off her sun hat and fan her face, which was coated with a layer of sweat and blotchy from the heat. She looked worried. She shielded the sun with her hand and looked down toward the lake.

"I don't aim to *swim*," Littlepaul said.

"Your Daddy's down there," Aunt Louise said finally. "You stay with him. Hear? Don't get any water in your ears, neither. I want you to go up and tell your Daddy I told you to stay near him."

"You, too, son," Mom yelled as Littlepaul and Jack and I ran down the hill full speed, but I knew she didn't mean it, not in the same way. Mom was different now, less strict than before, more like the parents in town, the ones at the parties where she laughed at jokes I knew she didn't understand and Dad stood around the other men with his thumbs hooked in his front pockets, sucking in his cheek where a plug of tobacco would normally be. These were the parties I didn't like much, that never felt right, where sometimes the other children would laugh and try to imitate something Claire or I said, like how we would say "yes, sir" and "yes, ma'am" even to our own parents. Still, by that summer the things in town didn't feel as strange anymore. It was beginning to seem normal to live in the new house right there in the city limits, with its small yard, central air, and water that tasted of chlorine. We were nearer to the schools and the new YMCA, where Claire and I took karate.

At the shoreline, Littlejubal and Pritchett were throwing a football. Claire sat watching, and Gator barked and chased the ball back and forth. The two boys looked a lot alike, both long-limbed and sinewy with patches of soft hair around their navels, and I thought of Eric Davidson's face in the tree house when, as proof, I'd pulled down my elastic shorts enough to show him the dark wiry hairs that had begun to sprout there. His look was less one of shock than of personal indignation, as if by this I had somehow betrayed him, moved on to some new fad without inviting him along, and I felt ashamed and sad for showing him.

Jack was heading toward the dock where his father, Uncle Jubal, stood with several beer cans at his feet. Some were full. Others had been drained and crushed. The younger boys were taking turns letting Uncle Jubal heave them into the lake like logs.

Uncle Jubal sipped from a beer can, then sat it down at his feet. He looked very tall next to the boys. His hair was wet and hung around his shoulders, and his red skin seemed to shine in the soft sunlight. A tattoo of a bald eagle in flight covered one side of his chest. He crouched as Jack stepped into his hands, and in one graceful motion Uncle Jubal jerked upright and flung his son off the dock. Jack ran and clawed in the air, his too-large blue jeans flailing at the ends of his feet like malformed flippers before he smacked backwards against the water. Uncle Jubal picked up his beer and held it loose between his thumb and middle finger. He looked up at Littlepaul and me. His eyes fixed on us for several seconds, and all of his muscles seemed to tighten. Under my feet, the grass was dry and gave me an uncomfortable feeling between my toes. The radio played behind me, and I felt a sick tightness in my gut. Uncle Jubal drew a cigarette to his lips, then released the smoke into the air.

"Them that's afraid better grow some nuts *real* soon," he yelled. "It ain't gonna stay daylight forever." He finished the beer in one long pull.

No one ever said it outright, that Jubal was a drunk or that he was dangerous even, but we knew you were expected to keep a safe distance from him on days like this, days he didn't have to work, when his eyes were wet and shiny and his voice took on a lazy slur. "Leave your Uncle alone," Mom would say. "He don't need you pestering him." Aunt Louise was more serious, and she would watch Jubal sometimes, a suspicious look in her eye. I never quite understood it then, what was behind it all. I'm not sure I fully do now, but as a father myself, to a child who seems to be growing impossibly fast, I think I know something about it. You want to keep them next to you, protect them every second from all the bad that seems forever at arm's length. And there was that dangerous part of Uncle Jubal, but there were other things too. The way he talked to you like you were another person, not just some stupid kid. How he would help anyone who needed it, work all weekend laying sod or repairing a roof and never taking a penny for it. I liked him most, though, because he was the only adult I knew then that was still willing to actually play.

I walked to the dock where Uncle Jubal stood waiting. Littlepaul didn't follow. I could hear him talking behind me. "It ain't that I'm scared," he said. "That ain't the reason."

The planks of the old dock were rotting and loose in places. I turned to check Mom and Aunt Louise. They were busy putting food away. Dad and Uncle Paul stood with their backs toward us. Dad spat a stream of tobacco juice and nodded at something Uncle Paul was saying. I turned back to Uncle Jubal, who opened another beer and smiled slowly, showing teeth like bright amber.

"They're just talking about them oranges." Uncle Jubal was whispering even though it was only the two of us on the dock. He tilted his head to motion me closer. "Same as always. I'll tell you something about them goddamn oranges, though," he said. He looked serious for a moment. "They can grow as many as they want to, make all the money they want to. But it don't necessarily matter none." He put down his beer and laughed. He looked straight at Uncle Paul and Dad and yelled, "It don't matter, you know!" They just watched him without speaking. Uncle Jubal laughed loudly. He mussed my hair and poked me in the chest with his finger, playfully, but it hurt. "It don't matter for shit, Ronnie," he said. "Not if it makes you try to be something you ain't."

He knelt and locked his fingers together, holding them low for me like a stirrup. I took a deep breath through my nose. The strong smell of his body and the beer together was like sweet cider. For an instant, we were close, my cheek pressed against his tattoo. Then I felt the lifting surge of strength beneath me and the sticky tear as our skin peeled apart. I was in the air, looking down at my floundering reflection that seemed to pause, just an instant, then advance toward me in a wild rush until we collided. Hard. Then it was quiet and wet and warm.

When I reached the shallows, the chicken fights had already begun. Jack was mounted on Littlejubal's shoulders, squaring off against Claire, who squeezed her thighs around Pritchett's neck so hard that his face turned purple. Her lips were slightly parted, and she stared straight ahead, holding Pritchett lightly by the hair and pulling the back of his head into her midsection for balance. It was a good fight, no advantages, until Jack caught the top of Claire's one-piece. He didn't let go, not right away. He pulled the elastic out and down on one side, just long enough to allow us a glimpse of the swollen tissue, milky-pale, except for the strange pinkish circle in the middle. I had seen them before, of course, lots of times really. She had a habit of finding a way to show them off when I had a friend sleeping over, but they looked different this time, not just bigger, although they certainly were, but different in other ways too, I suppose. Claire recovered quickly and readjusted her swimsuit. She connected with a backhand across Jack's neck, which sent both him and Littlejubal backward into the water like one felled tree.

"Come on, Ronnie," J.T. said. "We got winners."

Reluctantly, I steadied myself on J.T.'s shoulders. He was only a year older than me, but already tall and thick-chested like his father. Claire was more cautious this time. She guarded her top with one hand and grinned at me as I struggled to keep my balance. She threw an occasional jab, not really trying to hit me so much, just teasing. Each time she punched, she let out a high-pitched *kyai* like we were taught in karate. We circled. She managed to grab and control each of my wrists, pulling me about at will, but not letting me fall, having a pretty good time with it, I'm sure. It was like this until I felt J.T. step back just as Claire gave a hard tug of my arms. I lurched forward, falling. And then I was in them, trapped, my face wedged right between her breasts, stuck there in that fleshy softness and the smell of her wet skin, the sound of my cousins' laughter all around me.

J.T. finally collapsed, and I fell freely into the water. I stayed under for a long time, listening to the muffled laughter above the surface. I floated, safe and weightless, my hard-on pressed shamefully against my shorts, until my lungs burned and I rose slowly to the teasing faces.

Then came the cry, from the top of the hill. "Lord have mercy!" It was Aunt Louise, and she was trotting toward us, running actually, her whole body jiggling terribly with each tiny stride. She was headed toward the dock where Littlepaul was leaning against the railing, less than ten feet away from Uncle Jubal, who finished another beer and crushed it between his fingers, dropped it at his feet, and opened another. I don't know how or why Littlepaul made it out onto the dock, whether he'd fallen into one of his seizures or had in some way succumbed to the same draw of Uncle Jubal that I always felt. Regardless, he was there on the dock with him.

"You," Uncle Jubal said. "Paul Jr."

"Paul!" Aunt Louise yelled to Uncle Paul. She was out of breath and had to stop. "Do something before he drowns 'em!"

Uncle Paul looked up at her, not quite understanding yet. I waded toward the dock where Uncle Jubal now gripped Littlepaul by an arm.

He slipped the life jacket off Littlepaul and held it up in his other hand. Littlepaul made weak grabs at it, but Uncle Jubal held it just out of his reach. Littlepaul quit fighting and looked up at Uncle Jubal. "I cain't," he said. "I cain't swim. I always say I know how, but I really cain't."

"Paul!" Aunt Louise yelled.

Uncle Paul started walking toward the dock, but he was still a good bit away. Uncle Jubal lowered himself and looked into Littlepaul's eyes. He spoke softly, but I could hear. "You cain't," he said. "'Cause you ain't never had to. If you was to have to, really have to, you could."

Uncle Paul stopped at the edge of the dock. "You best turn him loose, Jubal," he said. I stood beneath the dock's edge, waiting in the water and looking up at Littlepaul. His legs hung like limp strings beneath him.

Uncle Jubal turned and smiled at Uncle Paul, who set his beer on the dock post. "It's how you learn, Paul," Uncle Jubal said. "Hell, it's how *we* learned. Look at 'em." He gave Littlepaul a slight shake. "Who ever heard of a white youngen his age who cain't swim. I don't care how much money you got. It ain't nat'ral."

"Turn him loose, Jubal," Uncle Paul said. He looked serious, his fists balled up and tense at his side.

Uncle Jubal shook his head. "I ain't one to tell a grown man how to raise his own boy," he said, "but what do you reckon our Daddy would've said about this? It's damn embarrassin'."

"There's other ways, Jubal. You're acting like a goddamn . . . ." Uncle Paul paused.

"A goddamn what?" Jubal said. "Go ahead. Say it."

Uncle Paul shook his head. "Like a damn fool, that's all."

"I'm just fixin' to teach the boy to swim. What's wrong with that?"

"You're *fixin'* to get your ass kicked if you don't turn my son loose in a hurry," Uncle Paul said.

Uncle Jubal was laughing now. "Maybe when *we* was youngens," he said. "Course, you still might have it in you. I ain't necessarily one to say. But you know as well as me, this boy's got to learn. He ain't never gonna get any better with you always babyin' him." Uncle Jubal dropped the life jacket and grabbed hold of Littlepaul by the back of the shorts and began rocking him back and forth like a porch swing. Uncle Jubal said, "In the name of the *Father* and of the *Son*."

I didn't like this—a bit. I was worried, scared for us, all of us, especially Aunt Louise who was nearing the edge of the dock where the footing was unsure. Even Dad, Mom, and the others were coming down the hill toward us.

"Fine," Uncle Paul said. "That's just fine, Jubal." He began walking fast toward Uncle Jubal and Littlepaul.

"And the Holy *Ghost!*" Uncle Jubal said.

"Jubal, don't you!" Aunt Louise yelled.

Then quiet.

Littlepaul didn't claw or squirm like the rest of us. He sailed through the air, doubled over and calm, almost graceful in a way, like he had practiced it for a long time, like he had given in to the inevitable and he didn't have to fight it anymore. He hit in a quiet splash and was under water only an instant before he broke the surface, changed. His eyes were wild as he bobbed and fought along in a clumsy panic. But moving. Slowly. And when I had waded out to my chest, I was able to reach out and lock fingertips with him, pulling him to me. He dug his fingernails into my neck until he realized that he could touch ground.

Uncle Paul stood at the end of the dock. When he saw that Littlepaul was okay, he turned around and threw a straight punch right into Uncle Jubal's mouth. It didn't make a sound like a sharp pop, the way it did on the TV and movies. It was a dull, pulpy sound, like the blunt end of an ax against the skull of a pig. Uncle Jubal took two steps backward and stopped. He didn't say a word, just smiled, his top lip darkening with blood, and sipped his beer. Littlepaul coughed and choked until a stream of thick vomit issued into the water.

"There went that one hot dog, I reckon," Jack said.

Littlepaul's face contorted as if he were about to cry. But, this time, he didn't. He spat. Then he caught his breath. And laughed. A line of mucus ran from both nostrils, covering his upper lip and dangling in the water like a fishing line. Still laughing, he looked up at Uncle Paul, who had both hands on the dock rail as he leaned down toward him.

"I *swam,*" Littlepaul said.

Uncle Paul watched him a moment. There was a strange smile on his face that I didn't remember seeing before, something approaching pride. Everyone else was quiet. "I reckon you did," he said finally. "I reckon you swam pretty good."

It was darker out. The water was green and shadowy, and scattered drops of rain began to splash around us. I looked up in time to see the sky turn loose altogether. Everyone ran toward the house except me. There was no lightning, so I stood awhile, enjoying the light sting of the rain.

HUDDLED TOGETHER on the empty back porch, everyone was drying off with towels. Mom engulfed me and began scrubbing away at my head.

Dad, who had been inside the house, returned to the porch with a lantern, which he lit and hung on a jutting nail. He said, "Let's put some light on the subject."

Uncle Jubal wasn't there. I had seen him climb into the cab of his truck with a six-pack of beer. The cement floor beneath us was dusty but cool and nice. I sat down in the corner with Jack and Littlepaul. They had a deck of cards, and we played three-way war as everyone stood around waiting. The rain roared against the aluminum roof, and the wind blew through the screen walls. I sat facing the open doorway that led back into the living room of the house. The smell coming from it was damp and stale. I looked into the dark room and could see the darker hallway that led to my old room. I imagined going to it, opening the door, and finding it the same as before, full of my things instead of empty like I knew it was.

When the rain let up, I heard Uncle Jubal's truck approach the porch, and Aunt Cheryl said, "Get ready, kids. Looks like we may be going home."

Uncle Paul walked out into the light rain, up to the truck window. He talked to Uncle Jubal for a long time, occasionally raising his voice. Most of it I couldn't make out because Dad had turned the radio on, but I heard Uncle Jubal say something about Uncle Paul's thinking he was too good and something also about oranges, then Uncle Paul saying, "That ain't got nothing to do with this, Jubal. Nothing at all!"

I CROUCHED BY THE FIRE and tried to light my sparkler. When the heat was too much, I pulled back and turned my face away, still feeling the sting against my nose and cheek and the dry hurt in the eyes.

"Bring that thing over here, Ronnie," Aunt Cheryl said.

I turned in the direction of her voice, but I could only see darkness and the waning orange image in the middle of my vision where the fire had been. I blinked and let the soothing tears roll down either side of my nose. I saw the flicker of Aunt Cheryl's cigarette lighter where Emmit, Jack, and Littlepaul had gathered around, the tips of their sparklers held to the flame. From further up the hill, there was the laughter and secretive voices of the men and older boys. I walked across the wet grass to Aunt Cheryl and joined my sparkler with the others. Emmit's lit first, then Littlepaul's. They were like white flowers, growing wildly, shooting out their tiny fire-petals. They sounded like quiet electricity.

"Go!" Aunt Cheryl was laughing and shooing the two away. "Don't just stand there. Go and play with 'em."

Dad's voice was coming down the hill. He was talking to someone beside him. "Goddamnit, you *will* stay down here, or else I'll take my belt off right now. We ain't in town." He came into the light, escorting Claire by the elbow. "You're lucky you ain't got your butt wore out already," Dad said. "Don't think you're too old for it."

I wanted Claire to say "yes, sir," to say she was sorry, and for things to go nicer, but I knew too that Dad was wrong, that she *was* too old. She was moving out of the world of belts and switches, away from karate and chicken fights, and I think, now, that even Dad knew this too, that we were all caught up in this same wave that would propel us blindly forward, and that there was little, if anything, that any of us could do about it.

He let go of her elbow. The firelight flickered over both their frowning faces. Behind them the Spanish moss hung low from the oak branches like thin dark ghosts.

"How come I can't watch them do the fireworks?" Claire said. "I was just watching."

"Because you cain't," Dad said. "And don't think I didn't see you and Pritchett take you a little walk down the beach, neither."

Jack's sparkler lit, and he was gone. It was only me left.

"Hold that thing still, Ronnie." Aunt Cheryl steadied my hand with her own.

"Claire Marie," Mom said. Mom looked stern, unblinking. Even then she must have had it, the cancer, keeping it hidden inside her breast like some secret vice. I was glad when I saw Claire walk toward her and sit between Aunt Louise and Rhonda, who were eating leftover grilled chicken. Gator sat whining, waiting for someone to toss him a scrap. Claire sighed and folded her arms. Her hair was pulled back into a ponytail, and she wore a Blondie tee shirt over her one-piece. She looked up and caught me watching.

"What are you looking at?" she said, giving me the meanest glare in the world. Someone tossed Gator a piece of meat, and I stared at Claire's pouting face, a face that was neither girl nor woman but straddling that delicate place between the two. I continued to stare, and her expression became less angry. No one spoke for a while, and I think we must have sensed it, that we were approaching the end of something, that we might never come here, all of us together, again.

A few years later, Dad, who had inherited the larger portion of the groves, was able to buy out Uncle Paul's and Aunt Louise's interest in the business, and while we still saw them and Littlepaul regularly, Uncle Jubal and the Taylors, never real relatives, receded more and more into memory. There were other things to take on: high school, the death of a mother, eventually college.

I have lived in many places over the years: dormitories, houses, apartments, now a large condominium in a fairly respectable section of Jacksonville, but I rarely think of those places, not in the same way I do the lake house. It appears with strange regularity in my dreams. Sometimes it is bright and full of things and people. Other times it's dark and empty, with secret passageways and hidden rooms. But the way I like to think of it is with us all together again. We are in the back yard, tired from a day in the sun. A warm breeze comes off the lake, and I make funny faces at Claire until she can't help grinning. She sticks out her tongue and turns away.

Aunt Cheryl held my hand steady, and I felt the prickly stings against my hand and looked down at the lit sparkler. I walked toward the other boys, dancing shadows between me and the fire. Their sparklers made white trails in the sky that lingered an instant before fading.
Whispered shouts came out of the darkness at the top of the hill. Then nothing. Then the bottle rockets came, tearing across the sky in airy streams of smoke. They hung above us an instant, dozens, then exploded in bursts of colored sparks. I stared up until the smoke cleared and only the stars were left. The women and girls all clapped and cheered. I laughed and made big white circles in the air.

"Look," Littlepaul said. He froze stiff in place and raised the sparkler over his head. "I'm the *Statue of Liberty!*"

"Watch this," I said, spinning the sparkler faster. "Watch me write my name."

KEROUAC'S GHOST

I HATE MY JOB, of course. Big deal. But last week, days before my manager left for a week in St. Augustine, I was promoted to shift manager at Suncoast Books of St. Petersburg. Now, at $9.25 an hour, I guess I'm part of the establishment, a team player, a career man. This is what I'm thinking as I stock *Drama & Poetry* in the rear of the store, working through a moderate hangover and trying to decide whether to make a face-out of *Death of a Salesman* or *American Buffalo*.

Everything's been slow today, even during the downtown lunch hour, typical for mid-July, when the heat has driven the snowbirds home and even the most adventurous tourists stay indoors during the hottest part of the day. The smell of baking cookies hangs in the air, chocolate chip, and I listen to the soft gurgle of someone steaming milk in the café up front. It makes me sleepy.

It's then that the cursing starts. It's Claire. I know that right off. She's somewhere near the registers. Her voice lifts high over the cappuccino machine and echoes through the building. I set down an armload of books and walk out into the center aisle in time to see her round the corner of *Self-Help*. She's limping, holding on to the bookshelf for support and carrying one of her sandals in her hand. We're actors, Claire and I—thespian buddies from college—and tend toward the histrionic whenever possible. But I can tell right away that this isn't just play-acting. I run down the aisle and meet her at the Info Desk. A few of her GRE note cards slip out of her shirt pocket and onto the floor.

"Jesus-mother-fucking-Christ-in-hell!" she says.

"Easy," I say. I look around for customers. "Just take it easy." A blue-haired woman peeks around the corner of *Romance* and gives me a wrinkled frown. I take Claire's hand, and she falls hard against me, grabbing wildly at my tie. I drape one of her arms over my shoulders and help her along. Her legs hang limp beneath her.

"You're not even trying," I say.

"Oh, Blake," she says, holding tight around my neck now. "She got me. The old decrepit bitch got me!"

It won't do, of course, her raising hell like this. It's not that I care. She could curse each of the saints in heaven, one by one, but Reese and Laura watch me from behind the cash wrap, waiting to see how I handle it, ready to tell all.

"The bitch!" Claire says.

I scoop her up, newlywed-style, and head toward the back room. She weighs like 105 pounds, so it's no great feat. I whip to the right, through *Science Fiction,* then *Men's Adventure,* taking a sharp left along the side wall where my shoes slip on the chalky tile. I might have fallen. That would be like me, but I somehow manage to keep my footing, Claire moaning in my ear the whole time, until we're safe inside the stockroom. I lower her down onto a Random House box, where she doubles over and pulls up the leg of her khakis. She grabs near her ankle, and I fight the urge to hold her again, whisper that it's okay, that I'm here. Soon, she settles down to a whimper.

"Ouch," she says. "Mother-*fucking* ouch."

"What happened?" I say. "Did you twist your ankle?"

Claire shakes her head and rocks back and forth. She throws her sandal across the floor. It slides underneath a low shelf. On the far wall the phone is ringing.

"What twist?" she says. "I got fucking run down. The crazy old hag drove right into the back of my heel."

"Jesus," I say. "In a car?"

The door flies open, and Reese walks in, pushing an empty stock-cart and sweeping his curly bangs out of his eyes the way he does.

"Don't worry, boss," he says. "I'll get the phone."

This is a jab at me, of course. And I don't blame him, but damn. I didn't ask to be promoted over him. He *has* been here longer than me, works harder in general, actually treats the customers well, but happens to be extremely and unabashedly gay, whereas I'm not, which may put me in a better place with our homophobe of a boss. Yes, very unfair, and maybe it could be a big controversy if things were different and we were more important people.

Claire sighs, weepy. She speaks softer now. "It wasn't a car," she says.

"What then?" I say. I move closer. I sit down on another box, leaning toward her. She tilts her head up toward me. Her pale cheeks have turned a warm pinkish, and her nose ring sticks up at a right angle. I flick it back down with my little finger and wipe away some of the tears with the back of my knuckles. "Tell me," I say.

"It was a scooter," she says. She pauses, thinking and twirling the corner of her auburn bangs around her finger. "One of those Lark wheelchair thingies. What do you call them, Rascals?"

Claire punches me hard on the shoulder, but I can't stop. I just can't. "Don't you even," she says. "Don't you even fucking laugh."

THE THING IS, I love Claire, have for a long time now. She knows. We drink in the same circle, so it comes up, never when I mean it to or can say it right, of course, but when I'm drunk enough to lose all credibility. The last time that I said it outright, she didn't even flinch. It was at the end of a closing-night cast party, both of us still in our makeup. She just looked at me with eyes shadowed in green and a strange, sad smile and said, "But, Blake, to whom will I run crying when we fight? Who will be my very best friend?" Okay, Claire. Got it, loud and clear.

Reese speaks into the telephone. "We're across from the old McCrory building," he says. "Yes, just a little west of First Union, on the north side of Central. There's a big sunburst painted on our window." Reese is over six feet tall with perfectly tanned skin. I swear he could be a model if he got braces and lost a few in the gut and ass. "Neither one," he says. "We're independent. We've been here for like forever."

I persuade Claire to let me have a look at her heel, but I have to turn away once I've seen it. I feel the familiar sick dizziness. Once, in Mrs. Rueman's junior high health class, I passed out during a film about the different types of wounds. I lost consciousness somewhere between laceration and amputation and, fool that I am, fell from my desk and hit the floor face first in front of everyone.

"How bad is it?" Claire says.

I turn back to the wound. It's bruised an ugly purple, and the skin is broken beneath, peeled down to expose the wet undertissue. I take a stack of hardbacks off the *New Arrival* cart and slide them under her calf.

"How bad, Blake?"

"I don't know," I say. "Worse than I expected, I guess. Picture a kiwi with a thin slice taken out."

"Oh, God," she says. "Do I need to go to the doctor? I've got no insurance, you know, no money."

Hearing her go on, I can't help thinking how I *do* have insurance. No, that's not exactly true, but I will in less than ninety days. It was one of the points highlighted in my manager packet. I haven't had insurance since '94, when my college graduation excluded me from my parents' policy. I wonder if this new protection will make me feel different, less vulnerable or quicker to take chances.

Reese is pointing at the wall behind me. I turn and see the plastic first-aid kit resting in its wall mount. I try to pull it out, but it's stuck. I pull harder and jiggle the box. Reese hangs up the phone.

"You have to unscrew the top piece," he says, just as the front lid springs open, sending a waterfall of products onto the floor. Reese bends over to clean up my mess. His formidable buttocks box me out of the way like I'm some troublesome kid, like it's too much for me to handle. I finger the cash register key in my pocket.

"Reese." I take the key and jab him lightly in the side. "Here, cover the calls, and I'll take care of things back here. I'll be okay. Your skills are needed elsewhere."

He drops a handful of bandages on the magazine counter and takes the key from me. "Oh boy," he says, holding it to his chest. He flips his bangs away and rolls his pretty blue eyes to Claire. "This could be the break I've been waiting for. You won't regret this, I promise."

Pompous asshole. He's an actor too, of the order that gives the rest of us a bad name if you ask me. "No," I say. "I've been watching you. I like your style, and I think you're ready. Now go away."

He sticks the key in his shirt pocket and loads his cart with *Nature & Pets*. "Oh, I'm going, sweetie," he says. "Don't you worry about that." He touches Claire on the shoulder. "Let me know if you need any help," he whispers, then backs his cart through the doorway.

I pick up a tube off the floor: *Bacterium Zinc Ointment. INDICATIONS: First aid to prevent infections in minor cuts, scrapes, and burns.* I gather a few other supplies and walk back over to Claire and kneel by her foot.

"Here we go," I say. "Now tell me who did this, and I'll ban them from the store."

"It was the old one," Claire says. "The really old one with the thin white hair."

I shrug my shoulders.

"You know," she says. "You can see the brown freckles on the top of her scalp when she rolls by the Info Desk."

I dab some of the ointment on my finger. "Could you be more specific?" I smooth out the wrinkle of skin the best I can. I feel only slightly light-headed.

"Ouch," Claire says. "Fuck." She squeezes my shoulder with her little hand. "Christ, Blake. She's the one who buys the baskets full of Silhouette Romances."

"The one that peed on herself last fall?"

"No, not her. I know you know who I'm talking about. She has a bit of a mustache. She's got a goddamned orange flag mounted on the back of her cart. It's on a five-foot pole."

Orange flag, this is familiar. "Mrs. Giffin," I say. "Yeah, she comes in with her husband usually. He was a professor of something at Columbia, I think. Mrs. Giffin ran you over? I wouldn't have guessed her."

Claire flinches as I apply more ointment. "It burns!" she says. "Oh man, that burns."

"Something like this was bound to happen eventually," I say. I bend over and blow on Claire's heel in short bursts. "It was only a matter of time, the way they speed around without a care in the world. Don't the engineers of those things figure in eyesight and reaction time? The elderly are meant to be slow. It's nature's way. You start fooling around with such simple truths as that, and the whole natural balance starts to break down." I keep blowing and open a roll of gauze. "The whole personal conveyance industry is out of control if you ask me."

I place a bandage square over her heel and wrap it into place with the gauze, feeling better with each layer between me and the wound. I cut off the wrap with the tiny pair of scissors and tape it down firm. It's not too bad a job, really. Mrs. Rueman would be proud. Claire pats me on the top of the head, like you would a young boy. "Thank you," she says. Her voice is almost a whisper. She leans forward and plants a hard kiss on my forehead. When she draws back, I can feel the place where her lips were on me, warm and a little damp.

It is always best at these rare times, when I can do something for her, when she needs help, or when she's sad, disheveled, like in the parking lot during that first week of classes, sitting on the hood of her car with a stack of textbooks beside her and her face in her hands because she'd locked her keys in her car. Then along I came, the awkward sophomore who'd managed to survive a whole year without making any friends to speak of. But she smiled so sweet, like I was just the person she'd been waiting for. Me. "This is not the way to start off the fall," she said. "This is not a good sign for me, I have to say."

Over the intercom, Laura calls for a manager to the register. Claire looks down at the floor.

"Come on," I say. I hold out my hand. "I have something that will help."

I OPEN THE RECEIVING DOOR to the gush of windless humidity and the faint odor of saltwater. A few pigeons scatter in fluttering retreat when we step out into the sun. I feel a tingling in my hands, like a weak electrical current, and the asphalt sparkles white in the heat. I leave the door ajar and carry Claire piggyback, down the receiving ramp, to the dumpster across the alley where we duck into the shade and take a seat, our backs against the old postal building. It's quiet except for cars passing in the distance and guitar music coming from the veranda of the Anderson Hotel one building down.

"Now, don't get the idea that I make a habit of this," I say as I take the plastic baggy and rolling papers from my wallet. "It's a freak accident that I even brought it to work today."

It's true. It's left over from last night, a fuzzy chain of events that began with a late afternoon poker game and ended with a bunch of us getting kicked out of The Pelican a half hour after closing, me on the arm of one Carlie, a Rubenesque hotel clerk and hopeful screenwriter, who was still asleep when I left this morning, curled up in my covers, entrenched in my world. I imagine her still there, folding my underwear and balancing my checkbook, shaking her head disapprovingly at the porn hidden in my bottom desk drawer.

I fill the crease with what's left in the bag and roll a nice thick one. A drop of sweat slips down the middle of my back in a warm tickle. I loosen my tie and stick the finished product between my lips. Claire produces her Zippo and lights the end. I take a deep hit, hold it a couple of seconds, then exhale slowly. The smoke creeps along the ground an instant, like a thin fog, before rising and dissipating in the dead air. I pass the joint to Claire. "Utilize this," I say. She smokes it casually, like a cigarette. Her eyelids hang half shut. I want to kiss them both.

Soon, we hear the unmistakable voice of Captain Lou coming down the side street, rough and hoarse, punctuated with shouts of laughter. I check my watch. He's right on schedule. His voice gets closer, and we scoot farther behind the dumpster, barely peeking around the edge when he and Doc come into view, maybe ten yards away. Doc is wearing a white tee-shirt that hangs loosely over his faded-green scrub pants. He lifts a lanky leg and begins scraping his tennis shoe against the corner of our building.

"What is he doing?" Claire whispers.

"Shh," I say.

Captain Lou stands in his yellow tank top and cutoffs. He adjusts a wide-brimmed straw hat and folds his arms across his thick chest. "Don't I always tell you to watch the hell where you walk around here?" he says. He shakes his head and looks up at his friend. "There's dog shit everywhere."

Claire giggles, and I shush her again. Doc continues scraping his foot. He moves sleepily and mumbles something to Captain Lou.

"No, I don't have a goddamned handkerchief," Captain Lou says. "And if I did, I sure as hell wouldn't let you wipe dog shit all over it." Captain Lou spits to the side and continues to shake his head, indignant. Doc lowers his leg and rubs his shoe against the ground until he's satisfied. They disappear, still arguing, around the edge of the building.

"Classic," Claire says.

"Straight out of Beckett, those two."

Claire yawns. "Yep," she says. She stretches out her legs and passes the joint to me. Her eyes are unfocused, like she's thinking of something far away. "I'm getting out of here, Blake," she says. "I have to. This place is literally killing me."

I take a smaller hit this time. "What do you mean?"

"Quitting."

"Quitting. Yes, but what will you do?"

"Work on an admission essay." She remembers her GRE cards and pulls them from her shirt pocket. "Other than that, I don't really care right now. You're allowed not to care for a couple of days. That's the rule. I'll find something. Something paying better." Her eyes widen. "Maybe," she says. She grins shyly. "Maybe, I could strip."

I choke on my smoke, on purpose, a variation of the old comedic trope.

"What is it?" she says. "You don't think I could make it?" She moves closer and puts her hand inside my thigh. She rubs her shoulder against me and whispers, "Hey, baby." She giggles. "How about a private dance?" She runs her tongue along the outside rim of my ear and takes the joint from my fingers. A cold chill runs all the way down my arm.

"Jesus," I say.

"What? I'm no good, am I?"

"That's not it," I say. "Not in the least." I want her to follow up, ask the questions, force me to explain—in words irrefutable—why we should be together forever. But she just scoots away, taking more small, petite puffs. She licks her lips. They look full and shiny-wet. She touches her bandage and sighs.

"It doesn't hurt so much now," she says. "I can sure feel it throbbing though."

Throbbing. I start to comment but change my mind. She looks up at me, pitifully. I want to pick her up again, hold her tight to my chest, use my newfound wealth to take care of her. I want to take care of her.

Self-absorbed drama queen Claire may be, but there's so much more to her, I swear. I watch her sort the cards, the joint secure between her fingers, deft fingers, that seem always so capable, and that once, years ago, even played the piano for me.

Usually, there were others hanging around, but that night it was just us. We had left a Friday happy hour at a local bar and bought sushi from the restaurant next door, which we took with us to campus. We sat on the lawn of the fine arts building. The sun had set, and the starless sky became a sheet of purple velvet; that's what she called it.

The door to the small auditorium was open, but inside we could only find the switch to a row of lights along the side of the stage. We took turns going to the podium and introducing the other to the rows of dark, empty seats. *We are very lucky to have with us tonight.* She had blonde hair then, long and soft. *Too many stage and screen credits to name here.* She still ate meat occasionally, mostly on pizza. Pepperoni was her weakness. *Not only as an eminent scholar and gifted actor, but also my very dear friend.*

Afterwards, she sat down at the piano. I didn't even know she played. But then there was music. Real music. Mozart, Beethoven. I sat down there on the stage and watched in the way you watch something unexpected and beautiful, her face in the half light, so focused, and her little hands moving so fast. A few times she stopped. "Sorry," she said. "I always fuck it up without my sheets." And soon she was done, and she turned to me as if it were nothing, like she hadn't done anything particularly special. I couldn't say anything. I just rose and clapped stupidly.

"Stop," she said. "Or I'll think you're making fun of me."

She came to me then, slowly, and—this is the way I remember it—her head down and shy. She rested her forehead against my chest and we hugged for a while, and I tried to say how amazing I thought she was, diminishing what I meant with every word.

"I'm not so good," she said. "I'm no prodigy."

It was just us, half drunk, in the dark and empty auditorium, and she looked up at me, and I thought this was the time for me to do something special, to match the moment in some tactile way. And for an instant I thought I might.

Claire tucks her note cards back into her pocket. It will rain before long. I can smell it in the air, like a wet chalkboard. A small flock of seagulls passes overhead. One drops a white splatter on the asphalt.

"How cliché," Claire says.

We sit for a while, not speaking. Far out to our left, over the bay, the sky is black with storm clouds.

"It's not so much that every day is terrible," Claire says. "I mean, don't get me wrong. I have good times. I like doing the little shows, drinking at the Pelican. Bullshitting with Doc and Captain Lou. I can't say we don't have good friends. We have *good* friends. But I swear, Blake, I have to trick myself into thinking that it's just a role I'm playing, method acting or something, like this time in my life doesn't really count against me in the whole scheme of things."

We smoke quietly, listening to the guitar and the soft sounds of thunder in the distance.

"It counts, though, doesn't it?" Claire says. "This, us, right here. This is actually life. It's happening right now." She pauses. "There, it just happened. A second I'll never get back."

I feel the cool tinge of the pot seep into my chest and neck. I say, "The bookseller has long been a respected component of the literary tradition," quoting the first line of our training manual.

Claire shakes her head. "You think I haven't tried that? You tell me what that means. I'm not Sylvia Beach. This isn't Shakespeare & Company. What, sell a shit-load of books this week and get another shit-load delivered the next? I'm twenty-fucking-eight years old, and I peddle bad literature here in Heaven's own waiting room, occasionally taking time out to get run down by a geriatric viper on wheels. This isn't what you dream about. It's not exactly Broadway, Blake. It's not how I pictured it, I have to say."

Claire fans herself with her cards as I try to remember how I pictured it, what I dreamed about five years ago, when we were students and the lead parts came easy, back when the parents were footing the bill, and no prospect was utterly ridiculous. There was so much time, and I guess

I had assumed it would happen for us eventually, slowly gestating à la *When Harry Met Sally,* until we were together for the rest of our lives.

"I think I know what you mean," I say. "It's like you forego certain things because there is always this hope for the other thing that you expect to become when you're really you. Then, one day you notice that your break *hasn't* come, and you realize that if you don't become this hoped-for thing by a certain time, you may be stuck being what you already are, which was really you all along."

"What are you talking about?" she says.

I try hard to think about it, to make it clear again. "I don't know. For a second I had it, but now I don't know."

We laugh. I drop the remaining nub of the joint from between my fingers and crush it under my shoe. *Au revoir, mon ami.*

"Is it all that hopeless?" I say. "What about Kerouac? St. Pete was good enough for him for a while. What was it he said when they asked why in hell he lived here? 'Everyone's got to be somewhere,' I think he said."

"Whatever," Claire says. "Jack came here to die, just like everyone else."

A group of skateboarders approaches. Claire and I share a cigarette and watch them attempt stunts on the receiving ramp. They seem, to me, more agile than ever before, little acrobats inside baggy costumes, long hair flowing wild in the sun. They are newly strange, almost impossible, and I wonder that I ever took them for granted as I watch them leave down the alley, the roar of their wheels getting fainter and fainter.

"I'm really feeling it," Claire says. "Yes, I am most definitely high." She rotates her ankle. "Much better, I have to say." She lifts the collar of her shirt and wipes the sweat from her face. She starts to get up, and I move to help her.

"I'm okay," she says. "Is your break over?" She looks at her watch.

"Who cares?" I say. She hobbles, barefooted, toward the back door. I follow, and the problem of going back inside stoned really hits me for the first time. I feel weak and sick to my stomach. "Maybe I'll just keep it going, quit right along with you. Maybe it's catchy."

"No," she says. "You're not the quitter type."

This hurts me. I'm not sure why, but it does.

"I could be a quitter," I say. "I could quit just as well as anyone else." I freeze at the foot of the ramp and stare off at an imaginary boss. "Sir," I say, enunciating from my diaphragm. "We will not be treated in this manner. Look at this woman." I pull Claire closer to me, then scoop her up again behind the knees and back. She squeals, then giggles. "Stricken

down in the line of duty," I continue. "Virtually maimed in your service!" I turn and start my way up the receiving ramp with her still in my
arms.

"We are educated people," Claire returns. "*Nous sommes les acteurs!
Artistes!*"

I stop at the top of the ramp and spin around quickly. Claire works
at my name badge as I look out over the tops of the buildings, where
the thunderheads encroach on the blue sky. She manages to unclasp the
badge and pull it free from my shirt.

"Fired?" I yell into the light. "You can't fire us. You can't, because we
quit!" I bump the receiving door open with my back, and Claire flings my
badge into the air. It seems to hang an instant, a flicker in the sunlight,
then hits the asphalt in a quiet clink.

I REALLY SHOULD QUIT. Start fresh. Update the résumé, maybe even go
to grad school like Claire. I adjust my tie in the bathroom, trying to
ignore the mixed aroma of industrial air freshener and excrement. My
face looks unfamiliar, a red-eyed stranger staring back at me. A man in
the stall farts and sighs in breathy relief. There is a trickle of urine, then
quiet. I wipe my forehead with a paper towel and walk out onto the floor,
stand under an air vent until the phone starts ringing. I make my way
down the main aisle. Everything is dark and cardboard-thin, like slides
seen through a View-Master viewer. I make it to the Info Desk and pick
up the phone.

"Suncoast. This is Blake."

The man on the phone sounds to be a healthy seventy-five, maybe
seventy-eight, still a few years from utter decrepitude with any luck. You
get a knack for telling after a while. He's looking to replace a book that
he lent out several years ago, to a good friend who unfortunately passed
away before she could return it. It was sudden, her passing, and as he is
sure I can understand, he never bothered to inquire about the book with
the family. The book, yes, it was a portrait of the historical Macbeth, not
the Shakespearean character, mind you, but the real-life figure.

I realize he has stopped talking and is waiting for me. I try to snap
back in focus. "Do you remember the title, sir? Well, how about the
author then? No sir, knowing the publisher doesn't really help us. Red-
and-black cover? No, you're right. That doesn't get us very far at all."

I squint and stare hard at the computer screen. My mouth is dry and
tastes like bile. I try to swallow. Can't. "I'm doing a keyword search," I

explain, my voice hoarse and strained. "'Historical' and 'Macbeth.' It will be just a moment while the computer sifts through the titles."

The man continues to talk as I shake my head clear again and start scanning through the store for Claire. Business has picked up a bit, but not so much. At the register, Reese and Laura ring up sales. One customer waits in line. Melanie comes through the front door, looking hurried and tired. She's late for her shift. She pretends not to see me, stares at the floor, and breaks into *Diet & Nutrition*.

Across the center aisle from me, a group of pale-faced teenagers lingers around *New Age*. They're all dressed in black. The tallest, a boy, wears a cape with red inlay. It has to suck, I think, to be a dedicated Goth in the summer.

In the café, someone is grinding coffee beans. I pull the phone book from the shelf below. I drop it to the floor and step onto it, trying to see over the bookshelves into the café, but I'm still a couple inches short. I read the computer screen and manage to call out a few titles that sound somewhat on target. The man doesn't recognize any per se, although the last one could very well be it. No, he doesn't want to order it, not without knowing for certain.

But did I know that Macbeth has gotten the bum-rap so to speak? Did I know he wasn't really the murderous usurper that he's been made out to be?

"Shakespeare does tend to take liberties," I say. "I don't think historical accuracy was really his goal."

The man talks on, about a collection of books that he still has stored up in Pennsylvania, how he really needs to have them sent down here to sort through. After all, he lives here pretty much year-round now. He's sort of a Floridian by conversion, so to speak.

Why is he telling me this? He's going too far with it, almost like he's poking fun at me, and it makes me nervous. I manage to force in that his lost book may be out of print. I give him a number of a good used-book store. I suggest the local library. He bites, long enough for me to wish him good luck and hang up before he can respond. And then I feel bad. I'm a reluctant asshole, really. Now I have to think about this poor old fucker, probably a widower, alone, just looking for someone to talk to, some human contact to break the silence of his empty condominium. And of all the clerks in the bay area, he draws me. I could almost cry. I'm still sweating like a wild man, so I pull several tissues from the box underneath the counter and wipe down my face and neck.

Sunlight filters through the front windows and casts light along the left front corner of the ceiling where there is also a water stain in the shape of a Volkswagen Beetle. I've never noticed it before. I look back down at *New Age* in time to see the caped boy slide a Wicca paperback off the shelf and drop it into the trench coat pocket of one of his cohorts, an overweight girl with thick features and a bad complexion. I could confront them, because I'm in charge here, but I think better of it. Besides, maybe I saw it wrong. The trench coat girl holds another book in her hand. She seems relaxed, not thievish at all. Maybe I should show her around the store, suggest some of my favorite titles, fill her pockets to overflowing.

I'm born out of time is most likely my problem. In the late '60s I would've had Kerouac at least, and that would be something, no matter what Claire says. They say he would stroll in here, drunk of course, looking like a hobo, nothing like what you'd expect. He would hang out in the fiction section, face-out all of his titles, and complain if we didn't keep them in stock.

And then he died. He died in the hospital right down the road. And afterwards, the strange things began to happen. Books knocked from the shelves onto the floor. Mysterious shuffling footsteps at night. Spontaneous face-outs of *On the Road* or *Dharma Bums*. That's what the stories say, and sometimes when I'm closing up and it's just me alone, the whole store dim and silent, I like to imagine I hear something too, that something is about to happen, something extra-normal that defies rational explanation. It's a silly thing to think about, or just sad maybe, the hipster of the open road resigned to haunt St. Pete, Florida. Kerouac's ghost moping through a humid, sun-drenched afterlife.

A redheaded woman, between fifty-eight and sixty-two, approaches the desk. Her tremendous hips undulate beneath her skirt as she walks. She hands me a half-empty paper coffee cup. "Do you have a trash back there?" she says.

IN THE CAFÉ, I find Claire. She sits facing the window, between Captain Lou and Doc. She has her bandaged foot propped up on a chair. I walk behind the bar and pour myself a glass of water with a lemon wedge. Captain Lou rises and walks toward me. His dirty tank top doesn't quite cover his gut.

"Come sit down, sport," he says, poking me in the chest. I rub the spot where his nicotine-stained thumb dug into me. I look down on his sunburned scalp where the freckles swirl in a pattern like a galaxy. His breath smells like Elmer's Glue, and his eyes are milky gray. "Sit," he says. "Tell this little girl over here she can't quit. Tell her we wouldn't know what to do around here without her."

"What *is* it that you do?" I say as we walk toward them. "What *do* you do around here?" Here I am being an asshole again. Captain Lou's okay most of the time, but I'd really like to have Claire to myself right now.

Doc laughs at something that Claire says. He runs his fingers through his gray beard and wipes the oil on his shirt. Claire seems content, gazing out on Central Avenue and sipping a cream-topped latte.

"Blake asks what it is we do, Boss," Captain Lou says to Doc. "He wants to know what we do all day. I think he thinks we're vagrants."

Doc laughs loud and hard until he drifts into a wet cough. Outside, the palm trees rock in the sudden wind. The sky is darkening, and a couple of people run to and from their cars.

Doc spits into a napkin, which he crumples into a ball and places on the table. "We hold court, Blake," he says. "We say the things that need said. We ask the right questions." From the table in the corner a homeless man looks up from his newspaper and nods, mumbling something beneath his breath.

"Jesus," I say.

"Blake," Claire says. She's still staring out the window, both hands around her cup, which she holds still against her bottom lip. "I'm at a loss. You tell me what to do."

I don't ever remember such deference from her before. "We've got Bard by the Bay tryouts next week," I say. "Maybe you'll get a part, something good."

"Do you really think so?"

"Yes."

"I won't, though. I know I won't."

"If you do, you don't want to be looking for a new job. At least stay here until you know."

"Okay," Claire says. "I'll quit next week."

"Now you're thinking straight, little girl," Captain Lou says.

"I just get so pissed," Claire says. She takes a long sip of her drink. "I feel like I'm in the middle of one giant nursing home. It sucks the life out of me. I swear it does."

Doc leans over toward Claire. "Honey," he says, his voice high-pitched and affected. "I think it's time to change my diaper."

She swats him on the shoulder, and we all laugh. "Listen to me," she says. "I sound so hateful. I've become this hateful person." She looks at me, and I think I can see a slight quiver in her lips. She fidgets with her nose ring, and then turns away. Captain Lou sits down, and the first drops of rain splatter against the window.

Claire jerks upright in her chair and points down the sidewalk. "There she is!" she says. "Man, look at her go. Pain on wheels."

Mrs. Giffin rolls toward us, her cart at full throttle. Her orange flag snaps in the wind. Her husband follows, struggling to keep up. The wind flattens his clothing against his gaunt frame. He looks like a hobbling scarecrow. They both stop in front of our window and prepare to cross the street. It's getting darker.

Captain Lou squints and stares out. "Mabel?" he says. "Mabel's the one that hurt you?"

"If that's her name," Claire says. "What, you know her?"

"He knows everyone," I say. "He *talks* to everyone."

"I'll be damned," Captain Lou says, turning to Doc. "Mabel Giffin, the dancer."

"Ballerina," Doc wheezes.

Mr. Giffin points Mabel to the curb ramp. The rain falls in big drops.

"What are you talking about, ballerina?" Claire says.

Captain Lou stares out the window as he talks. "Yeah, ballerina," he says. "She was huge in New York, back in the thirties."

Doc nods. "She brought a whole album of pictures in for us one time. She was a cute little thing. Looked just like a little marionette."

Claire looks up at me, her nostrils flared and eyes big. "Can I just hang myself right now?" she says.

"It's funny," I say. "It's like ironic."

"I'm serious," she says. "I'll stick my head in the noose if you promise to kick the fucking stool out from under me."

The Giffins cross the street, Mabel in the lead again. Mr. Giffin follows with a newspaper held over his head. They reach their gold Cadillac, where he fumbles with his keys and opens the passenger door. He helps Mabel out of her scooter and guides her gently into the front seat. He rolls the scooter to the back of the car and lowers an electric ramp. The rain falls, thick and slanted by the wind. It's harder to see him now. Behind me, the phone rings, but someone picks it up.

"A fucking ballerina," Claire says. "Perfect."

Mr. Giffin drops the useless newspaper and secures the scooter to the back of the car. He's getting pelted by the rain and wind, but he finishes calmly and struggles toward the driver's side. Mabel pops the door open for him just before he arrives.

"Kind of cute, aren't they?" Captain Lou says.

Claire turns back to me. "Cute my ass," she says. She tries to smile, but her eyes are all welled up. That's all it takes.

I do it.

I squat down and kiss Claire right on the lips. She's surprised at first, her mouth rigid and unmoving. But I feel her soften and begin to reciprocate. I pull her closer, feel her relax against me. Her tongue slips across my teeth like a tiny eel. When she pulls away, she wipes her eyes with her thumb and index finger. The phone is ringing again.

"It's about time," Captain Lou says.

"A grand gesture?" Claire says to me. "Is that what that was?"

"Sure," I say. "Why not?"

She reaches above my right eye and scrapes something from my forehead. She holds it between us, a piece of dried tissue paper. She flicks it onto the floor and smiles. "I suppose we're in love now?" she says. "Is that how it works?"

There's a bright flash of lightning, and a crack of thunder rattles the glass in front of us. Claire starts and grabs tightly to my wrist. I put my hand over hers, and our fingers lock as we all move away from the window. I pull up a seat and sit. I let the phone ring away. Claire loosens her grip. She adjusts herself in her chair and lays her torso and head across my lap. I think I can smell the dog shit from Doc's shoe.

"It's not *Antony and Cleopatra*," she says. "It's not *Anna Karenina*, I have to admit."

No, I think, it's none of those things. But for now, it's good. For now, we can take it like this. Right here. Right now.

We sit, the four of us, watching the downpour together.

MAKING WEIGHT

A Morning Run

INTRODUCING FREDDY CLEVENGER, senior honor student at Ridgedale High School, who on this Thursday morning, just two days before the District Four wrestling tournament, wakes a full six pounds over the weight limit for the heavyweight class.

Trouble for sure, Freddy thinks, standing naked on the bathroom scale, his nipples distended from the cold. The morning newscast has warned of a hard freeze, one of the worst Central Florida has seen in years.

Freddy considers one of the formulas from the list taped to the medicine cabinet: $\lim f(x) = +\infty$ (or $\lim f(x) = -\infty$). That is, the function $f(x)$ is said to become infinite as x approaches c, if $f(x)$ can be made arbitrarily large. Freddy feels discouraged but reminds himself that the AP calculus exam is still over a month away.

He steps off the scale, then back on again, watches the digital numbers return to 281. Better not to mention his weight to Ron Ramsey, the captain of the wrestling team, who is probably jogging toward Freddy's house at this very moment and who is himself dropping from a solid 170 to 152, where Coach Evans thinks he can be a real contender at the state level. Ron wouldn't understand Freddy's plight. And he would almost certainly judge him for being so heavy this close to the tournament. He'd shake his head, give him that look that wonders how someone can be so sluggish and undisciplined, so incontinent. He would remind Freddy that, as seniors, they're supposed to set an example, that it's not just about individuals this year. This year they could actually win as a team.

Freddy's calf is still sore in the spot where last night's cramp sent him shooting out of bed and onto his feet until the clenching pain relaxed enough for him to limp to the kitchen for potassium, half a banana and a mouthful of orange juice that he drank guiltily, straight from the carton, in violation of his mother's specific rule. But that had been it. Nothing else, then back to sleep, yet he'd still managed to gain a pound in the night. It's the cold weather, maybe. He's expanding in it, the way ice does as it forms. But that's different. There's no change in mass. Still, it almost makes sense. The human body is seventy percent water after all.

He looks longingly at the sink faucet, the dripping moisture. A small sip would taste very good, cool and refreshing in his throat. But water is weight at this point, and after Saturday he can have all the fluids he wants for a while.

In the full-length mirror, he's an overflowing mass of baby-pink flesh, hairless except for the small patch of brown now nearly hidden by the overhang of his stomach, and from underneath it the head of his penis protrudes only slightly, a small purple knob, an acorn, and he cringes to think that here's the image the other wrestlers see during his weigh-ins, what elicits the occasional snicker from behind.

He slips on his underwear and sweatpants. Yes, much better to be clothed, where you can pull yourself together a bit, tuck it all up in a way that's not so grotesque. Properly packaged, his fat is just a funny append- age, and there are decent times, even moments of triumph: his portrayal of Teddy in last year's *Arsenic and Old Lace,* or the night of junior prom when, dressed in a baby-blue tuxedo, he pulled Becky Millard out of her seat and into the dance contest, which they won with a performance anchored by Freddy's outrageous improvisations—moonwalking and Travoltaesque sky points—that eventually forced everyone else to the spectating margins.

Later that night, while couples necked in the cozy dark of the char- tered bus, a dateless Freddy convinced the driver to give him use of the speaker microphone and, to the amusement of all, narrated the ride home with spontaneous witticisms and jokes of local color. And if there was an aspect of being laughed *at* that came along with the role, he could deal with that. Overall, he was genuinely liked.

Three soft knocks sound on the bathroom door, then his mother's voice from the other side. "Honey? Almost done in there? I have to be at work early today. I have to wash my hair."

Freddy sighs. He doesn't like being rushed. He cups the underside of his breasts, the light areolas stretched large. Bitch tits, Ron Ramsey called them once. And yet—Freddy lets them drop—they're probably a full cup smaller than last year. He was forty pounds heavier then, before the Florida Athletic Board did away with the unlimited weight class and placed the high mark at 275 pounds. The board had cited safety concerns, a need to limit dangerous mismatches. But how do you not take it as a personal insult? It's as if you've grown into something untenable, an aberration or monstrosity. There's probably an expressible relationship there: The function of a wrestler is said to become freakish as he exceeds 275 pounds and is, *by definition,* arbitrarily large.

He may be a better athlete below 275, quicker and more agile than he'd imagined he could be. And there is even something different about him in the shoulders now, he notices, from all the push-ups, maybe. He is not muscular, and yet he does have muscle, faint lines of sinew running beneath the blubber. Why, then, does it feel like something has been forfeited in the trade? Freddy sucks in his cheeks and chews on them lightly, trying to build up a little saliva. He bends over the sink but can only expel a fluffy drop of foam. He slips on his tee-shirt.

In the kitchen he finds his mother in her flannel bathrobe and long johns, doubled over the sink and washing her hair.

"I'm done, Mother," Freddy says. "You could've waited."

She finishes rinsing and rings out her hair like a dishrag. She hasn't heard him. She wraps a towel into a sort of turban, hurriedly, the way she does everything, as if to say someone's got to be fast and productive around here.

"I'm done, Mother," Freddy says again.

"Oh," his mother says. She looks surprised to see him. "I didn't know, honey. Sometimes you're in there so long."

In there so long? There's innuendo there, but he will try to let this go. Lately, she has seemed more tired than ever. Older, too. She will work two jobs today, Wal-Mart until four, then a half-shift at IHOP in the evening. They could lose the house, she has warned. And while this seems unlikely, the lingering possibility is troubling. With Melvin Mearle, Freddy's stepfather, dead for three years now, money is tight. They could fall behind and have to move into a small apartment. Freddy has seen these kinds of apartments and imagines he wouldn't be compatible with the tiny toilet and tub, the claustrophobic hallways.

Freddy opens the kitchen cabinet and takes out a jumbo-sized trash bag. He finds the scissors in the end of the knife block.

"Oh sweetheart," his mother says. Her face looks slack, defeated. "Not this morning, please. It's still dark, and everyone's windshield'll be froze up. You're liable to get run over and knocked into the ditch. No one would even know you were there."

The ditch is prevalent in his mother's fears, and there's something hopelessly superstitious about it, he thinks, some ever-present netherworld ready to suck you in. It has its roots in Christian folk traditions, he bets, or even back in some pagan past. But he must remember to be patient with her. "I'm over my weight, Mother," he says. "I don't really have a choice. Plus, Ron Ramsey's running with me today. I'm sure he'll call you if I'm in *the ditch*." Freddy struggles with the scissors. The finger holes are too small for him. Carefully, he cuts arm slits along the sides of the trash bag.

"Ya'll are running together?" She says. "Honey, you'll need to tell him today, then. His daddy came through my line the other morning and was asking me if you had one of them little refrigerators for your dorm room or if he should go ahead and buy one for Ronnie." She's got that frazzled look about her as she speaks. "I didn't know what to say."

Here's the subject that will ruin his day for sure. Doesn't he have enough on his mind? "I'll tell him, Mother," Freddy says.

"Son, you know if it was up to me, you'd go to whatever school you wanted."

"Mother," Freddy says. "I know. I'll probably tell him today."

And this is possible. He might tell Ron today, that he's made the decision and there's just no way he can go with him to Chilhowee College in Tennessee, where they've both been recruited to play Division III football and where they've made plans to share a dorm room and have all sorts of good times. Chilhowee is a private school: That's the whole problem. Even with financial aid, it's too expensive for Freddy and his mother, and with Freddy's full academic scholarship at Florida State, Tennessee just isn't practical.

But Freddy has let the confusion go on so long that now it feels too big to broach, and Ron is someone you naturally want to please. That was always the way, even when they were kids—sleepover buddies and tree house confidants—and now that they're older it's even harder, Ron being one of the chosen ones at school, one of the beautiful people who, if they're good enough to let you into their circle, you want to do what you can to keep them happy. Also, Freddy likes the public notion of their heading out together as college athletes, breathing crisp Smoky Mountain air.

Freddy cuts a head-sized hole at the bottom of the trash bag. His mother crosses her arms. "You know I hate this losing weight foolishness," she says. "I just know it's not good for you, not like this, anyhow."

He slips the bag over his head and slides his arms into the side slits, but he gets caught up halfway in and for an instant is stuck. He feels vaguely panicked until his mother helps him work the bag down his torso. The bag is tight, but not as tight as it once was. He can almost tuck it into his sweatpants. He goes to the living room and sits on the couch.

"The season's almost over," Freddy says. He tries to sound soothing. "I've gotten pretty good, you know. I could win district this year. Wouldn't that be something?"

"Honey," she says. "Of course it would."

"In the finals they have you wrestle under this big spotlight. The rest of the gym is dark, and it's just you and the other guy in the bright light. It's pretty neat."

"Honey," she says. "I'd love to see that. You know I would. I wish I could see all your games. I just can't stand to watch you out there getting all twisted up with those big boys. I swear, the last time I thought I would faint for sure."

"*Matches,* Mother," Freddy says. "Wrestlers have *matches,* not games." But she has moved into her bedroom now. He can hear her rummaging in the closet. He puts on his shoes, which are also looser than before.

A light whistle sounds in the front yard as Freddy finishes lacing, and he goes to the front window, pulls aside the curtain. In his driveway, a shadowy Ron is doing jumping jacks, quick and jerky, double-time.

"Here, honey." His mother is behind him, and when he turns she is holding out an orange hunting cap, the wool moth-eaten and covered with lint. "Wear this, at least," she says. "You'll be easier to see."

"I'm hard to miss, Mother," Freddy says, and regrets it immediately. He's fat. He doesn't need to remind her of this. It's hard enough for her already. It's hard for her because she thinks it's hard for him, pain for his pain.

"This was your daddy's hat, you know." She is still holding it between them.

"Yes," he says. He takes the hat from her. "Thank you."

By daddy she means Melvin Mearle, who married Freddy's mother when Freddy was just five, and despite the fact that he and Freddy seemed constantly at odds in Melvin's last years—not despite but because of this, maybe—Freddy *did* think of him as a father. Melvin was a barber and a lay minister, and he died of an aneurysm while preaching at a tent revival in Gibsonton. Freddy's real father was a man named Jim Schick, a *long-haired hippy,* he once overheard his grandfather say, *a good-for-nothing who passed though just long enough to cause trouble and drop his seed.* Freddy has never met Jim Schick, but he sometimes imagines him returning to Ridgedale as a clean-cut cosmopolitan, successful and benevolent, the prodigal benefactor returned to make good.

Freddy kisses his mother on the cheek—she will be gone before he returns—and pulls on his winter coat. He zips it up to his neck and lets her pull the stocking cap down over his ears. He lifts the waist of his sweatpants high over his coat, just below his chest. He slumps his shoulders forward and does a sort of tap dance routine. He stops, spreads his arms dramatically. "How do I look?" he says.

"Oh good lord," his mother says, but she is laughing helplessly. She tries to fix his sweatpants. "Lord, Freddy. Don't do that. You look like one of them crazy old men." And then she isn't laughing anymore. She is looking at him in the sad way she does sometimes; it's a look that realizes a time has come or that another time is passing, a look of missing someone even though he's standing in front of you.

"Mom," Freddy says. "Don't . . . ."

"No, no," she says. "I'm okay." She pinches him on his chin, pats him softly on the cheek. "You're just so grown up. I'm just so proud of you."

OUTSIDE, THE WIND blows cold into Freddy's face. The grass is frosted white and glistens in the carport light. Ron breaks his set of jumping jacks and catches his breath with his hands behind his head. He is over-garbed like Freddy, artificially thickened, but on him the stuffing is good, makes him look more substantial.

"Hey, Biggen," Ron says. "How's your weight?" He widens his legs and stretches toward the driveway.

"Over by a couple of pounds," Freddy lies. "You?"

"One fifty-five," Ron says. "Coach is going to have my ass."

"You'll be good," Freddy says. "The rest is water."

"Water?" Ron says, looking up. "Remind me what that is."

Ron will make weight just fine. Freddy has watched him lose it in a steady progression that would graph as a gently sloping arc if not a straight line. He'll be an even 152 on Saturday morning.

Ron reaches into his coat pocket and pulls out a stick of Big Red. He hands it to Freddy. "Here," Ron says. "Just don't swallow."

"Same as your girlfriend?" Freddy says. And he thinks this is a pretty good one, but then he feels bad, remembering that Ron doesn't have a girlfriend anymore. He and Andrea Hogan broke up last week.

They run into the darker streets at a steady pace, careful not to burn out too quickly. It's not so much about conditioning at this point so long as you sweat. To move steadily, that's the thing. Starve yourself and dehydrate. Weigh in on the money, then hit the fluids so that you're really wrestling at least five pounds over the weight limit. This shouldn't be the way with Freddy. He has the fat to lose and maintain, but he's glad for the mutual effort.

Freddy chews the gum enthusiastically and thinks of all the things he will eat when the season is over. Lasagna is at the top of the list, then macaroni and cheese. Pasta of all sorts. And then a sensible diet. With work, he could make 230 by the beginning of the fall, step on the FSU campus as a new man.

When they pass Ron's house, Ron's father is easing his pickup out of their driveway. He backs with his head sticking outside because the rear window is coated with ice.

"He headed to the orange groves already?" Freddy says.

Ron runs with his head down. "Yep," he says. "He was there most of the night, too. Had my tired ass out there till damn near midnight." Ron exhales loudly and sucks air through his nose. "It's this fucking freeze."

Freddy waves to Mr. Ramsey, but Ron doesn't look up at all. It's only Ron and his father who live in the house, now that Ron's sister, Claire, is off at college. Ron's mother is dead. She passed when he and Freddy were in the eighth grade, barely a year before Milton Mearle. Freddy used to have silly thoughts, like their surviving parents would console one another somehow, that eventually they would fall in love and marry, and he and Ron would be brothers.

Freddy sends a stream of sweet spittle to the road.

"Nice," Ron says. "Get rid of those bodily fluids."

"Yep," Freddy says, steadying his breathing. "Good excuse to jerk off." It's an old joke, but Ron laughs anyway.

They run side-by-side in the dark. Ahead of them Mr. Cauper pauses at the end of his driveway in robe and pajama bottoms, holding his newspaper in one hand. He looks up the street at them as they approach, watches until they pass by: a straight man and his fat sidekick, Freddy thinks. Abbott and Costello. Tennessee Tuxedo and Chumley. George and Lenny. Later, they will be at school, cleaned up and in street clothes, and no one will know about this time. But Freddy will remember it. It will be a sort of secret.

"Did you ever send in your housing deposit?" Ron asks.

Freddy runs, a warm fear rising in his chest. Quickly, he says, "I think my Mom did. I'll check and make sure."

"There's a fine if it's late," Ron says. "You need to borrow some money?"

"No," Freddy says. "She probably sent it. I'll check."

Freddy works hard to regulate his breathing. He feels light on his feet, like a tap dancer. He feels that he can run for a very long time.

In Class: AP English

Mrs. Tyson writes the word "synthesis" on the chalkboard in large block letters. She underlines it twice. In the margin of his notes, Freddy sketches probable brackets for Saturday's tournament. He will likely be the first seed. Early in the season, to his own surprise, he beat Terrell Banks, the holy terror from Lake Collins High. A fluke maybe, because Lake Collins had gone deep into the football playoffs, and Banks hadn't had much mat time, had to wrestle with his football lungs, and Freddy won by tiring him out. Most people think as long as you're in shape, it's all the same. It isn't true though.

Just the thought of again facing Banks, who has beaten Freddy in their other five matches, is enough to sour his stomach. And who knows if Freddy can even make weight. It's definitely no given after today's lunch fiasco.

"First of all," Mrs. Tyson says, "what does this word mean, 'synthesis'?" She stands in front of the board, chalk dangling at the end of her short arm. She smiles. No one speaks.

Freddy shifts uncomfortably in his seat. His desktop pokes into his stomach, which has not felt right since lunch. He had dutifully eaten a light salad and the small baggy of dry Total Raisin Bran that he'd brought from home, but the hunger pains became so distracting as the lunch period wound down—so slowly the clock seemed to move—that he bought another ticket and went through the line again, this time getting the full complement, which he ate in a flurry of ravenous guilt—from the hamburger to the apple crisp—before the bell sounded. Now, he needs badly to defecate, or just fart at least. Something.

"Donna," Mrs. Tyson says, "what do you think we mean by 'synthesis'?"

Donna sits one row across from Freddy. He watches her in profile. She stares intently at the word. Today she is in jeans and a blue wool sweater, not her cheerleading uniform, which means there is no basketball game tonight. Her creamy legs are hidden, those muscular calves of hers that taper into petite ankles in a way that will just break your heart. She shakes her head slightly. "Not real?" she says. "Like fake?"

"Okay," Mrs. Tyson says. She switches the chalk from one hand to the other. "As in 'synthetic'?"

Donna nods hopefully. In the fall, she will leave for the University of Florida, just like Andrea Hogan, who broke up with Ron last week. Freddy wonders what breaking up feels like. He had a girlfriend once, in elementary school, but her family moved back to Pittsburgh, Kansas, at the end of third grade.

"That's related, Donna." Mrs. Tyson says. "But we're looking for a broader meaning." She circles the prefix, "syn."

"Anyone else?" she says.

Synthesis, Freddy thinks, a merging together, a making one. Like chemicals coming together to form a compound. Across the room, Ron props his arm under his chin. He dozes in and out, his eyelids occasionally falling shut and resting peacefully for several seconds, and when they reopen, they are wide and surprised. He blinks. Last night he was out late in the orange groves, helping his father battle the freeze. And it was a school night. It seems to Freddy an over-manly thing to do. A grown-up responsibility. Aren't they still kids, more or less?

"The prefix 'syn,'" Mrs. Tyson explains, "is from a Greek word meaning 'together.' The root, 'thesis,' is also Greek, meaning 'to put or bring.' 'Synthesis,' as we'll use it, is a bringing together of separate concepts to form a coherent whole." Now under the word she writes "primary text" and "secondary texts." Centered beneath those, she writes "you/reader." She draws circles around each of the terms and connects them with straight lines, forming a triangle. "You have all chosen your primary text. You've done outside research. Now your task is to make sense of it all and develop your own original statement about the book." She underlines the "thesis" in "synthesis," draws a line into the middle of the triangle, and writes the word "thesis" there. "Your thesis should take into account what the book literally conveys, what your outside sources say about it, and your own particular insights in light of both. You have to synthesize the three into a coherent, argumentative statement. Here's your chance to say something no one else has said before."

That was an elegant presentation, Freddy thinks. Synthesis. Well illustrated. He has to give her that. She makes it sound intuitive, not like calculus, where one little error throws off everything. He looks across the room to gauge Ron's reaction, but his eyes have relaxed shut again. He is tired from working for his father, who wants to know whether or not to buy a small refrigerator for their dorm room.

Mrs. Tyson moves to her desk and takes a seat on the edge. Her short legs dangle childlike. She's tiny, really. She can't even be 110 pounds. Freddy is sure he could bounce her on his knee. "For the rest of the period," she says. "We'll draft possible thesis statements. Remember we say 'draft' because it's rare to get it right on the first take. Start small. Then add to your thoughts. This skill will be important in college, where you'll be expected to take your ideas to the next level." She smiles, gestures for the class to begin, and there is a reluctant sound of shuffling.

Freddy organizes his note cards into piles on his desktop. He thinks about *Animal Farm,* about pigs morphing into something else entirely. He thinks about revolution and absolute power, about Stalin. Trotsky. He is not sure there is anything new to say, or maybe the problem is that there's too much.

He had almost chosen *Anna Karenina,* had pulled the thick book from the library shelf, then that first line catching his attention, something about all happy families being the same but all unhappy families being unhappy in their own special way. He had wondered if he and his mother were unhappy. Sometimes it seemed like they were. He'd thought about Melvin Mearle, and about Ron and his father, and Ron's sister, Claire, who never seemed to come home, even on holidays.

But then the book had moved on about people who were waited on by servants and who sat around in drawing rooms, whatever those were. He prefers the Americans from last year. In those stories people really did things, fought wars and drank absinth, fled dust bowls or rode down rivers.

Freddy's stomach makes a prolonged squealing noise, too high-pitched and low in the gut to disguise as a hunger pain, the sound of intestinal gas that, denied escape, was shooting upward in despair, reverse farting. Donna looks over to him. She grins and shakes her head. Freddy shrugs, tries to smile back. He writes a line on his paper: In the novel *Animal Farm,* George Orwell uses . . . .

MYRNA ON THE BUS

IT IS NOT A MIRACLE, Myrna realizes. She's quite sure of that now. For only a short while she was uncertain, the way the two boys make their running starts, then glide impossibly across the top of the shallow rain puddles like two imitation Jesuses. But it is only a trick, like most things. She checks her watch. The sun is low and bright, so the shelter gives no real shade, and the heat from the metal bench seeps through her clothes, to her back, her rump. The unlikely truth about the puddle gliders: It has to do with wheels that lie hidden in the soles of their shoes but that the boys can apparently summon at will, coast along on them above the shallow water, and retract the wheels again when they reach the end of the puddle. On a better day Myrna might laugh at herself, at her mistake, but she has a lot to do still, and the strangeness of the experience has left her feeling disoriented. At seventy-three, she thinks, one should enjoy a certain calm.

It has been different for her, getting around town this way, different from her first six years spent in Florida, when she and Walter would drive past in the comfort of a car. At the level of the street, things are coarser in detail, the heat more unrelenting than she had imagined. She adjusts her weight and leans forward so she can look far down Fourth Street. She still has good eyes, and she can see the front of the bus in the distance, high and boxlike, distinct from the other cars. It will be here within five minutes, she figures, which will be on time, and this will allow her to get to the Winn-Dixie by 4:45. She only needs a tin of cinnamon. That's all she forgot yesterday. It's for the apple pie, her son John's favorite, and she wants to have it cooking, the smell filling the house, when he arrives tomorrow afternoon. She knows just what aisle the cinnamon is on. It will only take a minute, and then she can catch the 5:15 bus home. That is the last one that runs on Sunday.

It's bothersome that she forgot the cinnamon yesterday, when the Giffins were kind enough to take her to the market with them, but Mrs. Giffin, with that little scooter of hers, flew around the store like a race-car driver. Myrna hadn't wanted to be a burden and was forced to rush, and at times like that it is hard to concentrate and anyone's mind tends to forget things.

Myrna takes a single dollar from her purse and smoothes out the wrinkles. If Walter could see her now, he would not approve, but she can't help taking a certain satisfaction in the thought, as if to say, look what it has come to for me. Or maybe, look what I'm able to do when push comes to shove. Still, if he were here, he would drive her to the store. He might frown or grumble for a while, but he would take her and use the chance to pick up some Oreos or Funyuns, and they'd be back home again in no time. Funny that back then it had never seemed like a luxury.

Myrna still has her license, but she thinks maybe her driving days are finished. Once, several months ago, she tried to take the Oldsmobile to a doctor's appointment, but she had paused too long at a green light. The cars behind her had begun to honk loudly, and right after, agitated, she turned down a one-way street and into traffic. Once in a while she cranks the engine and lets it run a while, but mostly the car sits quietly in the garage, an artifact from an earlier time, she thinks, mocking her. But it is not too much. The bus. This outing. And tomorrow they will be here: John and his wife, Crystal, and Myrna's two granddaughters this time, whom she has not seen since Walter's funeral. Can it be a year already?

When the bus arrives, the two puddle-coasters are there with Myrna, their breaths coming hard, their bodies smelling warm and something like salty. Behind them, Myrna takes care to climb the steep steps without putting too much weight on her bad knee. At the top she lines up her dollar, feeds it into the bill accepter, which sucks it greedily away. The bus is not crowded, though, and Myna finds a seat near the front, on the same side as the Winn-Dixie. She finds the yellow bar that she will need to press for the "Stop Requested" sign. Requested, she thinks. No guarantees. She prefers the buses that have cables to pull, something to grab hold of, tug. Inside the bus it is cool, the air conditioner a comforting hum, but above this a group of girls at the back has begun a sort of song, a chant really, and with it there is a kind of coordinated slapping of hands. Myrna has seen them do it before, their limbs moving about quickly, striking each other's palms, always in rhythm. African American, Myrna thinks, although she is pretty sure that black is sometimes okay too, but not colored, not Negro, and she reminds herself that she is no racist. In Burlington, when she and Walter were schoolteachers, they had been active Democrats. They had volunteered for McGovern. It is only the noise, the loud voices that she is not used to, that aggravate her nerves. People are people. There are good and bad of all types. And the young man who yelled out to her the one day, when she was waiting for this same bus, and him with half his body hanging out of a car window, his face all contorted with meanness and yelling—something—she wasn't sure what, just that it was a meanness and she thinks the word "grandma" a part of it but not in any nice way, he had been a white man.

The bus stops at Fifty-Fourth Avenue, in front of an apartment complex, and the two puddle-gliders get off with a few others. Who gets on is a woman carrying an infant. She digs into a very large purse that hangs from her shoulder. She says something to the driver in Spanish, then sits across the aisle from Myrna. The child has dark black hair, thick and wild, and is dressed in a light-blue singlet, and Myrna thinks again of John, who, unlike this one, had very little hair for his first six months, just a thin coat of blond fuzz, and now, although marrying later in life, he is a father himself, twice over, and bald once again. Tomorrow he will eat too much, unbuckle his belt and groan in mock pain, but he will save room for pie, for ice cream, before taking a long nap in front of the television, and Myrna will sit and watch him like that, take in all of him that she can. And some time after that, the next day, perhaps, when Crystal and the girls are at the beach, she might take up something he said recently, how Florida has spoiled her and she'd never last through a Vermont winter. How her blood has thinned and she would miss her ocean, her bridge friends, the senior group at church, and anyway, with his traveling for work he is rarely in town.

The thing she'll need to get across: She does not love it here. Yes, the winters are cold in Vermont, but that's what heavy coats are for. It had been Walter's idea to sell the Vermont home three years ago, not hers, and there is really little left for her here. Being around so many others her age—the talk of operations, estate taxes, bowel movements—only makes her feel older, part of some wretched herd.

By the time the bus passes Sixty-Second Avenue, Myrna is cold. It's more old age than Florida-thinned blood, she thinks, this tendency to chill. She brings her legs together and tucks her skirt under each thigh, and this is better. Outside, the world passes slowly: a dentist's office, a seafood restaurant that supports Desert Storm, an all-night laundromat.

She does not need her son's permission to move back to Vermont. There is money enough. She could rent a small apartment. That's all she would need, but she isn't used to making such decisions on her own, and it would be nice to have some support.

Myrna senses the problem before she realizes what is happening, the sidewalk receding away from her in a way that is not right. Then the bus is in full left turn. They are going west on Sixty-Sixth now, toward the Gulf, away from the Winn-Dixie. She turns her body sideways and surveys the passengers around her, searches their faces for some kind of confusion or alarm, something like she has seen in the faces of airplane passengers in unexpected turbulence. But Myrna seems alone in this, yet she is sure that she saw the number 19 on the side of the bus. The girls in the back talk and laugh. Myrna prepares to speak to the woman across the aisle, but the baby is crying now. The woman holds him close to her chest, pats his bottom and whispers something into his tiny ear. The woman's eyes close, and she sighs sleepily.

They move on, past the Presbyterian Church and the Springfield Center, where Myrna recalls attending a craft show once. It is almost 4:40. She will have to really hurry now. They move beyond these places, to an area Myrna does not know well, headed—she doesn't know—someplace strange and remote maybe, where she might have to get out, stranded. She has some change in her purse. She could call the Giffins, maybe someone else from the church if she could find a phone book. But what would she say? There are taxicabs, she knows, but she isn't sure about the men who drive them or even if they would accept a check. She has never been inside a taxi. They seem theoretical to her, the way buses once did. Or African Americans. Or widowhood.

It should not be this hard.

When the bus makes a right turn, Myrna is encouraged. A possible return to Fourth? Yes, a rectangular detour, she decides. The child has settled, and Myrna bolsters herself to speak. She has a soft voice, and the worst thing is to ask a question and not be noticed. She leans toward the woman, who throws her purse strap over her shoulder.

"I was wondering," Myrna says. "This is route 19, I think? Aren't we on the 19?"

The woman looks up at Myrna. She seems surprised by the sudden advance, and she doesn't answer right away. "Yes," the woman says finally. She pronounces the "y" with something like a "j" sound. "This is the 19." The woman stretches her neck and looks up the road in front of them. She pushes the yellow band, and the soft tone sounds.

"It's just that I don't remember coming off of Fourth this way before," Myrna says. "I need to get back to Fourth."

The woman looks straight ahead. "Yes," she says. "It *will* take you back to Fourth." Myrna doesn't like the tone of her voice. It says something like, I have my own concerns, old lady. Just go off quietly and be happy you're still alive. Myrna wants to tell her that she understands. You would think at some point a person would stop wanting, stop needing, but it isn't the case. It's not the way it works.

"I just have to get to the Winn-Dixie before the buses stop running," Myrna says. She looks at her watch. It is 4:46. She wants it clear that she has a purpose, that she is a mother too and people are depending on her. She says, "My son is coming to visit tomorrow."

The brakes make a high-pitched hum as the bus comes to a stop, and the woman stands with her child and her giant purse. She begins to make her way down the aisle, but pauses, seems to think a moment, before turning to Myrna. The woman's face is labored, as if this is a great effort for her, but she speaks to Myrna. "This is the 19 to Seventy-Second," she says. "It doesn't go any farther north. What you need is the 19 to Gateway. That takes you all the way down." She gives Myrna something like a smile before moving away, down the aisle, descending the steps and out into the daylight.

The doors close. The bus jerks into motion and begins to gain speed. It's cold. Myrna can feel it in her hands and feet. "I need the 19 to Gateway," she says. But the seats around her are empty, and there is no one she could be talking to.

HURRICANE PARTY, 2002

FELDMAN SITS on the carpeted floor of his apartment, unsuspecting, in the glow of the television, back slumped and pen suspended over a stack of student essays. The one he's grading: an analysis of alcoholism in two Raymond Carver stories. It's a competent argument, he supposes, but too skeletal, like checking off a grocery list. It needs more fleshing out, heart.

This is before the fistfight, before the bar and the whole mess with Mr. Riley, just seconds before Claire's unannounced visit. And when her first knocks come, loud and hurried, Feldman is startled. He pauses, a bottle of Afrin aimed into his left nostril. He listens to the following quiet, not quiet really but the sound of rain and wind outside the apartment, a prelude to tropical storm Jared. Just wait, Feldman thinks. Wait, and whoever it is will go away. The thought of another person—friend, landlord, or bug man—inside his home, walking among the considerable filth, is unsettling. He sprays the mist into his nose, inhales as quietly as he can. But the knocking returns, louder now, more insistent.

He stands, brushes off his khakis, looks around for the most embarrassing thing, and decides on the old bowl of cereal balanced on the ottoman, bloated Cheerios floating in a pool of sickish milk like fuzzy little corpses. He dumps them in the kitchenette sink and goes reluctantly to the door, which he opens to find—to his great surprise—his beloved friend Claire. She's wet and shivering, a bottle of lemon-flavored

Absolut in one hand. An extinguished cigarette dangles wet and limp from the other.

"You," Feldman says.

"Me," Claire says. She walks past him, stepping over a backpack and kicking a crumpled Extra Value Meal on her way to the refrigerator. She opens the door, shakes her head at the emptiness, and sets her bottle on the top shelf. Feldman takes a towel off the couch, sniffs it—something like mint, mouthwash maybe—tosses it to Claire. He watches her dry herself, her face first, then her short blond hair.

He hasn't seen her since Michelle and Dirk's wedding reception, early summer. And didn't the two of them kiss that night, maybe, a slow deep embrace outside by his car? They did, he remembers, and then she hadn't returned his calls for a while afterward. She's here now, though, and he wonders to what he owes this honor, this crossing of the bay with a potential hurricane on the way, her arriving here in North Tampa, unannounced.

"I got mother-freaking evacuated," Claire says. "Apparently, I live in a level four flood zone. Doesn't that flipping kill you?"

Feldman wonders at these new substitutions: "freaking" and "flipping." Maybe she has found religion again. She's back in grad school, he remembers, going for a teaching certification this time. She wants to mold young minds, she'd said. A year ago she was sure she wanted to be a midwife. Before that a stage actor.

She works the towel under her short black skirt. She dries her thighs, marvelous thighs, small but muscular too, dancer's thighs, Feldman thinks. They are both thirty-four, but she has held up better. "It's so typical," she says. "Just when things are starting to look up for me."

Feldman says, "There's really a mandatory evacuation?" But Claire isn't listening. She closes in on the television, which features a storm preparedness checklist.

"Do you have a flashlight?" she says. She lowers herself to her knees at the base of the screen. "Do you have a battery-powered radio? Extra water, a gallon for each person? What about a first-aid kit? David, I bet you don't even have a first-aid kit. Are you even prepared at all?"

"I think I have a box of Band-Aids in the medicine cabinet," he says. "I'd have to check."

She smiles now, seems to let her glance rest on him for the first time. "Let's get drunk," she says. "Totally, hopelessly drunk." She looks around the room, crinkles her nose. "But not here. Let's go out. Let's have a hurricane party."

Feldman would like to explain that it is not so simple, that there is a way of being that sets you out of sync with the rest of the world. He's become unstuck. But not in a temporal way. For Feldman it feels, what? Spatial, maybe. He's forgotten how to be a person among people.

"It'll have to be a tropical storm party," he says. "It got downgraded." He looks down at his socked feet, at the hole that exposes most of his left big toe—a terrible toe, he decides, wholly unattractive—too long and narrow, more like a finger really. "I don't know, Claire. I'm not quite sure I can go out tonight."

She drops the towel on the floor and moves toward him. "Why not?"

"I feel antsy," Feldman massages his sternum. "I think I'm having palpitations or something. Plus," he points to the stack of essays. "I have to grade."

"Surely classes are canceled."

"They haven't announced it yet."

With her fingers, Claire smoothes her hair into a neat part that makes her look almost boyish. She moves closer, seductively, he thinks. She hugs him tightly, presses the top of her wet head underneath his chin. He feels vaguely squeamish, unused to the close contact. But Claire's hands drop to his buttocks, and she squeezes playfully, alternating cheek-to-cheek, the way she once did when they were undergrads, drinking buddies, fellow potheads: for far too brief a stint, lovers.

"Shoes," she says, her face upturned now, grinning. Her breath is already thick with the vodka. It's a hospital smell, but also lemon drops and cigarettes. "What else would you do?"

"Plenty," Feldman says, and he lists the things on his fingers. "Wallow in self-loathing. Huddle naked in a dark corner, in the fetal position. Contemplate the absurdity of the human condition. You know, lots of things."

"You *see*." Claire squeezes him harder. Her nipples, erect from the rain and cool air, press against his ribs. "You always say the best stuff. My troubled professor friend." She is almost hurting him now, her thin arms constricting with disproportionate strength.

"Instructor," Feldman says. "Adjunct instructor."

OUTSIDE THE WINDOW of University Tavern, not yet 5:00, the light fades to near darkness. It rains softer now. The wind blows drops against the window. Feldman, with his back against the bar, stares out onto Fowler

Avenue, at the gray sky interrupted by an occasional SUV or semi-truck, one lonely U-Haul. A tin can skids quickly across the parking lot.

When Claire excuses herself to the restroom, Marcus, from behind Feldman, says, "She's cute, man. What the hell's she doing here with you?"

Feldman rotates on his stool and pushes an empty beer mug toward Marcus, who half-smiles amid a frame of dreadlocks.

"An off night for her, I guess," Feldman says. "She's slumming."

"I thought all white people stayed in till after eleven on Thursdays," Marcus says. He tilts the mug under the tap. "Thought you were all watching the Must See Tee-Vee."

"Right," Feldman says. He says, "Still in reruns." It's good to be here with Marcus. Old friend Marcus. High school band buddy. Homie.

"We're supposed to get surges from the outer bands tonight," Feldman says. "You staying open?"

"Tonight, I'm open," Marcus says. He lights a Kool and blows the smoke sideways from his mouth. "Tomorrow, probably. It's just a category one. Shouldn't be too bad. And it's turning west anyway, toward the peckerwoods in Texas."

"I thought it was just a tropical storm."

"No," Marcus shakes his head, and the dreadlocks sway gently. "It's definitely a category one." He points to the television above. "And the water's warm enough. Could be category three before it hits land."

Claire returns from the restroom. She slides onto the stool next to Feldman and places her hand on his shoulder. "You haven't said anything about my hair," she says.

"I like it," Feldman says.

"Better than when it was long?"

"I liked it long," Feldman says, "but I like it now too."

A student approaches and leans against the bar. His short hair is still wet, as if he just got out of the shower. He seems loose, comfortable, well-scrubbed.

"What's up boss?" Marcus says to the student. "Another pitcher?"

The student looks back into the poolroom a moment. He's grinning. He slips a foot out of an Adidas sandal and scratches his shin with his toe. "Please," he says. "And me and my friend back there want to buy a round for these two." He points to Claire and Feldman. "Whatever they're drinking."

Claire locks her arm inside Feldman's. She leans into him and says, loud enough for the student to hear, "I think it may be one of my young fans. I have them, you know, all over the Bay area." Then whispering to Feldman, "But don't worry. I promise not to ditch you tonight."

It's the brashness that annoys Feldman at these moments, not that he and Claire can look much like a couple. He'll grant that. Still, he doesn't like the brashness of the kid, who now offers his hand in greeting. Feldman accepts it, ready to squeeze with all his strength, but the boy's grip is surprisingly gentle. He smiles and slips his foot back into the sandal.

The boy nods toward the poolroom again. "My friend had your English class," he says to Feldman. Feldman turns around to see himself being watched through the wooden bars that separate the poolroom. The watcher: a thick stocky figure in a baseball cap. He stands beside a young woman and holds a pool stick at his side.

And Feldman recognizes this young man with the pool stick; the face begins to link with a composition class, last spring perhaps. Oh yes, the cocksure defiance, semi-literate personal essays dotted with anecdotes of high school football glory, the general classroom opposition. Feldman's gut feels thick and heavy. The student is moving away, carrying the pitcher toward his friend.

"A fan of *yours* then." Claire smiles, disappointed. "The guy in the back, I mean."

Feldman says, "His name's John Riley."

"You must have made an impression."

"I'm pretty sure I failed him," Feldman says.

Claire drinks through her straw. Her eyes tilt up and leftward as the clear liquid recedes from the ice. She swallows. "How *are* your classes?" she says.

Feldman starts to respond but the jukebox rises into play, and Claire sings along with the lyrics. Feldman doesn't recognize the song. A few more patrons enter, and he focuses on his new beer, which tastes faintly metallic, but cold and otherwise okay. But the presence of Riley has sent him off-kilter. As a child he was always bothered by encounters with teachers in public places, these school entities—not even people really—encroaching on his secular world. It occurs to him that now he feels the same way about his students. Seeing them anywhere but under the fluorescent lights of the classroom—the notion of them shopping, drinking, eating, pooping—is disconcerting. He finds his Afrin in his shirt pocket and squeezes short blasts into both nostrils. The salty taste gathers at the base of his throat. Behind him, beneath the music, he can hear the faint sound of pool balls smacking against one another. On the television above the bar, Storm Team 8 gives an update. No change in the projected path, but hurricanes are unpredictable. Stay tuned for continued coverage.

Outside, more wind and rain.

"What are you thinking about, darling?" Claire says, her favorite question.

"I was thinking that I hope they cancel classes tomorrow," he says, not untruthfully. He takes a cigarette from Claire's pack. "I really do."

"You're addicted, you know," Claire says.

"What? To smoking?" He lights the cigarette. "Not a chance."

"No." She points to the bottle of Afrin on the bar. "You're a big addict. You've been using the stuff so long that your sinuses are too f'd up to work right without it. It's true. I read about it in *Prevention*."

"What's with the PG language?" Feldman says.

"It's my new reinvention of myself," she says. "I'm linguistically inoffensive. But you're changing the subject. Typical addict maneuver."

"I have chronic nasal congestion."

"That's because you're addicted," she says. "Yep, you've got a huge monkey on your back." She ashes onto the floor. "What does it feel like when you go too long without a fix?"

Feldman drinks his beer and reads a list of local evacuation shelters on the television screen.

"What's the withdrawal like?" Claire says. "I want to know. Is it like the DTs? Do you shake? Do you hallucinate? Do you feel like bugs are crawling on you?"

"What are you even *talking* about?" He tries to sound perplexed, indignant.

"I'm talking about what it would feel like for you to go a day without your precious nasal spray."

"I don't go a day without nasal spray."

"I know, but if you had to be without it, for the whole day. Morning to morning."

"I don't really think about it, Claire." Feldman watches the television, the animated likeness of Florida, the green peninsula dipping phalluslike between the Gulf and the Atlantic. And the storm, an impressive depiction of swirling clouds, a well-defined eye in the center. Marcus was right. Category one hurricane. Feldman tries to will it northeastward, just close enough for a precautionary shutdown of the university. With the prospect of a long weekend, many things seem possible.

"Of course you don't think about it," Claire says. "But what *if* you had to go without it?"

"Jesus," Feldman says. His cigarette is suddenly disgusting. He crushes it out, pushes the ashtray away. "Imagine some giant elephantine fat-ass, some modern day Gargantua sitting on your face. Can you imagine that?"

Claire stares at him, her mouth slightly open, her eyes fixed and serious. "Yes," she says. "I'm quite sure that I can. Would it feel like that?"

"No," Feldman says. "Nothing at all like that."

FULL NIGHT NOW, and Claire has managed to coax together an unlikely group, faces shrouded in darkness, streaked with neon, looking smoother, more attractive, all laughing. Marcus is behind the bar, and seated are Riley, the guy in Adidas sandals, Claire, Feldman, and to Feldman's right two young women. Feldman sits at the corner of the bar, the point pressing uncomfortably into his stomach. He is the butt of Claire's current joke, the reason for the laughter.

Claire elbows his ribs. Marcus, who laughs hardest, silently, raises the bottle of tequila over the last shot glass, his own. He presses his free hand against his side as if holding something vital in place. An electronic dartboard bleeps in the background.

"No shit?" he says, catching his breath. "My boy was passed out on the toilet?"

Claire continues her story. "Unconscious," she says. "And we figured he'd been there for at least three hours before we found him."

"It was the shrimp in lobster sauce," Feldman says, but the words come out slurred. He swallows. "That and the Jim Beam."

More laughter from all.

This is okay, Feldman thinks. He finishes the tequila in his glass. This is fellowship, human interaction. Let these people hear he's a person with wild stories of his own.

The girl to his right, Jordan is her name, smiles at him. She wears dark-rimmed glasses that go nicely with her round cheeks. She reminds Feldman of some previous era, some vague time passed. Her friend: Jane? Joan? She smiles too, but she is less enthusiastic, typing occasionally on her cell phone.

Feldman studies Claire's face. He tries to think of the word that best describes her when she's this drunk. Puckish? He decides on Elfin.

"I'm sorry," Claire says. She pats Feldman's thigh. She's enjoying this. That's why she invited the others over, for an audience. Even when it's not about her, it is. Wasn't that why she kissed him this summer, to make herself central again? Force him to wonder, hope. She finds a way to get the attention she needs. Hear me. See me. Love me. Give me a little more consideration than you think I could possibly want.

Claire takes a sip from her glass and continues. "So someone took a picture of him like that, his pants around his ankles, dead to the world, just like mother-fucking Elvis!" She pounds her tiny fist on the bar with the last few syllables. "And for our whole fourth year," Claire says, once she's composed herself, "everyone called him *The King.*"

Renewed laughter from all, except for Riley, who does not seem won over and whose smile is more like derision, Feldman thinks.

"We're going to shoot some pool," Riley says to Jordan and her friend. "Come join us if you feel like it."

Riley and his friend move back to the poolroom together, but Feldman is happy to see that Jordan pays them no attention. Instead, she turns directly toward him. She brushes aside a wisp of hair from her eyes and loops it behind her ear. "So, David," she says, this Jordan. "You teach in the English Department."

"I do," Feldman says.

"Do you know Dr. Henry? I'm taking her African American lit class."

Feldman does not know associate professor Margaret Henry, not really. She's beyond his circle. He tries to think if they've spoken and remembers maybe a brief exchange at the mail cubbies once, something about conflicting meetings, some scheduling problem.

"Sure," Feldman says. "I know Meg."

Claire laughs and spits an ice cube back into her glass. "Sorry," she says.

Jordan smiles, dimples showing at the corners of her mouth. "Isn't she brilliant?" she says. "We're reading *Iola Leroy* right now. I think it's just beautiful."

Feldman does not think the novel is an especially beautiful one, all overwrought emotion and sermonizing, a syrupy tale of postbellum redemption. But he likes Jordan very much. "Oh," he says. He concentrates on his words, wants to sound something like coherent. "Yeah. That book, well it's seen a sort of rebirth lately. The sentimental novel in general, it's being reconsidered."

"Reconsidered?" Jordan says. She tilts her head slightly.

"Yeah," Feldman says, something like confidence rising in his chest. If she is a literature groupie, he may be able to interest her for a while.

To interest a nice girl would be something. "Critically, I mean. Books like that were . . . ." His head is cloudy and he can't think of the word he wants. "Popular," he says, finally. "In their day they were popular, but modern critics didn't like them much."

"If it wasn't ironic, it wasn't worthwhile!" Claire almost yells this, leaning across Feldman toward Jordan. "And if it was written by some damned scribbling woman, forget about it!"

"Right," Feldman says. "Exactly. Direct sentiment equaled bad literature. That idea is still pretty dominant."

Jordan removes her glasses, inspects the lenses. She is the type of girl some call plain but who is not plain at all, only pretty in a more nuanced way. "Yeah, I totally get the whole iceberg thing," she says. "But sometimes I think if something is sad or joyful it should just go ahead and say so, you know?"

"Amen, sister." Claire says. "Are you an English major?"

"I was," Jordan says. "I graduated in the spring. I'm applying to law schools."

"There's a book you might like," Claire says. "*Charlotte Temple*. It's another sentimental novel." She makes air quotes over the word *sentimental*. "It's gotten quite a bit of recent treatment."

Jordan slips her glasses back on and takes a pad and pen from her purse. She is a smart one, a serious student, the kind who tests out of Feldman's composition courses. He and Claire were like that once. So earnest. They would get drunk and read poetry aloud late into the night, debate Kant like it meant something. He is sure they did that, at least once they did.

Jordan makes a brief note.

Claire now has her knees up on her stool. "The author is Susanna Rowson," she says. "She was America's first professional person of letters."

Feldman thinks he should let it go, but he says, "Most still say that would be Charles Brockden Brown."

Claire keeps her eyes on Jordan. "That's because the literary canon was constructed by white men," she says. "Rowson was a bestseller almost a decade before Brockden Brown published a word."

"That's true," Feldman says. He tries to sound deferential, matter-of-fact. But he wants to show Jordan that he knows things. He has specialized knowledge. "But at that time she was an English citizen. She wrote *Charlotte Temple* in England."

"She was American-born, David." Claire turns slowly to him. "The book is *about* America. She moved back to the states after she got married and lived here for the rest of her life. Writing."

Jordan's friend keys at her cell phone. Feldman thinks he catches her roll her eyes.

"I think you're probably right," he says. "There's a case to make. Like I said, a lot of writers are being reconsidered. The climate is definitely changing."

Feldman looks to Jordan, then Marcus, who is bouncing a quarter on the surface of the bar. Feldman says, as if to apologize, "It's sort of a minor controversy in American lit. Who was our first professional novelist?"

"I can hear, fool," Marcus says. "I just don't care."

He's right, of course. It's all regurgitated dribble, anyway, taken from an undergrad seminar he and Claire had together: The Novel in Early America. When did their lives become so derivative? Once, Feldman thought he might scrape out a small niche for himself, rediscover a forgotten author, or suggest a new perspective of a known work. Contribute in some small way. But lately it seems to take all of his resolve just to get out of bed.

"Let's talk about something else," he says.

"That's right." Marcus lights a new Kool. "You don't want to offend the unschooled Negro bartender. What can he know about book learnin'?"

The women focus on their drinks. Feldman forces a laugh. "You just said," he begins, but he stops himself. "You shouldn't drink tequila. And you're not unschooled. You've got a degree in political science. For God's sake, you grew up in Tampa Palms."

"Tell me how that matters if I need to hail a taxi."

"Hail a taxi?" Feldman says. "In Tampa? I'd love to see that. That would be awesome."

"Mother-fucker," Marcus says. He stands with chest out and smiling. "I am o-pressed."

And okay, fine, Feldman is about to say, but Marcus is looking past them now, not talking anymore, then slipping around the bar and gone.

There's a fight in the poolroom, or rather a near fight, insults and posturing, several people yelling at once. On this side of the wooden bars Feldman can see a young woman, short and busty, maybe a cheerleader. Her hair is a blonde that's almost white. She stands, chest heaving, shouting at Riley and his friend. Two other young men stand behind her, but they are smaller than their counterparts and seem less invested. The cheerleader waves her finger near Riley's friend's face, and he, fists clenched at his sides and rigid all over, controls himself with seeming difficulty.

For Feldman there is a blurriness to the figures, not double-vision exactly, but moving in that direction. He closes his right eye.

"Jeez," Claire says as Marcus emerges among them, shouting something about the goddamned police, and then a slight calming among the students. "They're on their way right now!" Marcus says.

When Marcus is behind the bar again, Claire asks, "Are you really going to call the police?"

"Yeah right," he says. He dries his forehead with a dishtowel. "That's just what I need, for them peckerwoods to get the police over here, me and my drunk ass."

Feldman looks up at the television in time to see that university classes are indeed canceled. He lets his knee drift very slowly to his right, until it brushes against Jordan's, and she does not recoil in disgust.

WITH RILEY AND HIS FRIEND GONE, Feldman feels lighter. He works on a life plan. He is not wholly undesirable, he reasons, not without prospects. He had potential once. There may still be time. He will update his vitae, make detailed lesson plans, try to publish. He'll take better care of himself, get more exercise, work on his posture. He'll volunteer like he's been planning to, meet people of like mind. And no more fast food, that's a given.

But his Jordan, so charming and smart, will be leaving him soon, cutting short their flirtation. Not really a flirtation—he couldn't call it that—but a nice conversation at least. He senses her preparation, a yielding to the restless friend who has given her several pleading looks. Feldman searches for a reason to exchange contact information. He could write down his email address. That's less presumptuous than a phone number, no?

If he can ever be of assistance in any way, he can say. He's still working on his wording when Jordan stands. She addresses Claire first. Their hands clasp in front of Feldman. It was wonderful meeting her, Jordan says, and Claire says likewise and good luck with law schools. Jordan looks at Feldman now, and she takes his hand businesslike, shakes firmly. "I'm happy to meet you, sir," she says.

She does not release his hand immediately, and there is something in the way she pauses without looking away, a space of possibility for an interjection of some kind, something more than simple politeness.

"Indeed," Feldman says. He tries to speak deliberately, not to stutter. "Drop by my office some time. We'll talk sentimental novels." It is not the best line, not the embodiment of wit, but it could have been worse. It wasn't terrible. But when Jordan leaves, Feldman feels the possibility drain away, like the fleeting remnants of dream after waking. Marcus is busy rinsing mugs. Claire smokes a cigarette and makes a show of looking away from Feldman.

"What is it?" he says. "What's wrong?"

Claire's look is all wide-eyed surprise. "Nothing," she says. "I'm perfectly fine."

He doesn't say anything else, which is the best response—he's learned—at times like this, and soon Claire does seem fine. They drink, joke like before. He wonders about sleeping arrangements. He should offer her his bed. He isn't sure, though, when he last washed his sheets.

"What are you thinking?" Claire says.

"I was thinking I may become a vegan."

She doesn't respond. She puffs deeply, stares straight ahead. "I hate my life," she says.

"What?" Feldman laughs. "Why do you say that?'

Claire chews lightly on the end of the straw. "I don't know what's wrong with me. I've been stuck on Gooey Gumdrop lately."

Gooey Gumdrop. Feldman remembers the analogy, remembers playing Candy Land—a child's board game—in college, often quite stoned, but always at Claire's insistence, three or four friends usually, marveling at the bright colors, the design and layout, concluding that the creator *had* to be on psychedelic drugs. They played seriously, avoiding pitfalls like Lollipop Woods and Molasses Swamp. But Gooey Gumdrop was a particularly demoralizing hazard because it trapped you so far back on the board.

Claire takes a deep sip through her straw. "I guess I wish," she begins, but then stops. The words come out strange, and her lower lip quivers. "I'm going to throw up," she says. She looks at Feldman as if she's waiting for an assessment. "I'm totally going to throw up."
Feldman starts to offer his empty mug.

"Get her to the bathroom, fool!" Marcus says, and Feldman stands, feels himself sway to the side.

But Claire holds him off with a forearm, puts up an index finger. She shakes her head. She swallows. Burps. "It passed," she says. "But I think I want to go home now."

Outside, the rain has stopped. The parking lot glistens black and shiny under the lights. Feldman fishes in his pocket for Afrin. Claire, revived, dances across the asphalt, ballerina style. She is in mid-pirouette when the shouts come, nearby but slightly muffled. "Hey Miss. Do you know your boyfriend's a faggot?"

It's Riley's voice. Claire stops dancing and looks around, confused. From a dark Cherokee parked near the street a single arm hangs, thick and imposing, out of the passenger window. The door opens, and Riley emerges. He sets a beer bottle on the roof of the Jeep. His arms hang loose from his broad shoulders. His friend gets out of the driver's side and leans against the Jeep.

"Who is he talking to?" Claire says, still confused. "Is he talking to me?"

"I don't know," Feldman says. "Let's just go." He finds his keys. "Come on." He takes Claire's hand, moving toward his car.

"What's wrong, Professor?" Riley says. "It's true, isn't it?"

Now Claire stops, firm, tries to go toward Riley. Feldman can barely hold her back.

"Fuck off." She says. "Ass-*hole!*"

Feldman feels a cool instability in his legs as Riley steps toward them, his face creased suddenly with anger, and Feldman wonders if there is some rule he might evoke, some harsh consequence for harassing a former instructor in a parking lot.

Riley says, "It's true, you know." He points to Feldman. "He told us in class that all the writers were a bunch of queers that liked to go into the woods and butt-fuck each other." Riley sways slightly to one side. "Didn't you?" he says. His eyes are wide and insistent. "Didn't you?"

Feldman wants to yell back that he said no such thing, that it's a ridiculous notion, but his throat is tight and he's afraid he'll squeal. Also, there's a chance he may have an idea what Riley is referring to, something he says in class at times, a way of locating a work in a particular tradition. Just the fact that lots of American narratives include a kind of male escapism, the retreat to the river, the sea, the wilderness. A movement away from domestic space into a motherless, wifeless realm, a homosocial and—maybe he even said homoerotic—communion of men. But Riley has mixed it all up.

"How's it feel?" Riley asks Claire. "How's it feel to know your boyfriend's a big giant cocksucker?" Riley steps forward, but Claire moves in front of Feldman, between the two of them.

"If this is about your grade, Mr. Riley," Feldman says.

"Fuck the grade, faggot," Riley says. His torso seems to revolve in a small orbit. "You keep the piece of shit grade."

"Such eloquence," Claire says. "And a homophobe to boot."

"Claire, this isn't necessary," Feldman says.

Riley smirks. His friend makes no move from the Jeep. He only stands, smiling, watching interestedly.

"It's all terribly obvious," Claire continues. She seems suddenly sober, clear-headed and precise. "You're having feelings, Mr. Riley. Conflicts. Impulses that you don't quite know how to handle. Sometimes what we desire most is also the most terrifying. It's okay," she says. "Lot's of guys have those feelings. At least one in ten, I hear."

Riley's friend laughs loudly. Riley's face contorts, and Feldman knows he will have to intervene somehow. "Mr. Riley," he says. "John." His voice sounds tinny and embarrassingly frail, but he feels if maybe he could press through, clarify, he could still make things right. "It's just . . . ." Feldman tries to swallow. "Just a paradigm, an archetypal structure."

With this, the friend doubles over with more laughing. And it *is* funny, Feldman realizes. The whole situation is ridiculous, and it isn't about archetypal structures or his sexuality, or even butt-fucking writers, not for Riley. It's something more basic and biological, some unnamable need born of beer and rage, a thing with real inertia though, which is going to play itself out.

"It's okay to have naughty little thoughts sometimes," Claire says.

"Claire," Feldman says. "Please." He feels his sinuses closing up.

Riley takes another step. He's almost on top of them. "You want to know about me, little miss?" he says. "How about I show you right here?"

Riley reaches for Claire's wrist, the thick fingers closing in on her, and Feldman watches helplessly as his own hand slaps Riley's away.

Feldman backpedals clumsily, absurdly. "I never said that," he says.

Riley swings, a wide arching punch, but misses. Feldman sees the fist, feels maybe a brush of air as it passes right in front of his face. He tries to shout for Claire to get Marcus, but his words come out unintelligible. He feels dream-heavy, ineffectual.

"I'll call the cops," Claire says. "Leave him alone!"

Feldman is caught by the shirt now, just beneath the collar. He ducks under the next punch, covers his face and can feel the blows to the back of his head that, strangely, don't hurt the way he would expect them to, but that feel cold and dull. He falls, knees striking hard against the pavement; the punches go into his body now. His back. His ribs. He tries to call out. Can't. Sees, through his fingers, a single tennis shoe, and throws both arms around the supporting leg, drives his shoulder into the kneecap as hard as he can, and feels, inexplicably, Riley go down.

"Mother-fucking faggot," Riley says, and he is rising from the pavement. But Feldman is already up and has the angle now. There is probably enough time to break for his car, but instead he charges forward and drives his fist into Riley's face.

IN THE LIVING ROOM, on a patch of carpet now cleared of debris, Claire holds an ice pack to Feldman's head while they watch disaster footage on the television: mobile homes twisted like soda cans, houses gutted to the core, trees downed, and power lines exploding like fireworks. But these are old pictures, from Hurricane Andrew in '92, reminders of what *can* happen. A man on the screen stands before his roofless home. He fights back tears as he speaks.

Claire presses the ice pack firmly. "You really had him there for a minute," she says. "I mean, you were *totally* holding your own." She unbuttons the top of his shirt, which is spattered with blood, not all his. "It was." She pauses. "I hate to say it, and it makes me a bad feminist, but the way you protected me, that male defensive instinct, it was a little bit sexy."

"Thanks," Feldman says. A local reporter appears on the screen and warns that although it appears that the storm will miss the Bay area altogether, viewers should not become complacent in the future.

"I've never imagined you like that," Claire says. "I mean, fighting for Christ's sake."

"Who knew?" Feldman is fairly ecstatic. He *was* fighting. Actual blood was drawn. He is bleeding at this very moment.

Claire is silent. She retracts the ice pack and inspects his wounds. The blood pulses heavily at his temple. It hurts, yet it is also good. It's the swelling that he likes. His temple, knuckles, knees, lips. A general expanding, like the productive pain of growth. He shifts, feels a sharp pain at his hip joint. His fingers fumble around the carpet until Claire presses the Afrin into his palm.

There's something to know here, from this corporeality, a new kind of clarity, he thinks, that will descend upon him soon, if he's patient. He inhales the spray, watches Claire watching him.

"What's wrong with you?" she says.

"What do you mean?"

"You have like this huge smile on your face."

"Oh," Feldman says. "Sorry."

She grins, seeming unsure what to make of him, then reaches toward his face, touching where his lip is thick. He feels the small point of her fingertip, and there's a principle here somewhere, beyond Riley and the whole flesh and blood of it.

"I have to pee," she says. She stands, takes up her purse, and moves away.

A meteorologist now explains that while hurricanes can have devastating impacts, they play an important part in replenishing Florida aquifers. Feldman aims the remote carefully and clicks off the television. He listens to the growing wind outside. His body hurts, expands in this new, wondrous way.

Claire seems gone for a long time.

Finally, a flush in the background, then total darkness. She has turned off the kitchen light, and when she comes to him, she smells different. More patchouli and sweat, more earthy than before, and something vague, nostalgic. She lies beside him. He can hear his windows flex from the wind, and his eyes fall shut.

"David, I lied to you before," she says. "I wasn't really evacuated." She sighs. "I'm just a section two, not a four."

"It's okay," he says.

"I was just afraid I would fall to pieces all cooped up by myself. Isn't that fucked up?" Her voice trembles slightly.

"No," he says, but what he wants to say is don't cry or worry even, that he is beginning to know something new, that everything will be okay.

"Do you know what I mean, a little bit at least?"

"Sure," he says. "Totally."

"I'm naked," she says.

It's raining again. The sound is comforting. He feels empty, burned clean. And expanding. "I know," he says.

Her hand drifts along his stomach, stopping to work at his belt buckle. His eyes won't open, but it's okay.

"Don't you think?" she says, maybe noticing some reluctance on his part. "Don't you want to?"

"Sure," he says, turning toward her. But he is not sure because he needs to concentrate and to understand. They are together, kissing now, and this is okay because he wants her to be happy too, and it's good to be kind to one another in this way. The rain falls in earnest, a steady rumbling against the roof.

"This is right," Claire says, beneath him now, her legs locked and constricting. "Don't you think?"

"Yes," he says, and he does mean yes, that this can be a part of it, but only a small part, smaller than she can possibly know.

MAKING WEIGHT
An Unexpected Challenge

COACH EVANS seems in a particularly good mood today. He sits on the wrestling mat, legs spread wide apart. "Big days ahead," he says. He brushes something from his mustache and falls backwards, bridging high onto his head. His hips thrust upward, his body parabolic. "Big days, men."

Freddy stretches out his calf and watches Coach rolling on the mat in his tight gray sweat suit. The other wrestlers move about the room. They run and stretch or work moves against phantom opponents. Freddy seats himself on the mat, spreads his legs, and leans toward a knee.

"This is gut-check time," Coach says. "This is make or break."

Coach doesn't look like an athlete, not with his small frame and thick middle. He reminds Freddy of a smaller version of Gabe Kaplan from *Welcome Back, Kotter.* But in high school he was a Pennsylvania state runner-up at 112 pounds. Afterwards, he walked on at Penn State, where he made the team and backed up an eventual NCAA champion. Earlier this season, Coach brought in rolls of black-and-white projector film that showed him in high school, unimpressive in stature even then, making short work of opponents. Afterwards, some of Freddy's teammates had made fun of Coach's full-length tights or the fractured ancient film, but for Freddy it had been inspiring.

Coach relaxes out of his bridge and rises into a sitting position again. He springs to his feet and jogs over to the thermostat, raises it. He closes the door to the wrestling room, and already Freddy can feel the warming stuffiness that will only grow deeper, wetter.

Coach stands by the scale in the corner of the room, holding a clipboard and pen. "One fifty-three," he calls, and Juan Olmos springs up and trots toward him.

Ron Ramsey jogs in a small circle, then sidles up to Freddy and runs in place. He wears full sweats, and Freddy can hear the trash bag rattling underneath like cellophane. Ron looks at Freddy, conspiratorially, Freddy thinks. Freddy nods and matches Ron's stride. They run like this until Coach calls "one fifty-two." Ron sprints toward Coach while Freddy and several other wrestlers move over to watch.

Ron steps up to the scale fully dressed. Coach sets the balance at 154 and nods. Ron steps on, tentatively, like he's testing out cold water. He stands, bent-kneed and hunched, his palms upturned and fingers curled inward. The arm of the scale doesn't move. It stays flush to the top of the balance.

Coach's expression stays calm. He taps the weight, sliding it incrementally, just a fraction at a time, and his face moves slowly toward something like disgust, until the bar finally balances at 156¾.

"Sweet mother of God," Coach says. He looks at Ron as if he has just dropped a greasy turd in coach's own living room. "Did you go to Shoney's Buffet for breakfast?" he says.

Ron looks deflated. His shoulders slump forward. "I had a small salad at lunch," he says. He bends and begins unlacing his shoes. That's all I've had all day."

"Thousand island dressing?" Coach says. "With cheese and avocados?"

"No, Coach," Ron says. "Just lettuce mostly. I squeezed a few pickle slices over the top."

"What about last night?" Coach says.

Ron strips away his sweatpants. He's wearing red silky briefs. His buttocks are tight and shrunken, like two hard-boiled eggs beneath the fabric. Coach Evans resets the scale, and Ron steps up again. This time it balances just below 155.

Ron sighs. "Maybe I'm growing, Coach," he says.

Coach looks incredulous. He chews the end of his mustache. His good mood is ruined. "Get dressed," he says. "I want you at one fifty-three before you leave tonight. The district tournament's in two days, and you haven't seen one fifty-two once. You've got the rest of your life to grow."

When Coach finally calls "two seventy-five," Freddy steps forward, braces himself for a similar lashing. He considers telling Coach that Shoney's only offers the breakfast buffet on weekends. Melvin Mearle used to take Freddy and his mother there after church some weeks, but Melvin would limit Freddy to two trips to the bar. Freddy thinks of scrambled eggs doused with melted cheddar as he steps onto the small platform. French toast sticks. Biscuits and gravy.

The scale balances perfectly at 275, an utter surprise to Freddy considering his lunchtime indiscretions. It must have been the diarrheic explosion in the bathroom after sixth period that saved him, a rectal blast that left his intestines aching from the void. He hadn't expected it to be enough, but that is the thing when you're dealing with so much mass, he figures. There's more daily fluctuation, a wider standard deviation.

After Freddy weighs in, Coach blows the whistle, and there is a brief scramble as the wrestlers find their spots in line. Ron Ramsey is in the lead, followed by his co-captain, Leon Carnes, then the rest in order of weight class. They begin a circling jog along the mat perimeter, gaining speed until, at the same instant, as if somehow their minds are linked, Ron and Leon break from the line and into the center of the circle. They stand back-to-back, clapping in sync as Freddy and the rest continue circling, but side-shuffling now, and when the captains break down into stances and slap their thighs, the circle stops. The wrestlers stand ready. This is Freddy's favorite part of the practice, something like synthesis, the many coalescing into one.

IT IS VERY HOT NOW. Freddy's sweatshirt is fully soaked, and his legs burn with fatigue. Coach's whistle sounds, and Freddy sprawls his legs backward, hits the mat in a clumsy thud a half second after the other wrestlers. Another whistle, and he lifts his head, steps up with his right leg, pivots onto his left until he is standing with the others.

"Are you tired, men?" Coach Evans says. "Do you want to quit? Is it all just too much? Is it not what you signed on for?" Coach says this with the whistle still secured between his teeth so that his words have an airy lisp to them. "Well that's too bad," he continues, "because *play*-time is over. You can *play* basketball, or soccer, or baseball. You can *play* backgammon or even tidily-damn-winks." He pauses for effect. "But you sure as hell can't *play* wrestling."

He prowls slowly among them. "Men, the county tournament was just a warm-up. District is everything. If you don't place at district, you don't go to regional. No regional, no state. Want to stay in the hunt? Want to be a contender? Saturday's your day. Leave everything you've got on the mat. If you're not willing to give everything, then there's the door." Coach points to the closed door, which leads into the open gym where it is cool and breezy.

Freddy feels nauseated. He worries he may have to vomit soon.

"There's nothing to save it for," Coach continues. "Stake your claim Saturday or else that's it. Thank you very much for coming, better luck next year. Seniors, you don't have a next year. You can go off to illustrious careers in college and beyond or maybe jump right into the management track at Piggly Wiggly. You might go on to have loving families and achieve great things in the world. But when it comes to wrestling, it's now or never. This is your last chance. Coach moves over to Ron. "Ramsey, you ready to pack it in? You and Clevenger ready to head to Appalachia to play football and chase pretty little southern belles?"

"No, Coach," Ron says. He stands, breathing heavily, his hands locked behind his head.

"Carnes, Ramirez, Eliot, how do you want to remember this time in your life? Do you want to look back and think, gee, I coulda done something if only I'da just worked a little harder?" Here, coach uses his redneck voice.

Coach blows the whistle, and they all repeat the drill. Once Freddy is standing again, Coach is at his ear. His breath is cool and clean against Freddy's neck. "Clevenger, do you think you can coast through to the finals Saturday? And even if you do, don't you know that Banks is going to be ready to chew you up? You expect him to give out on you like last time?"

Freddy isn't sure how to answer. There were too many questions for a simple yes or no, so he says, "I don't take anything for granted, Coach," his words breathy and weak. His legs burn like fire, and he is fairly sure he could cry here and now, right in front of everyone, if he let himself.

Another short whistle sends him to the mat, then a long one follows, signaling the end of practice. He gets to his feet as soon as he can, but he's the last varsity wrestler to line up against the wall. Across from the varsity line are the potentially challenging JVs. This is wrestle-offs, the ritual before any match or tournament. The varsity wrestlers must take on any legitimate challenger, and the winner represents the team at that weight class.

Coach walks to the beginning of the varsity line like he always does, rests his hand on the knotty little shoulder of Juan Olmos. "Challengers for the one hundred three weight class," Coach says, a formality since none of the JV wrestlers are light enough to fill the spot. The first wrestle-off comes at 135, where Harry Stubbs steps out to challenge Ted Maglisco. This makes sense. The two have traded first spot a couple of times during the season. But today Maglisco won't have it. Less than a minute into the match, he has pinned Stubbs with an inside cradle. He stands nonchalantly and moves back into line.

The varsity line claps loudly in unison. Some of them whoop and bark. Coach suppresses a smile. This is what he's looking for, probably. He wants to see fire. Freddy claps and rests against the wall. His breaths still come shallow, but they don't hurt as badly anymore. No one steps out at 140 or 145.

"One fifty-two," Coach says, his hand on Ron's shoulder now. The JV wrestlers are motionless. Stepping out would be either a bad joke or blatant disrespect. Maybe both. No one challenges at 160, or at 171 where Carnes, shirtless, a muscular wall of glazed ebony, extends his hands palm-up and taunts the line forward with his fingers. The varsity wrestlers whoop louder.

"That's enough, Leon," Coach says.

No challengers step forward at 189 or 220. Soon, practice will end, Freddy thinks. He'll take a long bath. But when coach calls "two seventy-five," against all expectation, Mike Dozier steps forward to take on Freddy. Freddy inhales deeply, lets his breath drain slowly, and considers his stump-solid challenger. How to take this? While Freddy is no captain, he *is* a three-year letterman, one of the leaders in his own way—with one of the best records this year—and he can't help seeing this as a slight from the younger Dozier.

And yet he cannot take the sophomore lightly. In truth, he's a better overall athlete than Freddy, with more raw strength and quickness. He's a rising star on the football field, a division one prospect if he can grow a few inches and keep his grades up. If Freddy locks up with him directly, strength for strength, Dozier is every bit strong enough to get lucky with an upper-body throw. And Freddy is very tired. If Dozier has been planning this all along, the sneaky bastard was probably taking it easy during the drills.

The varsity line settles into rhythmic clapping when Coach directs the two to the center of the mat. Freddy accepts the green Velcro band and fastens it around his ankle. The extension of hands, the clench, then—after what seems like a long delay—Coach's whistle, and Dozier is a dark flash beneath Freddy. He has shot in for a deep double-leg, using the speed that serves him so well on the football field. Freddy tries to sprawl, but Dozier's hold is tight behind his thighs. Freddy can feel his balance giving way, so he turns to give up the takedown rather than expose his back. He falls to his elbows, then bases up only to have Dozier chop his arm away and drive Freddy's face into the mat.

"One, takedown, red!" Coach yells.

Freddy fights to control his anger. If he lets the match lapse into an uncontrolled brawl, he plays into Dozier's strength. Instead, he looks skyward, steps up with his right foot, pivots onto his left, and he is standing. He pries away Dozier's grasp and spins free for the escape.

Coach yells, "One, escape, green!"

The varsity line whoops and barks.

Dozier shoots low again, but this time Freddy sprawls hard. With his forearm, he drives Dozier's head to the mat and spins behind him for the takedown.

"Two, takedown, green!"

Freddy is ahead by one point. He arches his hips into Dozier, leans patiently with his full weight, knowing that the sophomore will eventually begin to fade. Freddy lets Dozier fight until he's almost free, then sinks the weight on him again.

"Work a move, Clevenger," Coach says. "I'm going to call you for stalling. You've got to show me some action."

When Dozier's strength begins to give way, Freddy can feel it, the body slacken beneath him. Football muscles, Freddy thinks. They don't exactly translate to the mat. Dozier's movements become clumsy and desperate, his breaths shallow, and on one of his awkward reaches, Freddy manages to bar his arm and then turn him with a basic half nelson. Nothing fancy, but Dozier allows his shoulders to be pressed to the mat in a way that feels, to Freddy, almost gentle.

Hungry and Cold in the Ramsey Orange Grove

Here's a Friday night in Ridgedale. The roads are mostly empty, the streetlamps straining, it seems, to cast out their pale yellow against the force of the cold. Freddy drives his mother to the IHOP, drops her off at the front door, then steers her car back into the streets. He approaches the McDonald's and slows. In the back lot only a few cars are parked and a handful of classmates mill purposelessly about. A couple of them spot Freddy in his mother's car and wave, but he decides not to stop tonight, mainly because of the wonderful smells that he knows would be swirling around in the air. Even now, with the tournament in the morning, the temptation could prove too much.

He turns off of Central Avenue and onto Scenic Highway, heads north, and soon the lights of the town recede. He makes a left onto Old Messer Road, and all is dark now except for his mother's headlights on the patch of pavement before him. He turns right onto a clay road, narrow and framed on either side by orange trees.

Spooky, Freddy thinks. He'd hate to break down here. It reminds him of Scooby Doo. *The Mystery of the Haunted Grove*. Or maybe, *Attack of the Fruitpicking Zombies*. Lots of possibilities.

Freddy turns carefully onto the grassy path, hoping this is the right one. He creeps into the grove and is relieved when a small clearing opens to his left and he sees Ron's Blazer parked next to a small fire.

"IT WAS FOOD I wanted before," Ron says. He rubs his gloved hands over the fire, which crackles with new dry kindling. "But right now, I swear all I can think about is getting something to drink."

Freddy can't drink anything either. He's two pounds over his weight. "I could go for some cold Gatorade," he says. "Lemon-lime."

"Or iced tea," Ron says. He's running in place now. "A big fucking vat of it."

Around them, the orange trees lurk in cold shadow. The engine to the water pump pulses rhythmically, and beneath that is the faint hiss of the microjet sprinklers. They send out their steady mist that coats the trees with a layer of ice.

Because the cold front has settled on Ridgedale so intensely, Florida Power is overwhelmed by the electricity demand. Periodically, they have to cut power to sections of town lest the whole grid overload. If that happens here, the electric pump will click off and the important mist of water will stop. The trees can last a while like this, but the pump will need to be restarted manually as soon as the electricity returns.

"Get my drift," Ron says, after having explained all of this to Freddy.

"So the ice actually protects the tree?" Freddy says. "You say the real damage starts around twenty-nine degrees, but the ice locks them in at around thirty-two. Is that right?"

"That's it in a nutshell, Biggen," Ron says. He talks without breaking stride. "You're a smart fellow. You're a fucking genius, man. But there's other things you've got to figure on. How long it stays at a particular temperature, how big and healthy your tree is, what its water content is."

"Water content?"

"Shit yes, water content," Ron says. "Trees get dehydrated just like us, only it's called water stress with them."

Water stress. Freddy likes the term. It captures much more than just "thirsty." *I'm in bad need of a drink. I'm under water stress.* He turns his back to the fire, feels the heat rise up the back of his legs. "What about tomorrow night?" Freddy says. "It's supposed to be colder than hell again."

"Tomorrow night is tomorrow night," Ron says. He spits at the fire, but nothing comes out. "Tomorrow night we'll be district champs. We'll get a bottle of Jack Daniels and celebrate." He laughs. "Don't you reckon?"

Freddy does not reckon. He nearly wretches at the thought. There was an incident over a year ago, when they had swiped a bottle from Ron's father, and Freddy still can't stomach the memory. But a case of beers would be good, iced down in a cooler. They could drink them out here, maybe with a few of the other guys. Freddy would like that.

Freddy starts to speak, but Ron interrupts. "I'm freezing my nuts off out here," he says. "Let's go sit inside the cab for a while."

By the time Freddy climbs into the passenger side of the Blazer, Ron already has the truck started and the heater blowing. From the stereo speakers, Axel Rose sings about a woman he once loved but, in the end, was forced to kill.

"Unhappy family, I guess" Freddy says.

"What?" Ron says. He is punching, throwing straight jabs above the steering wheel.

Freddy sees that in the back of the Blazer the seats have been folded down flat and a sleeping bag is spread out, along with two pillows.

Ron adjusts his seat so he can rest at an incline. He sighs long and heavy. He starts a new set of jabs, punching hard into the air, alternating hand to hand. "How's your weight?" he says.

"I'm close," Freddy says. "You?"

"It's damn near killing me," Ron says. "I'm almost there though."

"You'll be right on the mark," Freddy says. "You'll be the biggest guy in the brackets."

Ron smiles and stops punching. "It's true, Biggen. You're absolutely right." He stops punching and folds his arms across his chest. "You too, man. You ready for Banks?"

Freddy sighs. "I hope so," he says.

"You're ready," Ron says. "You've done everything you can. Don't overthink it."

"Just take care of business," Freddy says.

"Might as well, huh?"

"I reckon," Freddy says.

"I 'spect so," Ron says.

"I reckon-spect," Freddy says and laughs. After a pause he says, "You know the bus is supposed to pull out at 6:30. You sure you can wake up?"

Ron pulls back the sleeve of his jacket, then a sweatshirt sleeve beneath that, points to his watch. "I set the alarm," he says.

This seems like little insurance to Freddy. He says, "I'd sleep right through that."

"I never oversleep," Ron says. "I'm practically a farmer." His fists are flying fast again. He groans and finishes a final series of shadow blows before resting his arms against the steering wheel.

Freddy thinks about his own mornings, his mother's calls beginning as all sweetness but growing more urgent, until she has to threaten him. He must do better, he thinks. Get an alarm clock, take charge of his life, be more of a man.

Freddy checks his own watch. Soon, he will have to leave to pick up his mother from work. He looks again at the sleeping bag and pillows. It would be a tight fit, but the area is big enough for two people to sleep, even if one is very large.

"Listen, Biggen," Ron says. "My dad just paid me some money yesterday. I can spot you if you want, for that housing deposit I'm saying."

Again, the feeling of dread and fear, and Freddy knows that here is the moment for him to tell Ron the truth, which is a silly thing to let become so huge, but it is huge because it has gone on too long to be simple in any way. Here, though, in the partial darkness, it might be easier.

"No," Freddy says. "No, that's not it."

"It's not a problem. You can pay me back."

"Thanks," Freddy says. "But it's okay." He tries to steady himself, tries to begin to tell the simple truth that has become so large and unwieldy that he doesn't know where to start.

"Whatever," Ron says. "I just want things set up so we can hit the road with no bullshit."

Ron's cassette tape has ended, and it's quieter now without the music.

"Why?" Freddy says. "Why are you so anxious?"

"Aren't you?"

"Yeah," Freddy says. "I mean, I guess."

"You guess."

"No, I mean I am."

"Me," Ron says. "I feel like I'm getting out of prison after eighteen long years."

Freddy thinks about this. Leaving Ridgedale; it's like getting out of prison. He's not sure that he feels this way. There are too many things to consider over his life so far. He can't incorporate them into a unified metaphor.

"You have to get out right away," Ron says. "Look at the people who don't."

"Yeah, there's a kind of gravity, I guess."

"When the planets are lined up right, you can't fuck around and waste time."

"Right," Freddy says. "You'll get sucked into a black hole."

"A big-ass black hole."

"To continue the space theme."

"Yeah, yeah," Ron says. "I get it. You're a fucking astronomer, man." He squints and rubs his temples.

"You okay?" Freddy says.

"I get lightheaded," Ron says. "I feel like I'm stoned." He laughs. "One of the few benefits of starvation."

Freddy looks again to the bed of the Blazer. The air in the truck is warm and dry. He can feel it chapping his face. Also, he is hungry.

"I have to pick up my mother," Freddy says. He tries to inflect his regret, but Ron just nods. He starts his jabs again.

In the bed of the Blazer, there would be plenty of room for both of them, and thinking this does not make him queer, Freddy knows. It's only part of remembering times past, or of missing something before you've quite lost it, only a feeling of things changing in a way that makes you feel sad and afraid and excited all at once.

"Sorry I can't stay," Freddy says. "You need anything?"

"Yeah," Ron says. "A Big-fucking-Mac." He laughs. Then, "I'll pick you up at 6:15. Make sure your big ass is ready."

Freddy opens his door, and Ron stops punching, holds up a finger. He switches off the heater. His expression is serious now, and he rolls down his window. The cold seeps in at them. Ron sticks his head outside, then ducks back in and looks to Freddy. "I can't hear the pump," he says. "Can you? Sounds like they cut the mother-fucking power off."

Freddy closes his door and rolls down his window. He hears only wind, maybe the crackle of the fire. No pump or microjets.

Ron switches on his headlights, and in front of them is a patch of frozen trees that glow white in the new light, the flicker of the fire against them giving the illusion of movement. The icicles hang long and sharp, like emaciated fingers dangling over some place darker—an otherworldly place—and they are beautiful and terrifying too. This is a sight, Freddy thinks. This should be in a movie. The cold gathers in the cab, and Freddy shivers from the chill.

"That's a lot of fruit they're messing with," Ron says.

They sit there in the truck together, watching the weird frozen trees. The world around them is silent and still, and Freddy is sure he has never felt exactly this way before.

DECEMBER 1979

POPPY, WHOM THE WHOLE CHURCH prayed for today, sits with a TV tray in front of him because his wheelchair is too low to reach the dinner table. His chin sits against his Sunday shirt, and I can see the top of his head, which is shiny and covered with big brown freckles. His yellow ribbon is pinned to his shirt pocket. Dad kneels and takes one of Poppy's hands. Aunt Louise wears a ribbon too, pinned to the front of her green dress that's stretched tight in front across her two giant boobs.

We all got ribbons in church today, but I've already lost mine somewhere. Aunt Louise straightens the blanket on Poppy's lap. She's too big to kneel down, so she just touches Poppy on the shoulder and reaches out her other hand to take Uncle Paul's. I am in-between Mom and Claire, across the circle from Poppy. Behind him, the Christmas tree lights have not started blinking yet. We only turned them on a minute ago, and they are still warming up.

Aunt Louise prays, "Dear heavenly Father, we thank you for this day and for the chance to come together as a family in your name. Lord, we know that there are those today that cain't be with their loved ones, because they are being held against their will. This serves to remind us of how lucky we are to have our people safely nearby, and we thank you for this blessing. We pray for the hostages, Father. We ask that you comfort them and their families in this difficult time, and we pray that you may see it fit to bring them home in time for Christmas."

Claire is squeezing my hand so that my fingers are all smashed together. It hurts, but I bite my cheek and stay hushed. Aunt Louise says, "We ask that you bless this food to the nourishment of our bodies. Lead, guide, and direct us, Lord, in the way you see fit, for it is in the name of your precious son, Jesus Christ, that we pray, amen."

"She was squeezing my hand again," I tell Mom.

"I wasn't," Claire says, looking at me all surprised.

"Set down," Mom whispers. Her hair is pinned up and her face is tired with that Sunday-after-church look that wants you to just give her some peace. She dries her hands on her apron and looks hard at Claire like *"Stop showing your butt or else."*

Mom's fingers feel strong and sharp on my shoulder as she guides me away from the grown-up table. "Set down, Ronnie." Her voice is nicer now. "There by your sister and Littlepaul, and I'll fix you a plate directly."

I sit down by Claire and Littlepaul at our table, which is a card table set up in the family room not that far from the grown-ups. Mom piles Dad's plate high with fried fish and hushpuppies. I think I can hear the food crackle as she sets it in front of him, and the smell from it is warm and wet and good in my nose. Aunt Louise makes plates for Uncle Paul and for Poppy, who needs everything mashed up with a fork. Poppy looks down at his tray, and I think he says that he would like some dumplings. He talks from the side of his mouth and sounds like he's in the middle of a yawn. It's hard to visit with Poppy much anymore. I can hardly understand what he's saying, and when he looks at me, it's like he doesn't really know who I am, like he's mad or something, and I start to feel all funny.

Poppy was a tobacco farmer way back. Then he came to Florida to help build highways. I have seen the pictures of that, him and the other men leaning on their shovels with smiles stretched across their faces, which are thin and smeared with dirt. This was a long time ago, though, when Dad was just a baby and living with Grandmother, who I never knew, up in Georgia still. Aunt Louise wasn't even born then but was born later here in Florida. There is one picture of them all standing in front of a row of little trees, which later grew up to be Poppy's first orange grove. Dad and Aunt Louise stand next to Grandmother whose white dress flaps in the wind. Grandmother is tiny next to Poppy, who is clean and handsome, dressed in a fancy white suit and hat. Grandmother is in Heaven now. Also, she is buried in Georgia, where I have never been, but I know that the ground there is red and slick.

Claire kicks me under the table and smiles at Littlepaul. He laughs, glad she is not picking at him. On Christmas, Claire will be nice, though. Everyone is always nice on Christmas, even when the house is a mess with toys and wrapping paper strung all over the floor. Claire is nice sometimes anyway, but always on Christmas and for the whole day usually.

Aunt Louise mashes fish and some dumplings for Poppy. "Is this bluegill, Ray?" she asks.

"It might be some bluegill in there," Dad says. "One or two likely, but it's mostly specks." Dad looks a lot like Poppy does in the pictures, but older and fatter in the belly, which he calls his muscle. He lets me hit it like a punching bag sometimes when he's happy.

If there is bluegill on the plate, I probably caught it myself, in our back yard along the edge of the lake where they tend to bed. They'll strike a worm or a mussel, but I use crickets when I can get them because I like to watch them float across the top of the water and disappear in a quick splash. Speckled perch are the best fish for eating though, and to get them, Dad and Uncle Paul take the boat out on Lake Kissimmee. Sometimes I go. We eat sardines and soda crackers usually. Sometimes we eat Spam instead while we troll along with live minnows on about eight or nine poles and wait to hit a good spot. Poppy used to say to us that using all of them poles like that was cheating. You were supposed to give the fish a fighting chance, he said.

Uncle Paul cuts a piece from a big fillet. He holds it up on the end of his knife. "This here is Nile perch, I reckon." He offers it to Aunt Louise who makes a face and turns away. "Come on now," he says and smiles. A piece of fish hangs from his red mustache. "You never know 'less you try."

Aunt Louise goes back over to help Poppy eat, and everyone is quiet. The fish is not even Nile perch though. Uncle Paul is teasing. I think the joke is that only colored people eat things like Nile perch and coon and possum but that Aunt Louise would probably like just about anything, her being so fat and all.

Mom brings my plate with one fillet, two hushpuppies, and slaw. She gives me my dumplings and baked beans in separate bowls so they won't run together. Mom sets down a jar of honey in the middle of our table.

Aunt Louise feeds Poppy a spoonful of mashed dumplings while Mom pours everyone sweet tea. Poppy chews in a big slow circle. He looks small now, all hunched over and curled up on the side, one hand drawn up tight kind of like a claw. His face is skinny except for his eyes, which are big and red and shining. Dumpling gravy drips down his chin, but Aunt Louise scrapes it up and puts it back in his mouth, just like you do with a baby.

"Does Poppy wear diapers?" Claire whispers to Littlepaul. "I heard he does."

Littlepaul pours honey on his plate. Me and him are the same age almost even though he's smaller and is in the first grade again this year. I once heard Mom say that he was real sick with a fever when he was a baby and that's how come he's so pitiful now. After that I started to be mostly nice to Littlepaul, letting him have his way and all.

"Where do you sleep, Littlepaul?" Claire whispers. She twirls the end of her hair around her finger. "Do you sleep with Poppy?"

"Shut up," Littlepaul says.

"Okay." Claire puts her finger over her lips and smiles to quiet Littlepaul, who can be quick to tattle.

But I know that Poppy sleeps in his own bedroom. It's a room that used to be their den. I helped Dad and Uncle Paul the day they moved Poppy's bed out of his house, which is on one of the canals at the other side of our lake. Me and Littlepaul used to stay the night at Poppy's house sometimes. He would wake us up when it was still dark, everything quiet except our feet against the wet grass as we walked down to the water. Poppy worked slow, cutting up pieces of baitfish that he had caught the day before and let sit overnight. He tossed the pieces into the bait bucket, then washed the blood from his hands and knife in the dark canal water. With him, we always fished for catfish. We would cast our lines in the middle of the canal and let the bait sink to the bottom where the fish waited in that dark quiet place that is still a little bit scary for me to think about.

Poppy would sit on the ground between us, rolling a cigarette while we drank RCs and waited until one of our poles twitched and bent over. Then he'd whisper "mudsucker" and grab the hand net for us.

Everyone's eating now, and my teeth hurt from all the silverware scraping against the plates. Dad and Uncle Paul are the worst. They eat fast and serious like it's hard work, staring straight down without talking, breathing steady through their noses. Their food mixes together, and they use their hushpuppies to push it onto their forks. They are still chewing when Mom serves them pecan pie.

"I've got a feeling this may be a little dry," Mom says. "That oven's been acting up again."

Aunt Louise cuts a slice and starts to pick off the pecans for Poppy. I see that the star on the top of the Christmas tree is crooked. I start to say something but decide to just stay quiet even though it bothers me to look at it that way.

"Daddy," Dad says to Poppy. "I'm going to pick you a mess of greens so Louise can cook you some later on this week."

Poppy says something that I can't understand.

"Rutabagas, Daddy." Dad talks with a mouthful of pie. "I'm going to pick you a mess."

I am just getting my pie when Dad stands and rubs his belly, which is round from all the food. He walks with Uncle Paul toward the back door. Aunt Louise watches their backs with a look of thinking, like she is trying to decide something. Dad walks out the door, and Aunt Louise comes out of her chair and jogs across the family room. Everything on her starts to bounce, especially the boobs, which knock loose her yellow ribbon. It floats to the ground beside me like a hurt butterfly. She catches Dad and Uncle Paul not very far away from the door, which closes shut again. I don't understand everything she says, but I hear, "And you leaving him sittin' in there by hisself like that!"

Dad's voice is louder. "I reckon you'd have me push him through the garden with us? That'd be real good, Louise. Just put on the TV for him, and we'll be back in directly."

When Aunt Louise turns on the TV, it's a show about the hostages. There is a lady on the TV crying. Her husband is a hostage and a soldier. A lot of them are not soldiers, though. Aunt Louise pushes Poppy into the living room and up in front of the TV. A long time ago, Poppy was in a war, in a big ship. Poppy watches the lady who is young and pretty. The TV goes to a picture of some of the hostages. Their faces are covered up with blindfolds, and men with guns push them along. When the TV goes back to the lady, her face is wiped clean, but she is still red around the eyes. She stops for a second because it is hard for her to talk. Then she says she hopes her husband will be home in time for Christmas.

Mom and Aunt Louise work at putting away the food. Aunt Louise picks at the fish tray. She nibbles and talks quiet. "Lord knows I'm grateful, Mona. We could have just as easy lost him as not," she says. "I'm happy to have him staying with us instead of at some old home where he don't know a soul." Aunt Louise lowers her voice even more. "Lord knows I don't mind doing for him. But I cain't say it's always easy, even when it's someone you love. He ain't ever been an easy man, I reckon. It's a trial sometimes," she says. "Lord knows, it's a trial."

Claire is messing with the presents under the tree, trying to figure out which are hers. "Get away from there, Claire Marie," Mom says.

"Some of them're breakable." Mom waves her arm at all of us. "Go and play on the back porch," she says.

THE BREEZE RIPPLES across the lake and up the back yard, through the branches of the oak tree. It blows cool through the porch screen, and the three of us shiver. Ghost comes out of his doghouse and walks to the edge of the garden where his chain stops him. He whines at Dad and Uncle Paul, who are bent over digging with Uncle Paul's cigarette smoke floating up from their heads.

Me and Littlepaul take a spelling test from Claire, who is the teacher. Through the sliding glass door I can see inside the living room where Poppy watches about the hostages. I try to think about what dying is like. It must be like sleeping sort of, but only more dark and quiet, no dreams and by yourself, waiting for the Lord to lead you off.

"Pay attention." Claire smacks the table with a stick, which is supposed to be a ruler. She checks to make sure I'm keeping up with the words. But I have them lined up perfect on the left side of my page. They are easy for me, but Littlepaul can't get them and starts to cry, saying he doesn't want to play. He tries to erase one of the words, but the eraser is wore down, and the metal makes an ugly hole in his paper, which is all a mess with crooked letters. He starts to cry louder, and Dad and Uncle Paul stand up and look across the yard at us. Claire tells Littlepaul to hush and gives us some easier words, which quiets him down a little.

Dad and Uncle Paul turn away from us and shake the rutabagas so that the special black dirt, that we have to truck in every once and a while, falls off the roots. I watch it fall and think I can smell it in the air, strong and rich, different from Florida sand, which Poppy once showed us could be used as a cleaner.

"How can you clean with dirt?" I asked. "It's . . . dirty."

"Sand," Poppy said. He squatted by the shore, looking Littlepaul and me straight in the eyes as he scooped his hand into the water. He stood and dropped his big red knuckles underneath our noses, turned his hand over, and opened it slow. "Take you a pinch," he said.

We took some in our fingers.

"Close yer eyes," Poppy said. "Feel? In Georgia it's mostly red clay, slick as grease when it's wet. But here it's differ'nt. Like little pieces of glass."

Poppy dumped the bait in the canal. He filled the bucket with a little water and smeared sand on the side. He scrubbed hard with his strong hands, making rough scratching sounds. The daylight started to show, and we could see the red-black water in the bucket, which Poppy poured into the canal. He dipped the bucket one more time and poured it out by our bare feet. The water felt warm and nice splashing against my legs. He held the bucket so we could see inside, and it was empty and clean.

The sky is already gray when Dad and Uncle Paul finally come inside with dirt on their Sunday clothes.

"You could've at least changed," Mom says to Dad, who hands the greens to Aunt Louise. Me and Claire carry covered dishes outside, and Mom and Aunt Louise start to argue about who should keep the rest of the pie. Aunt Louise finally takes it when Mom promises it'll flat go to waste if she doesn't.

They bring Poppy out the front door backwards, Dad holding the chair from behind and Uncle Paul grabbing near the little wheels in front. They push him over toward Uncle Paul's van. It is getting colder. I can see our breath in the air like smoke.

"Ya'll are coming over Christmas day, right?" Aunt Louise says. "About noon?"

"Oh we'll be there," Mom says. "Lord willin'."

Uncle Paul pulls the wheelchair up to the open van door. "You ready, Mr. Ramsey?" he says to Poppy. "Just like before. One, two, three." They lift him up from the chair. Poppy groans quiet as they turn his back to the van. His blanket falls on the driveway, and his pants are a little wet in front.

"Step up, Daddy," Dad says.

Poppy lifts his leg but can't get it up on the step behind him. His eyes are open big, looking out at us, but not really seeing. His mouth hangs wide open and crooked with his tongue to the side. His foot keeps missing the step. There is a yellow ribbon hanging from the van's antenna. It's long and curly and blows in the wind.

"Lordy," Aunt Louise says. She puts down the pie and greens and runs over to them. Poppy gets his foot on the step, but they can't get him up like the other times.

"Here," Uncle Paul says. He puts Poppy's arm around Aunt Louise and climbs into the van, hugging Poppy around the chest and trying to pull him up. Poppy's pants slip past his hips, which look like they're sunburned.

"Okay," Uncle Paul says. "One, two, three." He pulls and Poppy is stretched out long. His back leans against the seat. His pants fall down to his knees, and I see he is wearing something that does look like a diaper. Part of his peter is sticking out, red as blood.

"Lord have mercy," Aunt Louise says. She tries to pull up his pants. Poppy's breath blows hard and quick out of the side of his mouth. He stares off.

"It ain't never been like this before," Littlepaul says. He looks at me then back at Poppy. "Not this bad." Littlepaul licks his lips, which are turning blue in the cold. I pull my shirt collar up under my eyes so that my breath is warm against my nose and lips. The sun is red and cut in half behind the tops of the orange trees.

"He's gonna die, ain't he?" Littlepaul whispers to me. He licks his blue lips again. He stares at me and waits. He waits like he knows I will tell him he's wrong, like I'm smarter and know more things and can tell him he's wrong.

Uncle Paul pulls again, and now Dad and Aunt Louise lift Poppy from behind the knees until he's up in the seat. Claire isn't laughing. She sees me looking at her, and she doesn't say anything at all but looks down and digs her shoe into the sand.

Mom picks up the pie and greens and walks over to the van. She talks to Dad who kisses her on the cheek. "I'm going to ride over with 'em," he says. "Give 'em a hand getting Daddy settled."

I walk over and lean against Mom's side even though I'm really getting too old for it. She lets her arm hang over my chest and pats my stomach with her hand. It is almost dark. Uncle Paul flicks on the van lights. Poppy is a dark shadow, bent over in his seat. I wave to him, but he doesn't wave back. Littlepaul climbs into the front of the van, on Aunt Louise's lap. I turn from him back to Poppy. I try to picture it out, the three of us fishing at the canal again. I think about our baits sinking real slow into the warm, quiet dark and wonder if maybe that's what it's like in that time before you see the lord.

RELEASE STATEMENT
OR
"CLAIRE RAMSEY, COME ON DOWN!"

GIVE ME A CHANCE and I'll explain some of the things I said upon my admission, try to frame them in a way that doesn't sound so crazy and that will—hopefully—mitigate some of the opinions you have naturally formed about me. I'll explain how it first got mixed up in my head, how it makes complete sense, really, that as a girl of four years I came to believe that Bob Barker and God Almighty were pretty much one in the same and how to this very day, when I have occasion to bow my head and pray, it's often his face I see—deeply tanned and regally handsome, his hair a glowing white nimbus—looking down on me with mercy.

But calmly, that's how things have to go here.[1] With calm lucidity I will render, record, and order some of those things I know to be true and telling, those things that, although their relevance may not be immediately clear, had some bearing on future events and circumstances that have led me to where I am today and which will surely exert their influence on future events. In the process I hope to satisfy my immediate audience that, as indicated in box "a," of your patient release form, I "have no compelling impulse to do harm to myself, other persons, animals, or property." Implicitly acknowledged, of course, is the fact that the

---

1. Some context for posterity: As I compose these lines, I sit, wrists bandaged and release pending, in the patient commons of the crisis unit at Emergency Mental Health Services of Tampa Bay (EMHSTAB), Clearwater, Florida.

present slice of memoir, as with any (re)presentation of lived experience, characterizes only a sliver of the overall story and hence can offer only limited insight into the subject (me) and to my recurring crises.

I'm never sure how much to weigh the socioeconomic aspect of my life. My family was never "dirt poor." We never went around hungry or tattered, nothing like that, but I do recall a vivid humbleness of means in my early years. We enjoyed very few extras. I think that's why the memory of our first colored television set, passed along by my grandmother who had bought a larger, nicer one, stands out so distinctly for me. This was around 1973, when it would still be a decade before the first cable providers would venture that far outside the city limits, ushering in screens of unnatural clarity, strange new channels, MTV. But for then (1973) we had the outdoor antenna that was mounted to the side of the trailer and rose above the roof. (Do not picture a trailer park but rather a piece of lakeside property outside of our small town, on which we would later build our own house.) To get decent television reception, two people were required: one to climb the ladder that leaned against the back of the trailer and manipulate the roof antenna, and another to remain inside to watch the screen and call instructions out the window.

Those were my first memories of Mr. Bob Barker and of *The Price Is Right*. Every day, religiously, I watched his show, and now in color. I watched it twice a day: in the morning when Dad was off at work and Mom was washing dishes or tending my little brother in some way, then again at night, freshly showered and in pajamas—feeling clean and warm, giddy with the sleepiness of the encroaching night. By far, my favorite part of the show was the beginning, when the first four contestants were called and told to *come on down*. I loved to watch them spring to life—all aflitter with excitement—and make their way down to Contestants Row.

I say that I watched the show "religiously" in way of a self-conscious segue, since organized religion plays its part in the story. Like many working-class families in the South, mine was steeped in evangelical Christianity. Specifically, we were Southern Baptists, but you shouldn't imagine snake handling or the drinking of strychnine although I once attended a tent revival, and I had an uncle who was a faith healer of some local renown.

A big part of the message we received centered on turning away from material desire and preoccupations with social status in favor of more spiritual pursuits. While this may be an admirable position in general, it does not well suit the needs of the adolescent girl, who wants more than anything to fit in like everyone else, to cause as little disruption in the social fabric of junior high as possible. Here I am digressing, but you'll allow me to relay a brief example of the indirect ways religion oppressed me. One of my more traumatizing moments takes us back to a Belk Lindsay department store, the occasion being the purchase of my first training bra. My mother, God rest her soul, failing to appreciate the inherent embarrassment of my situation, had me stand at the edge of the bin in the open store while she strapped the bras to me, one by one, on the outside of my blouse. As fate would have it, said events happened to coincide with the appearance of two of my Ridgedale Junior High classmates, Bruce Davidson and Chuck Bell, who chanced to walk by in their neon fluorescent shirts and skater jams, just as I stood modeling a pink brassiere, my most private shame made manifest to the outside world. Oh how I longed for the sweet relief of death that night, but Mom, in her efforts to understand me, just couldn't seem to comprehend what "all the fuss was about." Did I realize how lucky I was? She had to make her first bra out of an old pillowcase.

But back to the main narrative thread. It was several years before the above incident, on one particular Sunday. I don't even know the season although I remember it was warm, which could be almost anytime in Florida. I wasn't feeling especially well, and I was worse off when we got to church. Mom pressed her hand to my forehead and must have felt a fever because she kept me with her instead of sending me away with the rest of the kids, who would—after the opening prayer and pleasantries— rise at the same time and be led up the aisle toward "children's church." Every Sunday we would march, a precious queue of little saints, past the grown-up faces that were all smiles and adoration. I think there was even a certain song that went along with it.

I feel sure that I had been through an adult church service before this day, but this time it was different. Maybe some new cognitive stage had set in, or maybe my illness allowed me to fidget less and focus on the content of the sermon. I'm not sure. All I know is that the whole idea of salvation and damnation became much clearer that day. Reverend Carlyle, a handsome man with long thick sideburns, gesticulated and shouted as he drew, in metaphors of startling clarity, the contrast between the glorious rapture of the saved Christian and the hopeless despair of the eternally doomed. Most striking of all were the lakes of fire, repositories of the damned that would burn yet never consume you. Not being a particularly well-behaved little girl and having been told countless times about God and his record book and how each bad act would be a check against your name, I figured I had good reason to worry, to fear his just and terrible wrath.

The irrational fears of a child perhaps, but I wasn't alone in my convictions that day. During the invocation[2] many of the parishioners began to make their way out of the pews and down the aisle to where Reverend Carlyle waited on the small platform, hands outstretched and palms turned upward. "If you feel the Lord callin' you," he said, "come on down." He indicated the floor below him. "'*But preacher*,' he said, his voice affecting that of an old woman. '*I've been a member of this here church for thirty years. I'm a grandmother.*' I say to you, sister, it don't matter if you are!"

"'*But Preacher,*'" Reverend Carlyle said, his voice deep and manly now. "'*I'm a deacon, you see. I'm a Sunday school teacher.*'" Brother, I'm telling you unless you got the love of Jesus Christ in your heart right now, unless you know you're saved at this very moment, nothing else you've done matters and you are in danger of Hell fire. So I'll say it again. If you feel the lord a-callin' you, if he's tugging at your heart right now, won't you just come on down?"

I was a sinner. Not only that, I was worse than most. I couldn't shake the idea that I wouldn't make the cut. I was already prone to deception, selfishness, strange acts of cruelty. I often sassed, or lied. I had touched my baby brother's fontanel even though Mom told me explicitly not to, that I was to avoid it, this strange, round-red indention on the top of his fuzzy head, this soft spot that all babies had until they grow a bit. Touching it could "make him go away" so that I didn't have a little brother anymore. Wouldn't that be sad? (Parents, I plead with you: Always be precise with your children.) Early some mornings, I would wake up before everyone else, sneak into my parents' bedroom where he lay in his crib in the corner. I'd tiptoe over quietly and, whether he was awake or not, I'd tap that soft spot just like I was paging an elevator.[3]

By now, there was a steady trickle of parishioners making their way toward the front of the church, taking advantage of this free pass to Heaven. And I, Claire Ramsey, was among them. Mom had at first been confused when I began to extricate myself from my seat, thinking I was

2. Also called "altar call," this part of the service, practiced in certain Protestant sects, gives the opportunity for sinners to make a public declaration of faith and repentance.

3. An unsuccessful enterprise thankfully, as my brother, Ronald W. Ramsey, survived the peril of my fratricidal machinations and grew into a healthy child. Currently, he lives outside of Knoxville, TN, with his wife, Lenore, and daughter, Megan.

up to my usual trouble or that I had to go to the restroom. When I made her to understand that I was going to the altar, she shook her head. "No, no, Honey. This is for grown-ups." But as I persisted she eventually gave in (who was she to fight the tenacity of God's grace?) and we made the journey together.

Things weren't always so intense. All in all, I remember those years as good. In the evenings, Daddy would come home from the citrus plant, tired but usually in a good mood back then. Supper would be cooking and we would eat, and afterward he would climb the ladder to the antenna, and Mom and I would yell to him out the window: "No. That's worse" or "There! No, you passed it," then "Yes, right there, yes! That's good."

And I would wait anxiously for *The Price Is Right*. The beginning, as I mentioned, got me the most. The bright colors, the music, the happiness and excitement that seemed to race through the air: It all seemed so immaculate, perfect, and when the wall divided and Bob appeared, smiling and full of enthusiasm, I would smile too, no matter what else was going on. To me, he even resembled Reverend Carlyle, probably because they were the only two men I was accustomed to seeing in a suit. Bob, though, was different. Enhanced. Infused with something that made Daddy and the Reverend and all the other men I have known seem hopelessly earthbound.

Once the TV reception was clear enough, Daddy would climb down from the ladder and join us in the living room. He and Mom would sit on the couch and smoke cigarettes. Ronnie sat between them, chubby and quiet. Bob called forth the voice of Johnny Olson, and the camera panned as Johnny crooned out the names of the first four contestants who we watched spring to life, men and women of all colors and sizes. They ran down the aisle—jumping, smiling, tripping—and lined up in front to receive salvation. Usually, I would leap up and run too, celebrating with them as I ran laps around the living room, feeling the trailer floor resonate hollow under my feet. In those moments, the world was a safe and wondrous place, and I knew for certain that nothing bad could ever happen to us.

Bob's wife and soul mate, Dorothy Jo, died in 1981. A few years later, so did my mom. Both of cancer. John Olson passed in '85. On the sticky vinyl seats of Randy Mooney's Gremlin, I lost my virginity. Randy proceeded to tell everyone in school. In '88 Bob resigned as emcee of the Miss America and Miss Universe pageants after they refused to give up fur prizes. I became a vegetarian. In 1994, I had a grouper sandwich at a

seafood festival, but I have knowingly eaten no animal or animal byprod-
uct since. I volunteer once a month at a spay/neuter clinic. There was
Bob's affair with Dian Parkinson (one of "Barker's Beauties" aka Lying
Slut) in '93 and the subsequent controversy.[4] I graduated from college
with a degree in theatrical production, had an abortion, and flirted briefly
with lesbianism, hypersexuality, celibacy. None of it really took. In the
meantime I did community theater and worked retail (second shift, so
as to leave the 11:00 a.m. slot open for television). In '96, Bob made his
motion picture debut, appearing as himself in *Happy Gilmore,* where in
a golf course fight scene he kicked the shit out of featured actor Adam
Sandler. I watched it over and over again.

I can name the price of most supermarket products within ten cents.
I'm pretty good with durable goods too, but my weakness is probably in
estimating the cost of domestic and foreign trips. I am not a mindless
groupie. That's very important to know. It's nothing so cheap. I have
been in the audience a number of times, and I have even once made
it to Contestants Row; however, I refuse to allow it to be the defining
moment of my life. I have more to do. I have never stalked Bob Barker,
and I have only written an occasional letter. I am not delusional, despite
the flimsy diagnosis of one past shrink, Dr. E. M. Mayor: Delusional
Disorder of the Erotomanic and Mixed types.[5] But he was wrong. I
didn't want to fuck Bob Barker. I wanted to worship him.

But Bob Barker is not God. I know this intellectually, but once
you've internalized a certain paradigm, it's sometimes hard to shake.
Bob Barker is a man. I know this, although I'd put him up against most
any God. Don't people worship all sorts of things? Money. Possessions.
Fame. And I have uncovered some pretty compelling parallels: The
crowd = humanity at large, Contestants Row = The Pearly Gates, the
Price Games and the Wheel = Purgatory, winning the Showcase—well,
you get the picture. But I have since given up on such convenient cor-
relations.

4. After leaving the show in 1993, Parkinson brought suit against Barker for sexual
harassment. She claimed that he threatened the loss of her job in order to coerce her
into a sexual relationship. For his part, Barker denied coercing anyone, and in fact said
that it was Parkinson who seduced him. The charges were eventually thrown out of
court for lack of evidence.

5. *DSM-IV* 2003, which the fat orderly with the mustache—a wretched crea-
ture—has reluctantly let me reference, identifies Delusional Disorder as indicated by
"nonbizarre delusions (i.e., involving situations that occur in real life, such as being
followed, poisoned, infected, loved at a distance, deceived by spouse or lover, or having
a disease)" (275). The erotomanic variety of the disorder is manifested by "delusions
that another person, usually of higher status, is in love with the individual" (275).

I live, in most ways, a normal life. My feelings about Bob Barker do not prevent relationships. I date. And if I tend to "avoid intimacy" in part because these men are inevitably revealed as too un-Boblike, I don't think that necessarily makes me the one with the problem. Let's face it; people tend to miss the mark. Case and point: The most recent of the nonBobs to grace my bed sheets showed up at three in the morning two nights following our breakup, intoxicated and insisting that we get back together and further insisting that I must make a decision *now*.

When I refused and ordered him out, he walked causally over to my fish tank, took up the little net, and caught one of my goldfish. "Claire," he said, this until-now somewhat normal young man. "You may want to reconsider." He dangled the fish over his open mouth.

How does one respond to this? I could only watch in horror as in response to my silence he engulfed the helpless Sparky and swallowed him whole.

Yet I am the one who must make assurances that I'm safe to release into the world? Do I get sad about things sometimes? Who wouldn't? And how much of a stretch is it, really (although I am currently vigilant and devoted to the job of living) when faced with the absurdity of all things both cosmic and local, and with no discernable evidence of metaphysical design, that one might occasionally wonder if any of it is worthwhile, if, maybe, being nothing at all might be the better option? And then, if in a moment of resolve, one attempts to make said preference manifest, to retract into the self, implode, immolate. Is that crazy? Irrational? The easy way out?

Because of the nature of our system, the burden falls upon me to assure you, my immediate readers, that I am safe for release to the outside world. I feel thoroughly "stabilized," and I can assure you that neither I nor any other party will be endangered by my release. I have been interpellated into the discourse of illness by your psycho-medical gaze[6] and must rely on your judgment to align me once again with the "sane" world. I do not envy your task, and this is not only because I view the entire field of psychology as socially constructed and arbitrary. Many things do seem crazy to me. But let me say that I've never launched a war in the name of Bob Barker. I have never harmed another or threatened physical force in order to spread the influence of *The Price Is Right*. I don't claim it as the one and only true path to salvation.

I notice that my allotted time is coming to a close; therefore, I'll transition awkwardly to the episode involving Contestants Row. For a

---

6. See Michel Foucault's *Birth of the Clinic*. Also *Madness and Civilization*.

long time I couldn't talk about it, but now I can say that, yes, I made it there once, in 1998, while vacationing in L.A. with some college friends. I was sitting in the middle of the masses when I heard it: *"Claire Ramsey, come on down."* How I actually made it from my seat and down to Contestants Row remains a mystery to me, but once they rolled out that grandfather clock, my instincts took over. I knew the brand and model to sell for at least $1,800, so I bid $1,750, low enough to be safely under, but high enough, hopefully, to discourage some jerk from boxing me in at $1,751. It worked, and suddenly I'm up there with him, hugging him from the side and in the most respectful and gentle way.[7] I played the Match Game, won easily (a dinette set that was far too big for my studio apartment). Later, when it was my turn to spin the wheel, I had to beat $.70. I scored $.35 on my first spin, and I was surprised at the lightness of the wheel, how easily it turned. On television it seems weightier. On my second spin I scored $.40, and with a total of $.75, I sent sailor-boy packing. But my lead was short-lived as some Wisconsinite grandma, a blue-haired wonder who barely got the wheel around a whole time, hit $1.00 on the first spin.

And that was it.

I didn't even cry, not then anyway. I just walked toward Bob, never taking my eyes off his and gave him the softest, nicest hug you can imagine.

It's not even that I wish I had won it all. I know that there would have been no communion with Bob, himself. Just a brief congratulations and I'd be whisked off to some utilitarian backroom for processing. It would be all paperwork and logistics, and Bob would be long gone. And that's *it,* that's the thing I've been trying to get across, the crisis of faith I was trying to articulate during my intake meeting but couldn't make coherent. Whatever form you package it in, it's all the same thing, and it's all a lie. But it's a lie we manage to believe most all of the time. Believing, by its very nature, is crazy. But you do it. We're all hoping against the system, thinking that maybe, under the right circumstances, it could all work out although we know, in the end, it never will. But for those brief moments, you can be that little girl again, running around the living room, all hope and possibility: mother, father, brother watching you like you were something else.

7. Due to his advancing age and the sometimes-unbridled enthusiasm of contestants, it is made clear at the beginning of each show that physical contact with Bob should be minimal.

MAKING WEIGHT
Tournament Day

THE SCHOOL BUS makes its way through the gray half-light. Inside, Freddy is back in trash bag and overcoat, Melvin Mearle's hunting cap pulled down over his ears. He stands in the walkway, each of his hands clutching the top of a seatback, his legs running slowly in place. He goes until he can feel his heart in his chest, then stops, sits down in a seat, and tries to curl into himself, to become compact and hot, feed his own warmth enough to sweat away the two necessary pounds.

He doubts he has ever been so thirsty before. He is under water stress. Last night he dreamed that he was sucking on the end of an icicle that dangled like a stalactite from the headboard of his bed. The icicle was smooth and cool in his mouth and yet, no matter how long he nursed at it, his thirst never went away.

Several feet ahead, turned sideways in the aisle, Ron does jumping jacks, adjusting to the stops and turns of the bus without ever having to break off a set. In the front of the bus, Coach stares forward, too pissed at Ron and Freddy to look in their direction. In a few minutes they'll arrive at South Bay High School. Final weigh-ins end at 9:00.

From what seems like all sides, Freddy receives a cacophony of practical advice, tricks on how to piss, sweat, barf, shit. Carnes and Ramirez argue over a particular point, Ramirez insisting that Freddy should strip off the trash bag every fifteen minutes or so and dry the sweat from his bare skin lest it reabsorb through his pores. Carnes says that this is fucking ridiculous, that once the sweat's out, it's out, and Freddy is inclined to agree, but since his own body has proven to be a mystery to him, he wouldn't swear to anything for certain.

Ron speeds up his tempo. He hasn't stopped all morning. Freddy wonders about his night spent alone amid the scary orange trees. There's got to be a limit, Freddy figures, a point where the body says *no more*. This and not another ounce. Ron could collapse from exhaustion before he steps onto a mat. Freddy forces himself to stand again and begins his lumbering trot in place. He watches Ron's steady movement, his working toward the special number that will allow him to let loose on the competition.

Freddy has to agree with his mother on this one. It's not healthy. They could be developing eating disorders. In sixth grade Freddy read a *Weekly Reader* article on anorexia nervosa. It was a true story about a girl who wasted away until she died. There was a picture of her before, pretty, then another version, scarecrow thin, her chin and nose angular and oversized like a wicked witch. The image had given him nightmares, but he now thinks he understands the kind of thinking that could bring a person there.

If he makes it to the finals, he will call his mother to let her know. She has arranged the night off. She will bring his grandparents too. Freddy watches as Ron stops for a moment and puts his hands behind his head. Like escaping from prison. That's what he'd said. Ron, who was homecoming king finalist, who seems so well placed in Ridgedale. And yet he's scared too, no matter what he says. Why else would he be so bent on Freddy going to Chilhowee? Ron wants to bring something from home to ease the transition, one huge lump of Ridgedalean humanity. This is what Freddy has figured out, but this isn't enough. There should be more to know, to understand.

"Here's what you do, Freddy," Carnes says, leaning over the seatback toward him. "When we get there, find you a bathroom and take a seat in the shitter. Grab your pecker in your hand." Carnes holds an imaginary member tight in his fist. His expression is intense. "Spit in the palm of your other hand, and with it you rub in a slow circle over the head of your dick, right over your piss hole." He demonstrates the circular rubbing motion with a pained face. You'll think you can't stand it, but if you keep at it long enough, you'll get a nice solid squirt of pee every now and then. Do it as many times as you need to."

Freddy tries to tune out Carnes and his horrifying prescription, tries to think of something else. In his backpack he has his study guide for AP calculus, but he doesn't want to pull it out. He thinks that maybe today can be about just one thing.

When they arrive at South Bay, several other buses are already parked in the lot. Some are the fancy chartered kind that only football teams are awarded in Ridgedale. Outside, a few wrestlers are running in sweat-suits. Freddy and Ron sprint across the parking lot before Coach can say anything to them. Inside the gym, it's warm, the smell a familiar mix of sweat, mildew, and cleaning product. Three mats are already spread and taped down to the gym floor. They cover most of the court surface. A South Bay wrestler sweeps one with a dust broom. Other wrestlers jog around the gym perimeter. Ron and Freddy fall into line. They still have about twenty minutes before weigh-ins even begin.

And this is it, Freddy thinks. His senior district tournament. This is supposed to be big. And it does feel big, just not singular. Or maybe everything is singular at this point. Maybe that's the way it works in life, a gradual escalation of significance until you reach a zenith, a point of maximum singularity, and everything after that is a falling off of impor-tance, culminating in death, the ultimate exercise in irrelevance. But that is stupid. That is too much thinking, Freddy. He inhales deeply, lengthens his stride, and overtakes the wrestler in front of him. Ron pulls further away.

HE WATCHES THE 103s undress and line up at the first scale, a line of naked jockeys. They are beautiful in their smallness. Diminutive and yet some-how whole, some of them well-hung out of all proportion. Freddy sits on the bench in his underwear, vaguely listening to the young heavyweight from Garden Hills, who is going on about some idiotic thing or another. Here's the worst part of the process. It's like waiting for a variation of his worst nightmare, the public nakedness one, only here it's for real.

A referee mans each of the three scales, so the weight classes move by quickly. Across the locker room, Ron enters from the gym and begins peeling away the layers of clothing. Soon he's in his underwear, and he wipes the sweat from his body with a shirt. He leaves the pile of clothes and walks over to Freddy. The Garden Hills wrestler stops talk-ing. Freddy stands beside Ron. They don't speak. They just watch the other wrestlers weighing in.

In the end, maybe both will take first place. They'll wrestle under the light, an important dream realized, and the crowd will be a solid black of cheering and voices. Melvin Mearle would even appreciate that.

And maybe somewhere in the dark his spirit would be there, approving. That would be the way to play it out in a sentimental movie. Or better, with something tangible at stake, the family farm perhaps. Or no, with Jim Schick in the crowd, the prodigal father in the flesh, come to see the son he abandoned some eighteen years ago. It could happen, Freddy thinks.

At the call for the 152s, Ron gives Freddy a concerned glance before bending to drop his underwear. Freddy can make out the separate vertebrae along Ron's backbone. If he reached out, he could trace their bumpy path.

"Think light," Freddy says. Ron doesn't smile. He lines up with the rest of his class. They all look insubstantial next to him.

The Garden Hills wrestler starts babbling again, but Freddy doesn't even pretend to listen. He watches Ron on the scale, sees the referee shake his head and Ron step backward and onto the floor. The referee places the balances on zero and makes a small adjustment before nodding for Ron to step back on. Ron exhales, steps on the scale, body hunched and hands curled under, straining to take up as little mass as possible. And this time the referee nods. Ron has made weight. He shakes his fist once in triumph. Still naked, his penis swaying loose and carefree, he walks over to Freddy.

"Where do you want to go for breakfast?" Ron says. "I vote Burger King."

"Shut up," Freddy says. He keeps his eyes averted "Don't jinx me."

When a referee calls for the heavyweights, Freddy walks toward the scale in his underwear. He is in line behind the wrestler from Garden Hills, and in front of him is Terrell Banks, a man among boys, deep black and rippled with muscles, an all-state defensive end for Lake Collins and a highly recruited division one prospect. After he makes weight, Banks struts down the line of competitors, gives a wink to Freddy as he passes. The line moves forward. The Garden Hills wrestler strips down and steps onto the scale, ass cheeks wide and flat, looking reddish, chafed. He is fat and yet small for a heavyweight. Two-forty at the most. In their last match, Freddy pinned him in less than thirty seconds.

Freddy is up now, and he sheds his underwear, immediately feels the disorienting, dreamlike quality. Nothing to hide behind, bare-ass before the scrutiny of the world. This is the way it's done. No reason to fight it.

"Name and school," the referee says.

"Clevenger," Freddy says. "Ridgedale."

The referee checks his clipboard. He nods, something changed in his face, a new respect maybe. "The number one seed," he says. He sets the scale exactly at 275 and holds the bar against the top. "Step up, Clevenger of Ridgedale," he says.

Freddy steps onto the small platform. The metal is cold under his feet, and he feels crowded, wobbly. He's a spectacle, a circus elephant on a tiny pedestal. He wonders if he should do some trick, try to lift one foot off the ground, or balance a giant ball on the end of his nose.

The metal arm descends slowly and taps the bottom of the balance, then moves upward, to the top, clinking softly, and Freddy winces, but then the bar is falling again, not hitting the bottom this time, and then slowing, stabilizing right there in mid-air.

"You're dead on, son," the referee says. "You hit it perfectly."

The cool air gathers between Freddy's legs. It gives a sort of lifting sensation that feels nice. Right here, perfect. Freddy watches the metal bar floating magically between the two points, and he is almost afraid to move.

Under the Light

It isn't even close. Ron takes control of the West Bay wrestler from the start, working an underhook and overhook combination, then exploding into a throw that snatches his opponent from his feet, sends him through the air in a flashing arc and straight to his back.

The crowd responds from the darkness, and the wrestlers strain in the orb of white light. The West Bay 152 does his best to bridge and manages to hold out for a while, but Ron sprawls hard, drives his full weight into the pin, and it is over with more than a minute left in the first period. Ridgedale takes the overall lead, with Lake Collins now five points behind.

It's the only pin of the finals so far, and the crowd—a really big one for a Florida tournament—claps and stomps against the bleachers. This is good, truly. But already, as Ron's hand is raised, and as he then runs to Freddy and jumps up into his arms, Freddy lifting him high and then Coach joining in, the three a single mass of celebration, even now Freddy feels the pressure settle upon himself.

Because it is up to him now, him and Banks anyway, whether it will be Ridgedale or Lake Collins. If Freddy loses by decision, he will only forfeit three points and Ridgedale will still win. But a loss by pinfall—

that's worth six points—and Freddy could lose the tournament for the whole team. It's too much pressure. He steps away from Coach and Ron. He paces into the shadows alone.

CROWDS ALWAYS LOVE the heavyweights. There's something about the sheer bulk, two behemoths going at it, that lends an excitement, even more so with this kind of contrast, one fat and low to the ground and the other, Banks, all long muscles.

Freddy tries to listen to Coach's final breathy words in his ear, but the stomping on the bleachers is too loud. Over the loudspeaker he hears his own name, then a push from Coach, and it's into the bright light, Freddy darting to the center of the circle and planting his foot down on the mark. The crowd cheers and stomps. Somewhere in the darkness are his mother and his grandparents.

Banks, after his name is called, comes out slowly, cocky and egging on the crowd by lifting his arms and nodding. Asshole, Freddy thinks, although this is a hard thought to hold with Banks in front of him like this, the whole physical force of him.

The handshake and whistle, then—like Freddy expected—Banks locks up with him up top, the sudden smell of sweat and of another's body—but not foul—a soapy-sweet odor as if Banks has showered recently. And damn he's strong, yanking Freddy's head toward the mat, but Freddy recovers, matches the strength as best as he can. They struggle for position for some time until Freddy, thinking he sees a brief opening, goes for a standing headlock, misses, and is driven by Banks to all fours.

"Two, takedown, red!" one of the referees says, and Banks is chopping Freddy's arm, driving his face to the mat, and turning him almost for an exposure. The crowd responds, anticipates, but Freddy bases up, looks skyward, pivots until he is standing, but Banks is lifting him now—all of Freddy—off the ground an instant, and spinning him back to the mat. Freddy holds off the attack though, and knows he's lucky when, at the end of the period, he is down only 2–0.

Freddy stands and puts his hands behind his head, tries to catch some wind as one of the referees flips the wooden disk. Coach and Ron yell instructions from Freddy's corner.

Ron yells, "Suck it up, Biggen!"

Freddy tries to suck it up.

The disk lands on the side painted green. Freddy is green. He takes one more giant breath, then chooses neutral position because—he's not sure—because he needs a takedown is why, needs to catch up, and he shoots at the whistle, low and fast, but Banks sprawls hard, grinds a cross-face into Freddy's nose, the hard meat of his forearm forcing Freddy to retreat.

From the corner Coach yells, "Easy now!" which Freddy takes to mean don't get too aggressive and slip into a clumsy scuffle that will favor the better athlete, because then you're fucked. Your ass is pinned and Ridgedale loses.

Better to play defense, push and pull and if there's an opening to go for, then okay, but don't . . . don't get pinned.

But here's the problem with too much defense—it gives the guy too many chances—and here Banks slides behind Freddy, gets a tight hold, and before Freddy knows what the hell, he's back on the mat, Banks working a half nelson and turning Freddy's shoulders until it's a near fall.

It is possible, in wrestling, to surrender in a way that looks like your best effort. The fatigue can bring you to this low place, you gasping for air and with your blood so oxygen-sapped, limbs all dead weight and numb tingles. If it's done right, you can give in and that's it, pretend to fight all the way to your back, let the guy press your shoulders to the mat as if he's just too much for you, like you're being overpowered, which—in a way—you are.

And there's life after this match, everything really: college and experiences. With any luck, love and family. A good job of your own, with a degree in something like engineering or accounting so you can pay off your mother's house, buy her the whole damn block if she wants.

But Freddy can't think of any of this now. He only tries to breathe, bridge, hold out for the buzzer, which he does, but because of the near fall he's down 7–0. Banks, however, is the one who rises to criticism, his coach yelling how he should have finished it there and what the hell's wrong with him, just quit half-assing and pin the fat clown.

One of the referees cites the coach with a warning. Freddy double-checks the score. Seven points is too much to make up in a period. It would be impossible almost. He can only win with a pin. He tries to catch some breath and looks to Coach, who does not tell him that he has to go for a pin. Instead, Coach, half-lit at the edge of the light but big-eyed and crazy-serious, says, "You do not let him pin you, son. No matter what."

Ron just gives him a thumbs-up.

Freddy understands. Give up the three team points for his loss, but don't give in or do anything to risk giving away six. Ride it out, and Ridgedale wins the tournament.

Banks, glistening black and strong-faced, determined, chooses top position, and Freddy kneels to all fours, looks up at the referee, feels Banks settle behind him, one giant hand gripped at his elbow and the other wrapped underneath Freddy's belly. The whistle, and Freddy braces for the attack, which comes as another chop and thrust, but Freddy maintains his base. He's stiff, all firm defense, and the referee tells him he has to move.

But here's the thing. Banks is tiring too. Freddy can feel the drop in urgency, the thrusts still urgent and definitely strong but not as much so, and this is Freddy's chance maybe.

"Warning, green, stalling!" a referee says.

But Freddy knows that doesn't matter now. He has points to give away. He simply needs to hold on.

"One minute!" Coach yells.

One minute is a long time in a wrestling match, but Freddy knows he can do it now. He feels solid right here, immovable. And yet, there's more in him than this, maybe not enough for a full-blown chance but some kind of final death-throes effort, a sort of fight-to-the-end respectability, and here is Freddy bursting upward with all he has, on his feet now and spinning toward Banks, who chases too eagerly. Freddy uses the momentum, clenches Banks at the head and wrenches hard. And it feels as though Banks will go to the mat, straight to his back. The crowd—seeing this too—pounds and cheers, and Freddy wrenches hard with all that's left. Banks catches himself with an arm, pulls backward. Freddy, very nearly spent now, tries to hold his grip, but Banks' head is slipping, then popping free, and then Banks is behind Freddy again.

"Fifteen seconds!" Coach yells.

Not much left after this, his body all limp weakness and hardly conscious of anything except a need to hold on, fend off this last frantic effort by Banks. There's the buzzer finally, and Freddy, exhausted, plops spread-eagle onto the mat.

CHERUBIM

I FINALLY FIND THEM downstairs in the basement, my four-year-old daughter and the neighbor's boy, both naked and pinkish, their hairless bodies rosy-warmed against the cold by the churning dry cycle. They see me and freeze in mid-play, stare back with wide eyes and slight baby grins. For just an instant, I think Raphael, Michelangelo.

"What the hell?" I say. "What are you doing?" My voice is way too high, panicked. "Do you want to freeze? Put your clothes back on!"

They scramble to dress, fumble around like a couple of miniature adulterers. I guess this is what goes on while I'm in charge, what I let happen on my watch.

"It's time for you to go home, Billy," I manage, my mouth suddenly dry. I feel better when he pulls his elastic pants over his little pink erection. I help Megan with her zipper, and I try to think of what I'm supposed to do in a situation like this.

The dryer finishes with a loud buzz. Billy slips on his sneakers. He runs past me, shoelaces clicking around his feet. "Billy," I say. I push Megan's sweater over her head. I motion him back to me. He comes, and I tie his shoes.

Upstairs, I pull his cap down over his ears and walk him outside, watch him escape from my yard to his. He knocks on his door, is received by his mother, who waves to me and guides him inside. I give Megan a cup of apple juice and pretend to start the dishes. If she sees me get upset, I reason, it will only be worse. I watch her out of the corner of my eye, though, looking for some sign of trauma, some hint of secret shame, but she just sips away, takes up her coloring book as if nothing has happened.

Her eyes follow me to the phone where I page Lenore at work, the University of Tennessee, where she's finishing a master's in art history and where she teaches two sections of Intro to Humanities. The other thing: she's sleeping with one of her professors, the director of her thesis. She doesn't think I know, but I do.

Staring through the window above the sink, I wash a spoon under a stream of hot water. Across the road, two bundled Chilhowee College students are smoking cigarettes in front of their dorm. They have hoods pulled up over their heads and shift foot-to-foot to keep warm. In the distance, the sun has disappeared behind the foothills, which become dark rounded monoliths against the gray sky. I press my fingers to my neck, try to gauge my pulse. I'm sure that I'm not well overall. I feel like I'm slipping away. Or maybe stuck, the things around me moving, pulling loose toward some great corrective measure.

I microwave a bowl of Spaghettios, stirring them and testing with my finger before placing them in front of Megan. "Careful," I say. "They're a little hot." I cut a small green apple into four pieces, putting two next to her bowl when the knocks come, hard and fast, and both of us jump. The door opens, and Andy Wolfenbarger looms in the entrance. A twelve-pack of Michelob dangles from one of his long arms.

"Uncle Wolf!" Megan cries. She flies out of her chair, running into the foyer before I can say a word. Her spoon drops to the floor, and I'm picking Spaghettios off the tile when the phone rings.

It's Lenore. Frantic. Megan squeals as Wolf lifts her high into the air, growling and tickling her belly with his beard. I try to shush them, but they ignore me.

"God, what happened?" Lenore says. "Tell me."

"Nothing," I say. "I mean, nothing really bad."

"What do I hear? Why is she screaming?"

"It's Wolf. He just showed up, but that's not why I paged." I pull the cord around the corner and begin to explain. I can't find quite the right words for it—they all seem too ugly—but I manage to get across the basics.

"Christ, Ron," she says. "Where were you?"

"I went outside for like five minutes. I brought in the trashcans." I leave out that I also took a quick smoke, only half a cigarette. "I never thought I had to worry about them, you know." I can't finish.

"Playing doctor?" Lenore says. "I guess I'm glad that's all it was. Paging me in the middle of class? That says emergency, Ron. Do you want to kill me? Is that it? You want me dead?"

"She's four years old," I say.

"Exactly. It's not as if she's been *deflowered*. They're kids. It's called experimentation. That's why you have to watch them. All the time."

As I point Wolf and Megan into the living room, Lenore would like to know if she should tell her students that class is canceled because she can't leave her daughter alone with her husband.

"Nice one," I say. "We can't all be the model of parenthood. You're a real Joan Cleaver. Do you know that?" This stops her, but only for a second.

"June Cleaver," she says. She sighs into the phone. "Ron, I really need to go to the library tonight." Her voice softens a bit. "It'll probably be fairly late, if that's all right."

"It's *preferred*," I say.

The line goes dead, and I hang up. Anger rising now, the familiar heaviness in my chest. Generalized, mischanneled anxiety, according to the shrink we pay for me to see twice a month. I try to do my breathing exercises. I count to ten.

I pick up the twelve-pack left by the front door, pull out two beers, and slide the rest into the refrigerator. In the living room, Wolf and Megan play with a Nerf football. Wolf lobs a high pass that bounces off her fingertips and lands in the middle of the stacks of sorted photographs that line the carpet.

"Not in the house," I say. I set the beers on the coffee table and snatch up the ball, straightening the photos as best I can. Megan is overstimulated. She jumps up and down with her hands held out to me. I pitch the ball to Wolf, who tucks it snugly under his arm and affects the Heisman pose. I take Megan lightly by the wrists. "Go finish your supper," I say.

"I'm not hungry," she says, pulling toward Wolf.

"That's *one*," I say.

She looks to Wolf for help, but he just shrugs.

"That's *two*," I say.

Megan puckers her lips, glares at me. She turns and hops toward the kitchen. She always hops when she's mad. I take my beer and shake my head at Wolf.

"What happens at three?" he says.

"Time out."

Wolf chuckles.

"You can't just barge in like this all the time," I say. "Like some crazy person. You get her so worked up that she can't even sleep."

"Sorry," Wolf says, and he slides out of his jacket and settles onto the couch. He's wearing a faded-red sweatshirt with "Chilhowee Football" printed across the front in cracked yellowed lettering, then below that, "1990." It's the same one they gave us at the beginning of camp our freshman year.

"Damn, son," I say. "Fits a little snug these days, doesn't it?"

"You reckon?" Wolf flexes so that his bicep stretches against the old material. "Nine years of curls and bench presses. What can I say?"

I twist the cap off my beer and fling it into his gut. It hits just above the outline of his navel. "More like three years of Twinkies and sitting on the couch," I say. "You'd never make a linebacker now. They'd have to put your fat ass at O-line."

Wolf was the first person I met when I entered camp as an undersized cornerback out of small-town Florida. He was an all-state local, still walking gingerly on a bad Achilles tendon that he'd torn at the start of his last year of high school, an injury which forced him to sit out his entire senior season and ended any real shot of his playing big-time college ball. We were roommates for the next four years until I graduated and got married. Wolf graduated a year later, a Division III All-American. He's now in his second season as assistant linebackers coach for the college and teaches P.E. at Alcoa Elementary.

"You want to go to Sweeney's?" Wolf says. "Shoot some stick?"

"I'm babysitting."

Wolf rubs his face and takes a pull from his bottle. He squints, staring at the piles of pictures.

"We got a set of photo albums for our anniversary," I explain. "Lenore's been organizing all our pictures."

Wolf nods. He picks up my book off the table. He reads aloud. *The Hero with a Thousand Faces.* This for graduate school?"

I want to tell him to settle down, to quit fiddling with everything. "Yeah, sort of," I say. I don't mention that I'm taking the semester off or that I'm on academic probation.

He thumbs through the pages. "What's it about?"

"I don't know," I say. I take the book from him, set it back on the table.

"What are you going for again?" he says.

"Religious studies."

"What can you do with that? Be a preacher?"

"Not even close," I say, knowing where he's headed. "I might switch to something else."

"Reason I ask is I talked to Coach yesterday. Says they may be looking for a DB assistant this off-season. Told him you might be interested."

This is Wolf's new plan for me, but I don't want to get into it again. I click the TV to ESPN. "Did I tell you? They gave me a bigger route at *The Sentinel,* out in West Knoxville." I tilt my bottle and let the beer pour against the back of my throat, thinking about tomorrow morning, the muggy loading room, the smell of ink and cheap paper and the drone of Mrs. Vickers going on about the bursitis in her shoulder. I try to see past this though, to the afternoon. Lenore doesn't have school or work. Maybe she'll tend Megan, let me watch college football and doze on the couch in the comfort of daylight.

"Watch yourself on them roads tomorrow," Wolf says. "It's supposed to get down to the teens tonight. They're talking snow and ice." He sneezes and wipes his hand on his pant leg. "I'm just glad we play at home."

I think of Lenore, of what she said to me earlier, and about her fifteen-mile drive from UT, how she sometimes gets careless when she's tired and how an icy road and one little mistake could send her whirling away from us—an awful thought—into a ditch and out of this world forever. I picture Megan, motherless. Myself, a widower: the funeral, the tears, the gentle pity all around, the terrific simplicity of it all.

I leave Wolf in the living room and go to the hall closet, unzip my old travel pack and find a pair of my wool socks that Megan likes to pull up to her thighs on cold nights. I lay her pajamas and a towel on the top of the toilet and run a shallow bath with a splash of Mr. Bubble to help coax her in. I raise the hall thermostat and go back to the living room. Wolf is flipping through a stack of pictures. "Hell," he says. "I *have* put on some weight."

Megan hops down from her chair and is on her way to Wolf when I step in front of her. Her cheeks are glazed orange with tomato and cheese sauce. I smile. Not deflowered, I think. Kid stuff. Not the end of the world. "I've got your bath ready," I say. "Wash really good and you'll have time to visit with Uncle Wolf. He just told me we might get snow tomorrow. Maybe we can try out your sled."

She tries to go around me, but I shadow-block her. When she starts to cry in protest, I bulge out my eyes and make like I'm crazy. She grins, reluctantly. *"Meesta Bubble!"* I say. *"Meesta Bubble want you!"* She squeals as I sweep her up and blow fart noises against her belly on the way to the bathroom. I lean against the doorjamb as she undresses and climbs into the tub. I can hear Wolf laughing in that strange, high-pitched way of his. He leans back over the arm of the couch and looks down the hall at me, holding up a picture. "That's the damned worst beard I ever seen," he says. "You look like one of them Amish fellas."

I can't see it, but I think I know that picture. And he's right. It's a bad beard, weak across the upper lip. I'm in a bar in Aix-en-Provence, France, drinking beers with several others from the Grads Abroad program.

Megan holds up her washcloth and whispers something to it. I go to Wolf, look closer at the picture. Besides the beard, I'd say I look pretty good. Younger, thinner. I was different then: laid back, more comfortable with noise and crowds. But I don't remember when I started changing. Lenore is in the picture too, three stools down, smoking a cigarette and looking indifferently away from the camera. Her hair gathers around her shoulders in tufts of soft copper. We were both recent Chilhowee grads, from a class of barely 800, but at the time I scarcely knew her.

Sounds of splashing come from the bathroom, and I race back to the doorway. Children can drown, I have read, in only a few inches of water, but I find Megan okay, grinning as she sends a handful of foam splattering against the toilet and laughs. When I clear my throat, she starts and turns to me, repentant. A halo of white suds tops her head, but I keep my serious stare. "Get clean," I say. "Wash your face."

Wolf brings me a fresh beer, then goes back to the living room. I'm considering paging Lenore again, warning her about the roads. The tread on our tires isn't great, and the way she drives sometimes.

"Who do we play tomorrow?" I call to Wolf.

"Washington and Lee," he says. "The bunch of faggity-ass preppies. Rich fucking shits."

"Beat the *hell* out of W and *L,*" I say. "Do we still say that?"

Wolf gets up and joins me in the hallway. He brings some of the pictures with him. "It's a hell of a lot more work than I ever figured it'd be." He shakes his head. "I miss being on the field, Coach yelling at you and telling you what a worthless piece of shit you are, not having to think about it, just going after people and knocking their dicks in the dirt."

"Pursue and destroy." I say.

"Damn straight." Wolf looks at me seriously. "You're the one that ought to be coaching. You got the brains for it."

"Do we still run a straight five mostly? A cover two?"

"Double eagle. More stunts. You should do it. You weren't never worth a shit on the field, too damn short and a slowpoke to boot, but you could always see it, the whole big picture and all."

I think about it. I wasn't *that* slow, not for Division III anyway. I was as fast as he was. I think I was, but it seems like a long time ago, and I can't remember a specific incident to prove it. "I was a decent player," I say. "I was a good cover-man."

"You should call Coach after the season."

I try to imagine myself as a coach, the whistle and cap, the tight polyester shorts, me barking orders amid the chaos of a practice, right there in the wide-open field. "I'm not saying I was a superstar or anything," I say. "But I held my own. I didn't *suck.*"

Wolf squints at one of the photos. "That's the Louvre, ain't it?"

Lenore and I stand in front of the big glass pyramid. We wear baseball caps and daypacks, and the sun shines on our tanned faces. It must have been right after we toured the Rodin museum because her eyes look red and swollen underneath. She had sobbed quietly as we watched the blind man, who was allowed to touch some of the sculptures. He traced his fingers slowly along the rigid sinew while his companion explained, "collarbone, chest, abdomen, hip," and Lenore had stepped playfully on my foot for snickering when the blind man's hand wandered too close to the phallus. She got me square in the big toe, hurting me worse than she had intended, and it throbbed like hell while I walked through the rest of the museum, holding her hand and realizing that I was falling in love.

In the bathroom, Megan and I play *brr—brr, quick—quick.* It's a trusty cold-night after-bath game. She dances in a puddle of water and soap while I try to towel her chubby body.

"*Brr—brr,*" I say.

"*Quick—quick,*" she returns.

Then I'm shooed away so she can dress herself. Maybe she, too, senses my incompetence, realizes her second-rate father can't be fully counted on, a father who already allows her neighborhood coeds to lure her downstairs, seduce and undress her.

Wolf brings two new beers. We sit on the couch, Megan between us, and watch *RugRats.* Clutching one of Lenore's silk nightgowns against her face, Megan lays her head in Wolf's lap. Her hair, copper like her mother's but much lighter, hangs damp across her cheek. She blinks slowly, watching Tommy and Chucky, who have mistaken an open-bottom cardboard box for a secret doorway into a parallel world, where things are vaguely the same but also strangely different. It's a rerun.

WE HAD OUR FIRST FIGHT in Belgium, over a professional mime of all things. We met him in Paris, at *Sacre Coeur,* where he performed some kind of routine for tips. He joined us after that, a tall, thin Frenchman, handsome behind the makeup. The girls especially loved him, but there was something about him that annoyed me. I mean, a mime for Christ's sake. So in Brussels, drunk and jealous, I told Lenore that I wasn't leaving for Amsterdam the next day with the rest of the group, but that if she couldn't stand being away from Mr. Marcel Marceau for a day or two, that was just fine with me. She said that she couldn't care less about Laurent one way or the other but that I wasn't making myself very attractive at the moment either.

The next morning I woke alone, my mouth dry and chalky and a deep ache in my head. I found a note on the message board from her, telling me that she'd let me know where they were once they'd settled. Beneath the writing she had drawn a heart pierced with an arrow. The next day I got another message, this time asking me to please stay put and that she would come to me, alone.

Wolf slides gently out from under Megan and lowers her head to the couch. She shifts a moment, then resettles. We go to the refrigerator together. He frowns when I take out the jug of water and pour myself a glass.

"Here's something to wash that down with," he says, passing me a beer.

"I'm okay, actually," I say.

He closes the refrigerator door. "You trying to tell me to go?"

"No," I say. "Stay. Drink. I just don't like to have too much when it's just me at home with her. What if I had to drive?"

"I'll drive you anywhere you need to go."

"Oh," I say. "I didn't realize that. Why didn't you say so to begin with? I mean if *you'll* drive us, that solves everything." I take the beer from Wolf's hand.

We sit in the living room chairs and let Megan stretch out on the couch. I watch her breathing softly. Her pink eyelids remain shut. She's beautiful, really. It's not just my opinion. She truly is, this strange perfect little person, far too precious to be trusted to my care. There's so much to worry about: swimming pools, child abductors, car accidents, various cancers.

"I've got to get going soon anyhow," Wolf says. He nibbles off a piece of fingernail and spits it to the carpet.

IT'S OKAY TO GET a little drunk, I decide, to put some distance between me and this night. Tomorrow, I'll have a talk with Megan about private parts staying private. But tonight I want to sleep, calmly, no racing heartbeat, no walking through the house checking door and window locks.

The beers are finished, so I dig out the bottle of tequila from under a pile of frozen vegetables. I take two shot glasses from the cabinet. Through the kitchen window, I can see across the road and into the dormitory lobby. There's a blinking Christmas tree in the corner, and two guys are playing ping-pong.

Wolf approaches behind me, and I feel him standing there, can hear him breathing, and I know he's watching them too. I fill the glasses and pass one to him. "Think we could take 'em?" he says.

"Definitely," I say. I tilt my glass and empty it in a slow swallow.

"We should go down there," Wolf says. "Show the kids how it's done. Take 'em to school."

"Yeah," I say, enjoying the warm burn in my throat. "We should."

"I'm serious," Wolf says. "Not tonight, but next week. We could get a tournament going, like we used to. You want to?"

I turn to face him. I can already feel the shift from the tequila. I say, "I don't know."

"I ain't saying right this minute or anything, Ron." His eyes are narrow and insistent. "But some time. One of these nights."

"What did I say? I said I don't know." I'm irritated—and I know this is stupid—but I don't want to concede this to him right now. I need him to argue with me.

"You don't know," Wolf says. It's not a question. He takes his glass and turns toward the living room. "Don't seem like you know too much of anything these days."

I follow. "What the hell do you mean by that?"

"Nothing," he says. "Don't worry. Turn into a goddamned vampire for all I care."

"I'm *not* worried."

"Good." He tilts his head back and empties the shot glass, grimaces, his teeth bared, and lifts his coat from the couch.

I'm not sure why, but the thought of him leaving right now upsets me. "So I'm a vampire now, just because I can't go out every time you want?"

"I told you," he says. "Don't worry."

"I'm not worried, but you come out with this vampire shit. Because I can't go out every night?"

"Out?" Wolf says. He laughs. "You don't go *out* at all. Except to deliver them goddamn newspapers. You stay shut up all day, won't even answer the phone half the time. And you ain't been to graduate school for a long time."

For an instant I want to punch him, right in his big fat face, but when I think of actually doing it, it seems like the saddest thing in the world. I say, "I can't live like I'm a kid. I can't play dodgeball all day. I wish to hell I could, but I can't.

"No," he says. He looks genuinely hurt. "I don't reckon you can. You've got your papers to deliver."

"You don't even know," I say. "You don't understand."

Megan mumbles something. She rolls over onto her belly. Wolf puts on his jacket and shakes his head. "Hell, I know that Ron," he says. His voice is a harsh whisper. "How the hell could I understand anything, me, dumb as I am. I'm just a big kid, playing dodge ball all day. I'm just a big, dumb-ass kid."

"Fuck you," I whisper. I follow him through the kitchen. "That's not what I meant. You don't know." He walks into the foyer, opens the front door. Now I do want to let him go. I want to say nothing else, but I feel the words come anyway.

"The thing is, with my wife banging some guy at UT, it's hard to think about other things. It's hard to make ping-pong commitments."

And there it is. I've said it in words now, to Wolf and to me, and I'm ashamed—that he'd have to hear such a thing—that I couldn't hold it all together somehow. The cold air seeps inside. Wolf stands in the doorway, his back still toward me. He seems to sink, deflate, like he's been punctured and something vital is leaking. But I continue. "He's her professor. I heard her whispering to him on the phone when she thought I was asleep. Afterwards, I pushed the redial, and the fucker said his name when he answered."

Wolf shakes his head, turns. He stares at me, dumb-mouthed. We stand like idiots in the cold air until he remembers to shut the door.

"Jesus," he says. I can see him thinking. "And the whole time. Why'd you let me go on like a big asshole?"

"I don't know," I say. I want to take it all back, talk about football and ping-pong, have a few more drinks. "I shouldn't have said anything."

Wolf doesn't correct me. He shakes his head, looks away. "Jesus," he says. "Are you sure about this?"

"No, I'm not sure." I feel slightly relieved when I say this. "She was whispering. I only caught part of it." I don't mention the frequent hang-ups or that I found a condom wrapper in her car.

Wolf shakes his head. "Mind if I have me another one of them shots?"

We return to the television with the tequila where Mr. and Mrs. Brady are settling an argument between Greg and Marsha. It's the opening scene.

We sit quietly until he says, "I bet you it was some kind of misunderstanding."

"Yeah," I say. "Forget I said anything." I slam another shot.

The Brady theme song is playing, and the family grows box by box until all eight of them are there, looking up and down and across at one another from their respective squares, all smiles, until Alice appears in the center and it's through.

"Maybe she was just whispering so she wouldn't wake you up," Wolf says.

"Probably," I say. "It's probably nothing." I take a swig from the bottle.

We sit for a while, the silence now suddenly conspicuous and awkward. I could have avoided this. He's right. I don't know anything for sure. And hasn't Lenore tried too? More than most would? Didn't she send out copies of my résumé until I flat-out refused to go to the interviews? Didn't she stop talking to her own brother for four months after he called me a "spaz," right to my face, and at Christmas dinner?

I flip through the channels, looking for something, anything, to watch. I land on a documentary of the Vietnam War. Right now, Nixon is on the telephone, but you can bet that, eventually, they'll show that terrible footage of the Vietnamese girl, naked and running down a road, burns on her body. What kind of person would film such a thing and not try to help her more, pull her up into a jeep or something. And yet I remember she did make it out okay. I know this because I saw her a few years ago on a talk show, a grown woman, of course, and seemingly well-adjusted.

During the commercial, Wolf rises and pulls on his jacket. "I better get going," he says. He stands over Megan a moment, smiles. He starts to say something but doesn't.

"Kick their asses tomorrow," I say. "Maybe I'll come watch, if I'm not too tired."

He punches me lightly in the shoulder. "You best come," he says. "And don't bring a book this time, neither. Maybe we could play some pool after, talk or something."

"Maybe," I say. Then I add, "Really, maybe." He nods, turns, and makes his way to the door.

MEGAN SIGHS when I lift her. I'm still in the habit of supporting her neck, although I know it's not necessary. I lay her gently in the middle of our bed. She smacks her lips a few times, the way Lenore tells me that I do. I cover her with a quilt and raise the thermostat again before returning to the photos.

There are so many of them. I wonder if they'll look different once they're all transferred to the albums, safely sealed behind a layer of plastic. I wonder how Lenore will choose to arrange them, these glimpses of our years together, what story they will tell and how my character will come across. I spot a photo of *L'Auberge de Jeunesse* Van Gogh, the hostel in Brussels, where I waited after that second message. She found me sidled up to the lobby bar, drinking Duvels with a new Irish friend who had advised me to play it cool, not too eager. But then I saw her enter through the door, beautiful, in khaki shorts and hiking boots, her hair pulled back in a ponytail and the sweat bright on her forehead. She was carrying her backpack, which jutted far above her head, and I knew, right then, that I wanted to do anything she asked. She approached wearing the strangest expression. I stood, and she didn't say a word, just lowered her pack to the ground, reached into it, and pulled out something small and white. She smiled unsurely, holding the object between us in the top of her palm, and Megan made her first appearance on the scene in the form of a red plus-sign.

I flip through the pile until I find the one I'm looking for. We're in the same lobby, and I am on one knee, pointing up at Lenore's flat belly and smiling like crazy. That man is me; I can't deny it, but if he were here right now, I wonder how I'd explain things to him and if he could understand any of it.

I proposed, happily, right there in the common area with a rhinestone ring donated by my bartender. I bought a round of drinks. REO Speedwagon played in the background, and we danced, slowly, strangers watching and congratulating us, and all the time we whispered things to each other about our coming life and our baby, about love and forever.

It's not that I have regrets. Even now, I would do it again, only better. And Megan? You shouldn't be able to love another person so much.

I've never been able to explain it just right, not to Lenore or anyone else, why, for example, when she was a baby I would check her all through the night, stand over her in awe until Lenore called me back to the bed, knowing, I think, that I was hoping for the softest cry so I could lift her from the crib and rock her for hours—just the two of us—until dawn.

Some nights, when it was warm and Megan was restless, I would spread a blanket on our front lawn. I'd sneak her outside while Lenore slept, rest her belly-down against my chest, and we would lie there together, two gypsies under the night sky. On those nights I would sometimes forget myself, for seconds at a time. I would squint skyward, past the clouds, the moon, the stars, to a place before me, a hazy realm of silence and fog where I would hang an instant, unborn. No bills or responsibilities. No generalized anxiety disorder. Then it would rush back on me, all of it, and I was on the lawn again, a strange child breathing against my neck. And who I was seemed impossible.

I WAKE ON THE COUCH to the sound of keys against the kitchen counter. I scramble up, trying to fold my blanket, the dream images still with me, naked children, hundreds of them, wielding torches and lyres and prancing around me in a wall of terrible glowing faces.

Lenore stands at the end of the couch.

"They wouldn't let me through," I say.

She lowers her eyebrows, looks at me like I'm a fool. Strands of her hair have slipped from her ponytail and hang over her face like frizzy strings. She seems tired, almost old, but pretty even so.

"Who?" she says.

"Cherubs," I say. "I mean, cherubim." It all makes sense for an instant; for an instant, it is totally clear. Why doesn't she know what I mean? She shakes her head, annoyed, and the world comes back to me. "Sorry," I say. "Dreaming."

She glances at the beer bottles and the empty quart on the table, but she doesn't comment. I start to clear the mess, but she stops me. "Just leave it," she says. "You need to sleep." She sees a stack of pictures that I left on the table. She picks them up and sits down to look through them.

"I paged you," I say.

"I know," she says. "My beeper must have been on vibrate. By the time I checked, I was already driving home."

"There's supposed to be snow and ice."

"I heard that too."

I check the clock. It's almost 2:00 A.M. "Late night," I say, yawning.

"Late night," she says. "Lots of work."

"Naturally."

"What do you mean, naturally?"

"Nothing," I say. "I'm just saying."

"Ron," she says. She stares steadily at me. "I was at the library, then in my office for about an hour after, grading tests. That's the truth." She goes back to the photos and sighs. "Was she fussy at bedtime?"

"No. She was fine. I put her in our bed."

"What did you say to her about the thing with Billy, the playing doctor business?"

"Nothing."

"Did you call his parents?"

"You said it was no big thing."

Lenore stops on one picture and looks awhile. "I know," she says. "I know I did, but then I started thinking about it."

I'M BRUSHING MY TEETH when Lenore enters the bathroom. She comes at me so suddenly that I step back in defense until I realize what she's up to. I let her slip my boxers to my ankles and watch her down there, half wondering if I'm still dreaming. I spit into the sink and set my toothbrush down. She rises, and I help her out of her jeans. We giggle because she has failed to remove her left shoe, and her jeans are stuck on her foot, hanging inside out like some stubborn molting.

I grab her from behind and pull her to me. She lets me lift her shirt over her head and pushes her bare back to my chest. She's warm against me. She leans forward to take hold of the counter. Her soft pale shoulders dimple at the top. We do it crouched over the sink, quietly, out of habit, but with a long-missing resolve. The booze is still in me, and I feel like I can last forever. Cold sweat bubbles up on our skin. We both look straight into the bathroom mirror. Our faces, focused and stern, stare back at us like stone.

"Remind you?" Lenore gasps.

And it does. We returned to our Paris hostel to find our rooms filled with sleep mates. We had to slip into the upstairs WC that very first time. I remember it. Legs tired from a day of walking, the smell of fresh pastries still in my nose. My toenail sore. Both of us worked up by the barrage of art, the naked forms frozen in eternal perfection, unmoving ripples of muscularity. Gods and warriors. Lovers, heroes, angels. Saviors and saints. The constant flashes of marble tits and pricks. We held each other afterward, trembling and spent, naked together in a community toilet, an ocean between us and home.

Lenore straightens and presses her back to me again. "The stuff on the phone," she whispers. "I shouldn't have said it. I know you watch her close." She reaches back and strokes my hair. "You always have." My hips ache and I feel myself about to lose it. I end in a flurry, managing to elicit a few high-pitched squeals before I finish inside her.

AT 3:28 I SWITCH OFF the alarm. Megan is a warm pod wedged between Lenore and me. The room is cold, so I tiptoe into the hall and raise the thermostat. I dress in the dark. No time for a shower. I get my coat and ski cap. I finish washing my face and hear whispers in the bedroom. In the mirror, I stare at myself and think *Aging vampire paper boy. Cuckold with drinking problem.*

They are waiting for me in the hallway, both wearing long coats and slippers.

"She woke up," Lenore says, handing me the scraper for the wind-shield. "She wants to see if it's snowing."

I turn on the porch light, and we walk out together. The cold hits us, and we stand, huddled, staring into the clear darkness.

"It's not snowing," Megan says. Her cheeks are pink in the light. Lenore crouches beside her and uses her own sleeve to wipe away a trace of snot from Megan's nose.

"No, honey," she says. "Not yet."

I kneel between them and hug. I feel simultaneous kisses, warm and moist, on either cheek.

"*Brr—brr,*" Megan says.

"*Quick—quick,*" I say.

As I stand, Lenore holds tight to my sleeve, rising with me and keep-ing herself close. She looks closely at me, grips my jacket. "I'm going to leave you," she whispers. "I'm so sorry, but I am."

We separate, and I look into her face. She's waiting for my response, and there is something almost submissive in her eyes, as if she wants me to take control, dispute it, say that I won't allow it. And I should do this, fight for us, for the people we once were, the ones we could be. But it's not enough, I think, not now. Love, whatever, it doesn't always translate, disperse evenly over life in a way that works. I feel drunkish, distant. Tired.

"I just can't do it anymore," she says. "You'll make me crazy."

"I know," I say. "I know I will." I watch her. I wait. This is it. Not the end exactly, but part of the end. I'm so sleepy. I want us all to go back to the bed, to rest under the warm covers, sleep through the whole day together.

Megan wipes her nose with the back of her hand. Lenore looks as if she is about to cry, but it might just be the cold. "I'm sorry," she says. She swallows hard. She touches Megan on the shoulder. "Tell Daddy bye," she says.

"Bye, Daddy." Megan yawns slowly. Her little mouth forms a small dark oval.

"Bye, Sweetheart," I say.

"We'll see you in a few hours," Lenore says. She shivers. "We'll talk."

I reach the car and start scraping the ice from the windshield. It's not very thick, and it comes off easily. They're still watching me, shadows now, silhouetted by the porch light. They see me pause, and they wave as if to encourage me on, like they know I need it. I wave back as the first snowflakes drift to the earth.

THE MOST WE CAN HOPE FOR

IN THE HITCHES' GUEST BEDROOM, Catherine lies prone beneath the breezy cool of the ceiling fan, its steady rhythm—*thick-thick thunk, thick-thick thunk*—soothing. She wills movement, in her legs first, draws her knees to her chest, then sits upright on the edge of the bed.

She has been faking a migraine for an hour and a half. A pity, she thinks, that at forty-one she should resort to such a thing. It's best to be honest. She had always taught her son that. But today she truly needed this time alone to remind herself, as the muffled voices continued outside, that it was her own choice to be here, in Tucson, Arizona. She can't truly blame Toby, who took pains to let her know that, although he would like to have her with him, the decision was entirely up to her. No pressure.

The light through the silk curtains, burnt-orange, is softer now. Catherine rises, moves barefoot into the house, through the kitchen and to the open doorway that leads to the back yard. She pauses here. Outside, Mike Hitch stands in profile, squat and portly in his khaki shorts and Hawaiian button down. He points a pair of barbeque tongs at his wife, Linda, who sits at the table sipping a margarita.

"My wife, the neocon," Mike says.

Toby sits across from Linda. He looks up and sees Catherine waiting. He smiles, big and honest. He strokes his dark goatee, a thick patch of bristle that he thinks hides his weak chin and that Catherine has begged him a hundred times to shave.

She squints in the soft light, tries to appear puffy and pale, drained, like someone who has been in physical pain, and she realizes that this is probably exactly how she looks. She steps outside. The gravel is warm beneath her feet, and beyond the yard is the open desert, an army of giant cacti, low green bushes, even some trees. So much life. She had expected sand dunes, dust storms, desolation. Further off are the mountains, the Catalinas. She inhales deeply, tries to draw strength from the view, the fading sunlight that casts strange colors over the surface of the stony peaks: auburns and pinks. Violet, maybe. A hint of yellow.

Mike pivots on his heel and turns to see Catherine, his eyes hidden by a pair of large sunglasses. His broad smile reveals the straight wall of unnaturally white teeth, and for a moment Catherine considers returning to the bedroom.

"There's our Cathy," Mike says. "How's that headache, babe?" He sets his margarita down on the cocktail cart beside him.

"I feel much better," Catherine says. "Thank you."

Toby pulls out the chair next to him, pats it with his hand, like he's calling some household pet. Catherine moves slowly across the gravel. The air is cooler now, the breeze soft and pleasant. She sits next to Toby, lets him rub the back of her neck. His hairy fingers work their way into her spine. His touch is like nails on a chalkboard to her today. Like a skipping CD.

Mike turns back to the grill. He lifts the clear plastic bag that holds the raw steaks. Inside, they marinate in a creamy sauce, a milky mass of viscera. Flames flicker in the grill. Mike takes up his margarita and drains the glass. He says, "Cathy, I was just telling Toby how I married a neocon." Again, he points the tongs at Linda. "And I never even knew it."

Toby laughs, but Linda just shakes her head. Catherine doesn't know exactly where this is headed but bets it has something to do with Maria, who was married yesterday, which was the main occasion for the trip. But Catherine has spent the last three days with Toby and with Linda and Mike. The three of them, along with the lovely Maria, were college friends in the early '90s, and it has been difficult for Catherine: the nicknames, the stories, the inside jokes, and all of it so relentless. She's sorry she cannot soak it in more eagerly, be that kind of girlfriend. Other women pull this off. She has seen it done, but she can only think about tomorrow morning, when she and Toby will fly back to Kansas City, back to her crummy job at the news desk of *The Star*, to their new apartment, boxes still piled in the corners.

"Don't get me wrong, Lin," Mike says. "I think it's great. Conservatives of the world unite."

Linda sets her drink down against the glass table, hard enough to startle Catherine. "That's my whole point, babe," Linda says. "It doesn't have to be a conservative position, especially if you look at the science of the thing."

Linda has discarded the straw hat from earlier. Her brown hair is pulled back into a ponytail, showing just a little gray at the temple. She is not pretty, Catherine has decided, and yet there's a certain freshness about her, a kind of groomed bohemia.

"Of course, babe." Mike slides his glasses above his forehead. With his thick fingers, he lifts one of the steaks from the bag. "The science of the thing," he says. He lays the steak gently on the grill. It sizzles.

"Yes, the science," Linda says. "Even an atheist biologist will tell you that, at the very least, there's a continuity between fertilization and the fully separate organism. A lot of them will say that, *biologically* speaking, life begins with conception. We don't have to like it. I, myself, don't care for the implications, but you can't ignore the science because it's convenient politically."

Catherine watches Linda, who is herself a scientist, an ecologist, and an expert on the giant cactus, which is called saguaro, the "g" pronounced with a "w" sound.

"So your argument is?" Toby says. His fingers have moved down Catherine's back. His nails—too long—poke her uncomfortably.

"My argument *is*," Linda says, "that it's possible to be anti-abortion on the grounds of civil rights. That's liberal. It's a liberal stance. I'm not saying it's the correct stance, or that it's mine even, but you can't exactly call it conservative."

This is the thing that is killing Catherine, exactly this right here, the arguing without conviction, or perhaps, conviction without belief. And Toby, the man she is supposed to love, is the worst of the three. *So your argument is?* Who says that? It all seems so self-indulgent, wasteful even.

Catherine shifts under Toby's hand. He seems to understand and stops his massaging. He takes a sip of his margarita, then offers some to Catherine, which she accepts gladly. The drink is cool and tart. She takes another deep swig.

Mike pours some of his drink onto the hot coals and closes the lid of the grill. He joins them at the table, next to Linda and opposite Catherine. His eyes are outlined by a light mask in the shape of his sunglasses. The rest of his face is red.

Mike says, "I get what you're saying, babe, I do." He fills half his glass with tequila and tops it off with margarita mix. The glass is beaded with water. He turns it in a circle on the surface of the table, lifts it, then sets it down again. "I'm just saying, and I know we agree on this, that it was no good reason for her to get married or to do anything else for that matter, not if she didn't want to."

And there it is: Maria. Intelligent, beautiful, perfect Maria. Although no one has said so, Catherine is fairly certain that there was once something between Toby and her. She watches his face closely, but he doesn't betray anything in particular. Maybe Maria is, for him, the one that got away, the standard all the rest are judged against. Catherine wonders how well she survives the comparison.

"There's no reason to think she's anything but happy," Linda says. "Don't you think they looked happy, Toby?"

Mike waves his hand as if to dismiss any response. "Ask Cathy," he says. "Cathy's more objective."

Mike began with the "Cathy" business sometime yesterday, and he probably thinks the familiarity is flattering, but she doesn't approve of the diminutive. It makes her think of the comic strip, the noseless bachelorette. Mother issues.

"Did who seem happy?" Catherine says. There is only one person they could mean, but she can't resist.

"Maria," Mike says. "At the wedding. I didn't get the sense that she was that happy."

How could she be, Catherine thinks, with her one true love Toby in the pews. She says, "Happiness is tough to gauge sometimes, but I guess she seemed happy enough. Of course, me not knowing her, it makes it harder."

She smiles. She does not really want to be rude. These are Toby's friends. They aren't bad people, not really. There are far worse people in the world: murderers, arsonists, corporate embezzlers. She wonders what the Hitches would think about her own past marriage, her own unplanned son, twenty years old now and studying engineering at KU. It's hard to believe, her child grown and progressing toward a clear and bright future while she, approaching middle age, is still trying to figure things out. It's not always easy, life. It can be complicated, actually, not reducible to a *so your argument is?*

Toby places his hand over hers. His forearm brushes against hers. Mammalian. That's a way to describe him. He's a bear, Catherine thinks, a wooly mammoth. But she's just irritable is all. This will pass. She loves this man, seven years younger than she, but a good man, the only reporter at the office who ever treated her with any respect, who ever had anything to say to her besides *get me this* or *file that.* He'd even encouraged her when she went back to school, sat with her at the desk and worked through quadratic equations. When she gets home, she must cancel the lease to her old studio apartment, make a leap of faith. Probably, she will do just that.

Linda places the tequila bottle back on the cart, and Catherine accepts the fresh margarita. She stares toward the open desert, at the saguaros. Linda says they can live for two hundred years and grow up to ten meters. At first, Catherine couldn't picture what ten meters was, but a meter is a good bit longer than a yard. Ten yards. More than thirty feet. An impressive plant, she has decided.

"I'm just saying," Mike says. "I'll say this, and I'll shut up. To me, there seemed to be something not-quite-right about the whole thing. I mean, that guy, Jorge. Nice enough but . . . ."

"But what?" Toby says. "But he's a construction worker?"

"That's not what I'm saying," Mike says. He pauses, wrinkles his sunburned forehead like he's trying to think of something smart but can't. "I'm a little drunk, Toby, but I won't let you make me out as a classist. I don't look at people that way. That's not what I'm saying, and you know it."

Linda shakes her head. "He's not even a construction worker, anyway, not that it matters. He's on the business side of it. He's like a builder."

"A contractor," Catherine says. She'd spoken to Jorge briefly at the reception. He works mostly with commercial buildings, he'd said, but recently his firm had built a couple of churches.

"See," Linda says. "He's a contractor. You guys need to listen better." She smiles to Catherine as if she's appealing for some female solidarity, as if to say, *"these boys of ours."* Catherine responds with what she means to be a normal smile, but it feels stiff on her face and she is not sure. She will try harder. Tomorrow at this time she'll be home.

"I guess it's the whole *situation* that bothers me," Mike says. "So conformist. I mean, Maria was an honest-to-God revolutionary. Her parents marched with César Chavez. She could quote Marx by heart."

Catherine drinks deeply.

Linda says, "I will admit, Jorge's not the one I'd have pictured her settling down with."

Mike wipes his forehead, flings the sweat from the end of his fingertips. He stands and returns to the grill. His balance seems tenuous.

"No," he says. "Too conventional, for her." He turns to Catherine. "She turned us into protestors, you know. And back then *no one* protested."

"People protested," Linda says. "People always protest."

"Yeah, but still," Toby says. He tightens his grip on Catherine's hand. "Mike's right. She radicalized us."

Catherine tries to conjure an image of the young, radical Toby who attracted Maria.

"It seems like a lifetime ago," Mike says. Gently, he turns over a steak.

It's his eyes, Catherine thinks. They're too small and close together. They make his head seem even larger than it is.

Mike says, "Maria would show up with a bottle of Southern Comfort and a box of colored chalk. She'd drag us onto campus and have us marking sidewalks with political slogans. What did we write, guys? 'Free South Africa'? 'No Blood For Oil'?"

"'Murphy Brown for President,'" Linda says.

"Yes," Toby says. "'Hate is not a family value.'"

"We put on dark clothes," Linda says. "We wore hooded windbreakers, and we took flashlights and tiptoed around like cat burglars. We would hide behind bushes when the security golf carts would come near, duck into shadowy corners and take nips from the bottle. We thought we were so subversive."

It sounds like fun to Catherine, but she remembers those years differently, recently divorced with a son who seemed always to need something else: soccer cleats, Boy Scout dues, Ninja Turtles.

"And *laughing*," Mike says. "Oh, man we laughed so *hard*. Guys," he says. "Can you remember laughing like that, so hard you were in physical pain, so hard you thought you might die? Do any of us ever laugh like that anymore? I mean, I never laugh. I see things that are funny. I say, that's really funny, give a little chuckle, maybe, but I never really laugh anymore." As he says this, he gestures widely, the utensils still at the end of his hands. He almost loses his balance and has to catch himself. Catherine worries he will fall, land on the knife or launch it dangerously into the air, create some complication that will force them to stay longer.

"I'm feeling a nice guffaw coming on, right now," Toby says.

"Poor Mike," Linda says. She smiles, but there is irritation in her eyes. "He's having a mid-thirties crisis."

"Okay, okay," Mike says. He sits next to Linda. "I'm drunk, yes, and maybe talking out of my ass a little. Someone else talk for a while. Talk about something serious."

The rest of them are quiet. The stillness moves over Catherine's ears. She listens for the howl of a coyote, the scream of a mountain lion.

"Can I just say this?" Mike says. "This is a totally dorky thing to say, but." He sighs. "I love you, Toby. You too, Cathy. I know I haven't known you that long. But I love you, just the same. I'm going to miss you guys when you leave."

Catherine feels her face flush.

"Mike," Linda says. "Mike. That's sweet, babe, but you're going to scare her away. You're going to smother her." She stands and takes Mike's margarita from him. His fingers trail after it, and Linda moves toward the back doorway. "We want them to come back again," she says as she enters the house.

Not very likely, *babe,* Catherine thinks, but she will not say *never.* Life puts you in the strangest places.

"Lin's right," Mike says. He looks hurt, like a reprimanded child, and Catherine actually feels sorry for him. There's something so earnest about him. She's just not the right audience right now. "I'm sorry," he says. "I just want us to be good friends. Cathy, you're very mysterious. Tell me something about you. What are your hopes and goals? Are you guys getting married? Do you want kids?"

"I have a kid," Catherine says.

"Right, right." Mike slaps his forehead. "I knew that."

"No kids for me," Toby says. "I have an aversion. A fear really."

"You're scared of kids?" Mike says. Linda is still inside the house, and Catherine is surprised to find that she misses her.

"Terrified," Toby says. "But not of the actual child. It's the triangulated relationship between child, parent, and world. It's too intense and crippling."

Catherine has heard this bit before. She wonders if her headache should come back, if that would be pushing it.

"Babies," Toby continues, "are reminders of the fragility of life. Wrinkled, screaming, defecating little capsules of death. A mysterious illness, a short fall, something sharp thrust into a fontanel. It's ridiculous for something to be so vulnerable. And the most horrifying part of it all is that when it comes down to it, we're no better off, just bigger." Toby takes a drink. He seems satisfied. Linda returns with a cup of coffee, which she sets in front of Mike.

"Go on, Toby," Mike says.

"On one of my first feature assignments with *The Star,*" Toby says, "I was doing this story on childhood drownings. They're the number one cause of accidental death in toddlers, by the way. My editor wanted a follow-up on an incident from the previous spring. There was this young suburban couple. Their son had been three. First, when I called, they didn't want to talk with me. But I eventually convinced them with the angle that maybe their story could help raise awareness, save others. Finally, they gave in. I think they were just too beaten-down to resist.

"Their story was basically this. It was a Sunday afternoon. The mother was out shopping, and the father was home with their three-year-old son. But pops fell asleep on the couch, for no more than five minutes, he said, and somehow the son slipped out the back door and made it all the way to the neighbor's pool. The pool was guarded with a fence. The fence was almost always latched, but on this particular day, it wasn't."

Toby pauses. He offers no more for now, part of his master storyteller routine, and Catherine feels she could pretty happily scratch his eyes out. He will absorb her eventually. It's what men do, what she allows to happen. He will pull her in, engulf her until she's lost in a curly black hairball, never to be heard from again.

"And the son?" Linda says, finally.

"The dad found him at the bottom of the deep end," Toby says. "He dove in and pulled him out, but the boy was lifeless. Dad began CPR and rescue breathing. When the paramedics got there, the boy had no pulse. Basically, he was dead, but they were able to revive him on the way to the hospital."

"He didn't die?" Mike says.

"He did die," Toby says. He strokes his goatee. His face is pale and serious. "Two days later, he died again, this time for good."

Catherine watches Mike and Linda, their reactions: sad faces and reverent silence. This is a kind of game for them, Catherine realizes, one they have been playing for a long time, and she, coming in late, is just now learning the rules.

"But I'll tell you the thing that got me more than any of it," Toby says. "It was the feeling I got in that house, with that couple. We were drinking coffee in their living room, and I noticed that on the mugs there were these little designs along the handles. At first I thought they were strawberries, but as I looked closer, I realized they were ladybugs, and right then, sitting with this sad couple, their middle-class respectability and their year-old grief a palpable presence in the room, I suddenly had to get out. I felt like I couldn't breathe." Toby places his hand over his chest. "I swear to you, ever since that day, I decided no kids for me. It isn't worth it."

Well-done, Catherine thinks. She once took a composition class at the junior college and learned how to structure an argument: main point, supported by an illustration, followed by an explanation. The bit about the strawberry ladybugs, that was Toby's own touch, part of the game. Bravo.

She remembers how one of the things that she first liked about him was how he could talk and talk. But listen too. He'd pull up a seat next to her in the office, ask her questions about her job, her son, her life. Who? What? Where? When? Why? He had a way of making her feel interesting. And his whole point about kids? He's not even wrong. They are constant worry. A child, even an adult one, is always with you in a way that makes everything else secondary.

"That's a little crazy, Toby," Linda says. "But I can relate in a way. Too many bad things can happen. You'd always be waiting for something terrible. That's how my family was."

Mike takes a bottle of bourbon off the cocktail cart, unscrews it, and pours some into his coffee. Linda pretends not to notice, but Catherine sees her jaw clench.

"When I was a girl," Linda says. "my maternal grandparents lived about a mile away, so any time they heard a siren they would call us, worried. I'd hear the ambulance or police or whatever pass down the main road, and, without fail, the phone would ring, and it would be my grandmother. 'I heard sirens,' she'd say. 'I thought I would see if everything is all right.' And I would sigh and say, 'Yes, Grandma, we are all fine here.' It was pathological the way we worried."

Mike is back at the grill. He clamps the tongs into the edge of a steak and makes a careful incision. He bends over to scrutinize the insides. Catherine begins to feel hungry. "Did anything ever happen?" she asks Linda. "Were any of you ever not okay when she called?"

"Never," Linda says. "We're still all fine, including Grandma and Grandpa. They're both ninety-one. It's as if all the worrying kept tragedy at bay. But the thing that I never expected—and this may go against what I've been saying—is that I miss those calls. Here, in the valley, I hear sirens all the time. But no one ever calls, and I don't call anyone."

Okay, Catherine thinks. Okay, it's about a lesson at the end, like a fable, only more ambiguous. That's how it works with them. There's a sort of method to it.

"That's why we *do* want kids," Mike says. He sits and drapes his arm over Linda's shoulders. "What I was saying about Maria, it's all jealousy. I'd love a house full of little hellions. For a long time I didn't want kids, but now it's all I can think about. Sorry, Toby, if that makes me selfish, but I want progeny."

"I can understand that," Toby says. "I didn't mean there was anything wrong with wanting that." Toby glances at Catherine, then back to Mike. "You should meet Catherine's son, Kevin. An absolute delight, a fine young man. He's getting an engineering degree."

"I *should,*" Mike says. "Cathy, I want to meet your son. Aren't children a blessing?"

"Yes," Catherine says, and she suddenly wishes Kevin were here. It would be good to show him off. But he doesn't much like Toby. Once, he told Catherine she was too pretty for him, that Toby looked like her ugly nephew. But he had been laughing when he said this, and Catherine knows that his standards for her will always be high.

"Children are our best hope," Mike says. "It's not like Linda and I haven't been trying like hell."

Linda's eyes, cautionary, move from her drink up to Mike. She stares hard at him.

"It's okay, Lin," Mike says. "We're all good friends here. It's not like you're the one with the problem, anyway." He draws his coffee mug to his lips. He looks to Toby, then to Catherine. "Linda got checked out last month," he says.

"Michael!" Linda says. "That's enough."

Mike doesn't look at her. He keeps staring steadily across the table. "We're friends, right guys? I mean, we're buddies, right?"

Linda says, "I'm sure they're not interested in our reproductive challenges."

On the contrary, Catherine would like to say. She takes a gulp of her margarita. She would like to hear more about this indeed.

"Her ovaries are pristine," Mike says. "She has the uterus of a twenty-five-year-old."

"And now you're just being vulgar," Linda says.

"Lin," Mike says. Then lower, "Linda. I'm sharing, that's all." He smiles at Toby, at Catherine. "I switch to boxers. I ice my *cojones.* Nothing. Next week I'm going to give a specimen, just like the men on the sitcoms. I'll go to one of those rooms that have the start-you-up pornography, and all sorts of confusion and mayhem will ensue."

With this, Catherine laughs before she can stop herself. The image is too much. Mike is thrilled, his smile wider than she's ever seen it.

"Michael," Linda says. She points to the grill. "The steaks."

WHEN THE FOOD IS FINALLY in front of her, Catherine realizes that she is no longer hungry. She mixes herself another drink. She cuts the steak into small pieces and arranges it on her plate. She had been a vegetarian once, for years. She can't remember actually deciding to eat meat again, how it started. A little fish at first, maybe, then a slice of turkey here and there. She wonders if this might be how true love works, not a spontaneous burst of emotion but rather a gradual wearing away of resolve, a sort of love by attrition.

"It wasn't always like this," Mike says. He has been talking about the evils of the Internet, and before that the effects of Wal-Mart on small businesses. "I can remember a time when it was different, you know. It was like we were at this end pass; there was the sense that we were on the cusp of something cosmic. I remember this made-for-TV movie in the early '80s. It was called *The Day After,* and it was about nuclear war."

"A documentary?" Toby says.

"No, no," Mike says. "A dramatic miniseries. A four-hour television event. My mom told me not to watch it. She warned me, but I didn't listen. And boy was she right, too. I couldn't sleep for a week. It all seemed so inevitable. Mushroom clouds on the horizon. Two vowed enemies stockpiling missiles, enough to destroy each other several times over. I felt like we were being dangled over a fire. At any moment we could be food for fission. But nowadays, with the twenty-four-hour news cycle, everything gets hyperexposed. We're not allowed to stew over things through the night. There's so much coverage that everything tends to dissipate. But back then, events still held a certain heft."

"Food for fission," Linda shakes her head. "That's a good one. You're practically a comedian."

Catherine remembers the drills in school. Crawl under your desk, curl into a ball, the tight-knit fear and exhilaration. Her father, a career navy man, watching the television solemnly. Always a reservoir of canned food on hand. But even this was after missiles in Cuba. She wants to tell Mike they all missed the worst of it.

Mike's face is serious. His little eyes look wet and shiny. "Somewhere around that time I got this idea—no, it was more than an idea—it was an honest-to-God premonition, that I would never be a father, that I would be dead by the time I was thirty. When Reagan and Gorbachev started making nice, I started to think it would be AIDS. When I got my first credit card, I charged indiscriminately. I only paid the minimum balance. I never thought I'd have to account for it. And yet, here I am. Here we are. On Wednesday, I'm going to beat off into a cup. I never thought I'd be that guy."

"Honey," Linda says. She takes the coffee mug from him. "Settle down. Eat your food and you'll feel better."

"It's all good, buddy," Toby says. "You made it. You're thirty-six."

But Catherine wants to tell Mike that he's right. She wants to tell him that even though he's mostly an idiot and doesn't know how to express it all, in some way he is exactly right.

They are all eating silently now, and Catherine is glad for the quiet, the chance to enjoy the rising chill. The mountains are a deep blue. The saguaros are silhouetted, keeping their two-hundred-year watch. They plan for a time beyond the four of them, beyond their children even. These are the things she will talk about when she gets home. Postcard images. The beautiful weather and landscape.

She slips a piece of steak into her mouth along with a bell pepper, chases them with a cherry tomato. Eventually, this day and the next will pass and they will be home and other things will happen and this will become that one time when she went to a wedding in Tucson, and the memory will make her sad that Toby is gone, or call up a certain fondness that only time can bring about. Or she will be married to Toby and maybe she will know Mike and Linda quite well, will come to adore them and their children, which she knows they will have because, if one thing is for sure, life will find a way. Things will move forward no matter what, and maybe the important thing is to try, to make an effort.

Toby smiles at her as he chews. A drop of salad dressing is stuck in his beard. "Tomorrow, back home," he says.

And Catherine knows what he means. Work to do, things to unpack. Decorating. She remembers him before they left Kansas City, sitting on their new couch in their living room, sweaty from a day of moving. "This is great," he'd said. "*Our* place. Me and you." Catherine had smiled, nodded, but she had felt miles away. She'd gone through the whole thing before, this playing house, and she wanted to warn him, ask him to curb his expectations.

Her life stretches out in front of her like a tape measure. There was a family, a mother and a father, and there was a childhood, transient but happyish, a particular teddy bear, a prom date, eventually a serious boyfriend and a child and a marriage. Along the way there was pain, but also love. There are no gaps. She can trace herself all the way here. And yet, there should be more that she's taken from it, something else that she should know.

"Steaks are delicious," Toby says.

"Yes," Catherine says. "Very good." It's even cooler now. Soon, she will need to put on shoes. The breeze moves across them all.

Linda is looking at Catherine as if something confuses her. "I'm afraid we've put you off, Catherine," she says. Her voice sounds tired, but there's also an edge of annoyance. "All of this going on of ours," she says. "I'm afraid we've annoyed you terribly." Her look is harsher than her words. It says, *You aren't fooling anyone.* "I hope you won't hate us forever."

"Oh," Catherine says, surprised by the sudden accusation. "Yes. I mean, no. I've just been listening, that's all." She's caught, but she wants to start new, now that she gets it and likes them all a little better.

"I've ruined the night," Mike says. He holds up both hands. "I've spoiled it all."

"False," Toby says. "It's good times. No worries." Then to Catherine, "You okay, babe?"

"Yes," Catherine says. "No worries, babe."

To Linda, Mike says, "I'm sorry babe. I'll shut up now." And to Toby, "Toby, tell us another story. Something happy this time."

But no, Catherine thinks. Let me play for once. "I have one," she says, surprised to hear her own voice, and surprised, too, because she does have a story. Maybe she does. "It's about a place I lived once. In Florida."

They all look to her. They wait.

"My dad was in the Navy," she says. "He was stationed in Orlando for a while, but we never lived in the city. We stayed in a small town about an hour southwest, where the cost of living was cheaper." It's just her talking now, her voice only, and they're all listening. She waits, but they don't speak. They eat, chew. Wait. "In many ways, I hated it," she continues, not sure exactly where she's headed, where it will go. "The summers were hot. There were terrible thunderstorms. And the girls at school hated me. They knew I was just passing through and so did I. Plus, if you wanted any real social standing, you had to be able to trace your roots back about four generations to one of the founding families. I would read a book during pep rallies.

"But I liked our house," she says quickly, remembering. "It was a small house, but it was on a lake and we had a sailboat, small too—practically a dinghy—but still, nice. This house, it was outside of town and sort of surrounded by woods and orange groves, and there weren't many other houses nearby. In the evenings, I would take long walks with my black lab."

"Sadie?" Toby says.

"No," Catherine says, taken aback by his memory. She plants her hand on his thigh. "But this was one of Sadie's puppies, Skippy. He was used to leashes and sidewalks, so he loved it there. He was in heaven. I would walk him down the clay road, and he would jump in and out of the brush. Chase rabbits or whatever. No one cared.

"One early evening I had a fight with my mother or something, and I walked really far. Skippy had darted after something he saw off in the distance. It was cold, I remember. It was around Christmas. When I finally caught up with him, he was sniffing around some garbage cans at the end of a long driveway, in front of a house that I'd never seen before.

"In the yard of the house, there was this family gathered around. Two families maybe, because one group was leaving. Except, there was this problem." Catherine waits to see if someone will stop her, but no one does. Mike, Linda, and Toby nod like this is the most interesting story in the world. "The problem was they were trying to get this big old man—Grandpa, I'll call him—out of his wheelchair and into the van of the family that was leaving. Only he wouldn't go. Couldn't, I should say. They could stand him up okay, but each time they tried to maneuver him into the cab, something would go wrong, and they'd have to sit him back down into the chair. All of my grandparents had died by the time I was four, so I never really spent time with old people, and I guess it was kind of fascinating for me.

"On some of the later tries, Grandpa's pants were sort of falling down and you could tell the others were starting to get troubled. There were several people working at this: two or three men, a couple of women, maybe even a kid or two, and I'm there with my dog, and it's getting dark. I'm crouching behind their garbage cans, watching—rooting for them, you know—waiting to see if they can pull it off, get big Grandpa into the van."

Catherine can feel her breaths coming quicker, her heart pulsing. "I remember thinking that this old guy must have been a terrible liability, a huge inconvenience, and yet there they were, doing whatever was necessary, dragging him to family functions, keeping him a part of things. And I started crying right there by the trash cans, because it was all so terrible and sad, and so beautiful, and sometimes I think that that's the most we can ever hope for, to be cared about like that in the last part of life, when we're no longer useful."

Catherine finishes. She can't remember ever speaking so many words at once, and the effort has left her lightheaded. The others are quiet for what seems like a long time.

"That's it exactly," Toby says.

Catherine turns to see if he's making fun of her, but he isn't. He puts his hand on hers, and she leans into his shoulder. She can hear his breathing and also the sound of the desert, which is mostly quiet. In the distance she can still make out the dark outline of the mountains.

Mike watches them, his little eyelids suddenly heavy and half-shut. "Did they ever get him into the van?" he says. "Big Grandpa?"

"Yes," Catherine says. Toby squeezes her hand, and she squeezes back. "It took them a while, but in the end they got him in okay."

"That's good," Mike says. He nods slowly. "That's good to know. I'm glad."

TRUE KIN

Ron

Ron was already one hundred miles south of Valdosta when he noticed the smell, a faint burnt-toast odor that seemed to come through the air vents and into the cab of his pickup. And the rise of the temperature gauge too, barely measurable at first and maybe a normal fluctuation, until he studied it more closely and noted a definite increase, the needle rising, slowly, but rising.

He stopped at a convenience store, hurriedly added oil and water, bought extra of both and then drove south again on I-75, into the heat of this unreal morning, the air conditioner switched off now and him sweating and yet cold also.

He had known that this would be something very bad the instant he heard his father's voice on the line, hoarse and breathy, straining through a cloud of whisky. Or he knew it sooner, maybe, with the first rings that broke the stale quiet of his living room where he slept on the couch in the glow of the muted television. Below, on the floor, Wolf lay prostrate, snoring in irregular bursts.

Out of his blanket and onto the floor, Ron had crawled through the over-cooled air, past emptied beer cans, with the twinge of dread already in his chest because the phone was ringing and it was dawn, an hour only for the report of very bad news.

His first fears had gone, as they always did, to Megan. This could be the morning a parent fears. He was not immune. The singular phone call that would change his life forever, the blow from which he would never recover because if that were to happen, the worst of all conceivable things, he would not want to recover, would not want to move forward or cope, start a foundation or raise awareness, or in any way live, although most parents did—continue to live on at least—and that had always amazed him.

But if not the worst possible thing, maybe something nearly as bad. She could be sick or gravely injured, in need of a blood transfusion or bone marrow transplant and here he was drunk, and couldn't that complicate such a thing, taint his own internal supply and disqualify him as a donor?

He held the phone to his ear, spoke hello, and here was Ray's voice, starting and then stopping, silent now except for his breathing.

"What is it?" Ron said, then waited, allowed the man, this Ray-father, to form the words.

"It's about your sister," he said, finally. "It's about Claire."

The temperature gauge seemed stable for the moment, the burnt-toast smell not as strong. The wind came through the open windows and swirled around the cab.

Claire.

He allowed the word to settle inside him, and he bit down hard on his lower lip—a test—to feel the pain, remote, like pain felt from a distance, yet real, not the counterfeit hurt of dream wounds. He was awake, and this was real, and he was driving to St. Petersburg where there had been a car accident, Ray said, a collision with a telephone pole or something. Claire is dead, son. He was so sorry to have to tell him this. And when could he come home?

It was possible. Such things were in the news every day. And yet? Sometimes there were mistakes. He had heard of such cases. Mix-ups. Mistaken identity. Ray was drunk, too, and might have misunderstood. So Ron was not headed home to Ridgedale, not yet. He had the address of the medical examiner, which is where they had the person they thought was Claire.

He tried to focus only on the space of interstate before him, slowed at the appropriate times, avoided the other cars, peopled with drivers speeding carelessly past billboards that advertised products, theme parks, hotels, as if this were any other morning and life were everlasting.

He had to stop once more for gas, entered his PIN and pumped, then drove on, and when it came lurching out, the non-dreaming force of knowing, it was each time all new again, as if freshly learned, and at these times it was hard to catch his breath, and he was very cold, a prickling numbness in his face and arms, and the far away but very real pain of teeth on his bottom lip.

IT WAS RAINING when he bypassed Tampa and exited onto the Howard Franklin Bridge, which took him south and over the bay, its surface alive with the downpour. With his windows rolled up the hot engine smell was worse, the temperature gauge rising near the section marked with red.

In St. Pete, by the time he found the address, the rain had stopped. He parked in front of the building marked Pinellas County Medical Examiner. Morgue, he thought. That was more honest and true, the lobby when he entered looking like any normal waiting area—fake normal, though. Here was misery.

At the desk were two women. The older one greeted him, a grandmotherly figure, kind-faced and portly. She pushed a Danish discreetly underneath the overhang of the counter and swallowed the bite she was already chewing.

He told her who he was, stating his name clearly, sensibly, passed his driver's license to her. She did not look puzzled though, as he had hoped. Instead, she nodded. She smiled a smile that was not happy but one of practiced condolence. She picked up the phone and rang someone. "Mr. Ramsey is here. I'll bring him in now." Then she hung up the phone and said, "Please come with me, Mr. Ramsey." She led him to an elevator and got in with him. He was conscious, suddenly, of his sweat-soaked clothes, slept-in and disheveled. He should have worn something more appropriate, or thrown some things into a suitcase. There had been time for that.

He and the grandmotherly woman were in another room now, and a young man greeted him. He wore a shirt and tie, but his top button was unfastened and the tie loosened. An introduction: grief counselor. Here for him, to support him in any way he could.

And yet there were blunders sometimes, cases of mistaken identity. Then down a hallway and into the next room, the smell like alcohol, forced sterility, becoming more distinct until he was at a curtained window, a man standing by the curtain. This was Doctor Benedict, the grief counselor said. And the doctor asking now, was he ready for the identification? There was no hurry. Would he like to prepare himself? And Ron, no, no, no; just let's do this thing.

Then no curtain and her, Claire, on the other side of the glass, lying on a sort of stretcher and covered to the chest with a papery sheet. No mix-up. And he like a damn fool beside the glass in wrinkled tee-shirt and shorts, sockless, his feet wet with sweat and there forming a sort of slippery grime mixture in his shoes that had been warm in the car but that was now turning cold in the air-conditioned building. He was still trying to be sensible despite the cold working its way up, past the thighs, into the chest, the face.

He was on a knee and on either side someone held him by the arm, his body all cold needle pricks, and he was scared because this was not a place he knew. A voice asked if he was okay, and then they were easing him onto his back. He stared up into a face. "It's okay," the face said. "This is what happens. This is difficult." But it did not make sense yet. He was lying on a cold floor, had been standing and now was on the floor. He hadn't passed out, though. No, he had only grown faint. He had grown faint and was lying on the cold floor—of the morgue—and beyond the glass window his sister lay dead forever.

OUTSIDE, HIS TRUCK STARTED only after a terrible grainy struggle, the engine's warning lights and gauges leaping back to life. He was headed downtown, toward the bay, because he needed to drive a while, look at things, add some context so that maybe he could order it all out a bit before he had to frame it for everyone else—goddamnit—the people he hadn't seen for three and—he counted silently—over three and a half years, because of no good reason really except that he was busy and his marriage had faltered, then ended, and he had felt so different from those people, his family, and even so there was also that kind of guilt that compounded upon itself, and even though he'd meant to write that letter or make the call because every single day he'd think of it, of all of them, still he did not, and it grew on itself and everything was harder, and now this was the way he would have to return, under the worst circumstances. And the pills, which he had to admit had helped him lately, evened him out so that he wasn't so anxious all the time: he'd left those in Valdosta. So he needed to drive and look at things, get some distance from the place were he'd seen her and grown faint, but not to Ridgedale yet, not until he could pull himself together a bit.

When he reached the water, he turned north and soon hit the narrow brick-paved streets of the Old Northeast section, arriving before he realized it in front of the pink stucco building with the crumbling Spanish tile. He stepped out into the heat. The sky was clear now, the sun casting a sparkle over the shiny-wet world. Warm mist rose from the street and hung thick and palpable in the air. He didn't feel right, still dizzy-nauseated, legs trembly as he walked toward Claire's apartment, unsure of what he would do, how he might get in. Maybe he could call Megan here. Just to hear her voice would be something. It would remind him to hang on, stay in the world. And other calls to make, necessary business to attend to. And there was his truck to think about too, smoke seeping now from the hood.

He passed through the front gate and into the small courtyard, which was overrun with tropical plants and plastic lawn furniture. He pushed aside an earlike leaf and watched the water fall and dissolve into the cement. He was thirsty. His mouth was very dry and a soreness grew at the back of his throat.

Not in denial now. He had seen her and it was finished. He wouldn't expect to find Claire inside the apartment, explaining that there must have been a mistake because she was clearly fine. Not this, and yet something, an unspoken prayer as he turned the knob—it was unlocked—and pushed open the door and then the falling feeling when he stepped into the one-room studio, the smell of patchouli and litter box. A large cat was crouched on top of the neatly made bed, and it stared mistrustfully at him. Nausea again, worse now. Sick. He stepped back outside and leaned against the building.

A voice from above: "Ronnie?"

He regrouped. Stood—stupid cold numbness in the face—and looked through watery eyes to see, on the opposite balcony, someone watching him, leaning forward over the rail toward him. "Is that Ronnie?"

"Yes," he said, his voice weak and hoarse. "Ron."

The small figure disappeared behind a wall and emerged on the other side, hurrying down the spiral stairwell. He blinked and cleared the moisture from the corners of his eyes. She landed barefoot on the cement in front of him, a young woman wearing cutoff shorts and a yellow bikini top. Her small breasts bounced in unison and sprang to a halt.

"I'm Gina," she said.

He could smell a sort of buttery sweetness coming off of her. Her eyes followed something behind him, and he turned to see the cat bound across the courtyard and up the same steps that she had just descended.

"Is it really true?" she said. She had been crying, he could see, her eyes red and face swollen. She watched him. "It's true, isn't it?"

He was no good with tears, maybe because they'd had no currency in his family. They weren't forbidden or even actively discouraged, but crying wasn't part of what they did, so much so that even when his mother had lain dying, the rest of them had hardly cried. They had hurt, to be sure, as much as any family or more because there are a million ways to hurt and feel, but they hadn't cried much.

Gina stood before him, waiting. She was talking about Claire, wanted to know if it was true. He had the answer for himself, had seen it on the other side of the glass and was working on a way to understand it. But it was something else to voice it to this new person, a stranger who had called him by name and who was already beginning to cry again and he wishing she wouldn't. If he said the thing about Claire to her, there would be no turning back. He could feel something heavy welling in the center of his self, and he did not know what to say to this Gina, who stood too closely to him, the tears running shamelessly down her cheek now, and her sweet odor, something like coconut.

"No," he managed, and he shook his head emphatically, but that wasn't exactly what he meant. He fought to control his stomach. "I just need. You have to go." He braced himself against the side of the building, doubled over, and vomited at the foot of a banana tree.

Gina

It was 2:00 A.M. and Gina leaned against the balcony railing. She reviewed what she knew. An accident on 66th Street, a single-car fatality according to the news, which Gina had watched only because Cybil had called— worried and asking about Claire—because Laura from work had passed by the aftermath on her way home, saw the small red compact being loaded onto the wrecker and, while it was hard to say with all of the damage, it did look something like the one Claire drove.

This and the fact that, at this late hour, Claire still wasn't home.

That morning they had had a fight, but it was the heat of anger that made things go the way they did, and Claire would know this of course, that it was just one of their spats soon forgotten between friends.

Gina stared at Claire's apartment below, the windows dark and silent except for the occasional meow from Sophie, who must be getting hungry. For now, Gina could only wait, rehearse her side of the morning's events, how she had awakened to the sound of Claire's stereo, which rattled the windows at seven in the morning and, for God's sake, when you lived in a community, you can't just disregard others that way.

When Gina had drawn her curtain and looked down, she'd seen

Claire exit her front door carrying two giant garbage bags stuffed full. She held one steadily in each hand, and moved slowly across the court-yard and toward the gate. And Gina, slipping on shorts and flip-flops, hurried downstairs and stood so that when Claire returned from the dumpster, sans the garbage bags, Gina was waiting for her, eyes still adjusting to the morning light.

Claire looked up, startled in that way of hers, like she had been some-where miles away and as if Gina had rudely intruded. "Hi," Claire had said. Just, "Hi." So typical.

Gina stood unspeaking, gestured to Claire's open door, out of which the music echoed, then threw her hands up in exasperation, and gave Claire a look that was meant to ask *what the hell?*

"Sorry," Claire said. "I'll turn it down." She stood with her hands on her hips. She was wearing purple surfing shorts that reached just below her knees and hung low so that her hip bones jutted out like twin foot-hills. She was fucking adorable.

Gina clenched her jaw. "It's seven in the goddamn morning," She said. She had to remain firm. You had to show resolve with Claire or else she'd lull you into timidity before you realized it, then plow right over you.

"Like I said, Gina. I'll turn it down."

Claire looked pale, peaked, like someone who had just had a fright. Her lips had that sort of drained quality, and she was doing her passive thing, the "little old me" hurt look in her eyes. She started toward her door but Gina caught her arm as she passed, spun her so they were facing each other.

"Claire," Gina said. "What is it? If there's something going on, if I can help."

"I'm fine, Gina," Claire said. She pulled her arm free, gently. "I'm okay; you're okay."

Dismissive now, another of her techniques. Don't try to help me. I'm too tragic. My problems are larger than you can comprehend. Fine, Gina thought. Let her do whatever she has to do. And that would have been best, to leave things at that, but instead Gina had pushed forward.

"When's the last time you slept?" she asked.

"I don't see how that concerns you," Claire said.

"You weren't at work yesterday. You didn't even call," Gina said. "Even if you've decided to quit, you could at least call. Even you could do that."

Claire had her hands on her hips again, those genetically skinny hips, which she cocked in that way, and she smiled. "Is that a message from Blake? Are you speaking on his behalf now? Are you speaking as my boss?"

That one Gina should've seen coming. Fucking-A, but Claire had a way of turning things on you. "This isn't about Blake," Gina said. And this was true. It was, after all, Claire who had called it quits with him over six months ago. It wasn't like Gina had done anything wrong. Why did Claire wear her hurt like some badge of honor? Why did she take everything as some monumental personal insult, require every comment to be filtered through her own ego?

"The world's not out to get you, Claire," Gina said. "You're not the only one with problems."

Claire walked into her apartment, and the music lowered to almost nothing. From inside, she called, "I have your money, Gina."

Money? The twenty dollars that Gina had all but forgotten about? Gina felt her face flush, her teeth begin to grind. Claire would have her apologizing in the end. But not this time. She slid her hand into her shorts pocket. Her keys were there, and before Claire could come out again, Gina walked out into the steamy street, the wet heat gathering around her bare ankles. She got into her Corolla, and as she was speeding away, she yelled "fucking bitch!"

It was 2:15 A.M. now, and Gina leaned hard against the railing. She was tired, and probably it was best to go to sleep. Maybe, when she woke, Claire would be home, and Gina would apologize, for the way she had acted, and hopefully Claire hadn't heard the last insult, which she didn't mean at all. Still, "fucking bitch." She had yelled it loudly, but she was halfway down the block by then and Claire couldn't have heard.

Ron

There was a picture, framed, and it was all of them, he and Claire seated on either side of their mother, all dressed in '70s pastels and Ray standing stiffly behind them, smiling uncomfortably. Ron set the picture down and switched the wall unit to HI COOL.

Claire, he thought. No waking relief would come. Her and their mother both. He hadn't thought of it in that way yet, how it linked the two in a sense, the events separated by so many years as to seem individual and distinct, yet both of them gone in a sort of unified way. Only he and Ray left, the men.

On the couch he closed his eyes and tried to move backward, before the glass window, her pale-coldness—the wound on the forehead patched with gauze. And so, he tried to work backward before that time. The apartment was getting cold, and he shivered, the loud labor of the air conditioner muffling out the outside as he sat in her apartment. He would work backwards, make her all over again, in every detail and in a million ways. The basic things come first: the fineness of her hair, blonde and always seemingly windblown. Her hands, small like everything about her and yet strong in their way.

She is with him in his home in Tennessee, before his divorce. His wife and his daughter are there too, and Claire takes Megan to the park to fly a kite. He had gone along, had watched. And long before then, in Ridgedale, Claire teasing him in church: *"Susie Ledbetter likes you,"* she says. *"See how she looks this way? You two are going to get married and have a hundred babies together."* Claire laughs like this is the funniest thing in the world. *"Ronnie and Susie, sittin' in a tree . . . ."*

Their mother had died. It seemed implausible now, but it happened, and afterwards that difficult time of silence, none of them knowing how to act, and he and Claire both blaming themselves silently for angering God and bringing it on, and some evenings lying in bed together, but not in any way that was wrong or dirty, only as a small comfort to one another.

His bedroom lamp clicks on, and she stares down at him, mascara wet and smeared under her eyes. He's startled and shifts sleepily. He has *Star Wars* bed sheets even though he is thirteen. He doesn't speak. *"Remember this, Ronnie,"* she says. *"Because before long you'll be a man yourself, and you'll need to remember and know this."* She's wearing a white terrycloth robe, open in the front so that a deep "V" of pale skin runs between her breasts. She smells like the ocean. *"No woman wants some beer-stinking slob on top of her, some idiot sweating and grunting like some kind of sick animal. Do you understand what I'm saying?"* Her voice is deep, and the space around her eyes is so dark. *"Mom's real sick Ronnie, and she's not going to make it. I think it's important for me to tell you certain things. Women need to be loved, touched in soft ways, treated special. Can you look at me and promise you understand and will never grow into one of those terrible kinds of men, Ronnie? Can you look at me and say this.*

And then, days later, as if Claire's saying it called it into being, their mother died in her hospital room, and none of the family there with her, instead he and Claire having neighborhood kids over to the house, which wasn't allowed when they were home alone. But this was not a

memory he wanted. This was sin, what you tried to push aside and forget and not know anymore, their father coming through the back door
in the middle of the day, unprecedented, and there upon them before
they could all get dressed even, the playing cards arranged on the carpet,
and Ron with only his shirt removed, but little Candy Wideman, whom
they had all sort of ganged up on collectively, stripped down to bra and
underpants.

He curled up on Claire's couch. He was reaching further back,
toward older memories, when he heard the quiet rapping, barely a knock
at all, and looked up to the slightly cracked door and a thin line of Gina
on the other side. He sat up but didn't speak. He watched her watching
him through the thin space.

"I just wanted to give you her keys," Gina said.

The door opened slightly, and he watched, still said nothing. Keys.
What keys did she have? She was spoiling the whole thing. What hor-
rible, real-world keys did she have, terrible earth-things that required she
break in on him now? And yet, he motioned her inside. She had added
a gray tee-shirt and a pair of thong sandals.

"I keep her spare keys," she said. "I didn't know if you had a set." She
began another series of toe raises but stopped herself and stood still in
place. "There's no way, really," she continued. "No way to say how. How
terrible." Her words began to falter. He thought she might cry again, but
she swallowed, recovered. "I'm just so sorry."

And she was. He could see that now, something in the way she looked
deep into him, that same searching, but with something like knowing,
too. But what was he to do with sorrow from this Gina, keeper of keys
and feeder of cats? She had nothing to do with what was next, which
was to go home, amid tragedy, and his daughter who would be a comfort
now, hundreds of miles away. He had to think about these things when
all he wanted to do was curl up and hurt forever.

"I'm her brother," Ron said. "But you knew that already."

"We've met before," Gina said. She took a careful step forward. "A
little over a year ago. You were visiting."

He looked closely at her face and tried to match it to one from that
night, the last time he was here. He had barely recognized Claire when
she met him at the airport, her hair cut short and dyed black, piercings
not just in her ears and nose but also her eyebrow, a thick stud through
her tongue. Ron was fresh off of a finalized divorce, on the very short
end of a custody agreement, and Claire had taken him to a dusty little
theater to see a play that was performed by her fellow actor friends.

"Are you an actor?" Ron said.

"Sometimes," Gina said. "Mostly I just work at a bookstore."

Claire had taken him to the cast party afterwards, where, uncomfortable among the unfamiliar artist types, he drank too much, and ended up smoking marijuana in the bathroom with an enormous and beautiful black woman named Cybil. He'd kissed this woman there in the bathroom—some kind of an attempt at post-divorce spontaneity—their tongues dry and rusty from the smoking, and he had tried for more, but she had pushed him away with sturdy arms in a way that said that's enough, white boy.

Gina folded her arms across her body.

"I don't remember you," Ron said. "I'm sorry."

"No," she said. "I mean, you wouldn't. There were a lot of people there."

When Ron and Cybil rejoined the party, Claire was nowhere in sight, and he didn't see her again for hours, not until she burst through the front door and into the living room where a few late-nighters were dancing and where Ron dozed on the couch. He squinted sleepily to see her raising the volume of the stereo and then moving toward him. He was angry. This was classic Claire, in the bad sense. "Where were you?" he said.

"Where were *you?*" Claire said. She raised her eyebrows and grinned, then pounced on him, one of her pointy knees striking his thigh.

"Get off," he said.

"I will if you dance with me."

"I swear to God, Claire."

"Okay," she said. "Jeez." She rolled off and to the floor. She squatted at eye level. She had a lollipop in her mouth. "Let's have a dance," she said. She took his hand and stood, pulling until he gave in and rose to his feet.

"You left me," he said. "With no car, no mention of where you were going, when you'd be back."

"Just dance," she said. She pulled him closer and laid her head against his chest and he was still angry but not as much so. He felt the sweat from her hair seep through his shirt as he kept her steady and they danced.

"Know what this reminds me of?" she said. "Eight tracks. Dancing in the living room at the lake house to Mom and Dad's eight tracks. Remember?"

"I remember," Ron said. "Charlie Rich."

"Yeah, Glen Campbell."

"The Bee Gees."

"Do you remember doing the bump?" she said.

"I remember. You knocked me clear across the room the one time. My head hit the corner of the coffee table. I had to get stitches."

"I'm so sorry, Ronnie."

"If you look close, you can see the scar running through my eyebrow."

Claire lifted her head. She looked at him, slowly. Sadly. And he was sorry he'd said the last part.

"Was I a monster? Was I like the worst sister ever?"

"No," he said. "Of course not." And this was true, but there was more to say than this, so much, and he felt it right there inside him but too large, no way to break it into working pieces, no way to start. This was his sister. This was Claire. And she had a thick rod through her tongue. She had left him at the party for God knows what reason, and maybe she was in trouble, needed help, and it could be him maybe to help, but he was divorced now, easily excised out of a family and sent into the world alone. Soon he would be moving to Georgia, by choice, hundreds of miles away from his daughter. His confidence was shot.

"What are you thinking?" Claire said. She tapped him softly under the chin. "Don't be sad. Everything will be okay."

"I know," Ron said. But he didn't know anything. So he was quiet, and they danced until the first threads of daylight cast a grayness in the room.

Gina held out the keys, and Ron took them, the warm metal heavy in his hand. She watched him. She was waiting.

"I have to make phone calls," he said. "Arrangements, you know." There was still the taste of vomit in his mouth and the dry hurt in his throat. He couldn't quite swallow.

"Of course," Gina said. "Let me leave you alone. I'm so sorry. But if there's anything I can do. If I can help. Any little thing."

"Thanks," Ron said. He forced something that he meant for a polite smile, but it felt strange and awkward on his face. He closed the door behind her. He was alone again. He tried to call Lenore but got instead her boyfriend, Brandon Stockdale. Lenore was out, he said. And Megan was at day camp. They were both out and Ron wondered, if this was the case, why Brandon was there in the house, the house that was his once.

"Just tell Lenore I'm in Florida," he told Brandon. "Tell her I'm headed to Ridgedale. Yes, Ridge-dale. There's been a family emergency."

"Oh," Brandon said. "Do you have her cell number?"

Ron said that he did, somewhere, but he took it down with a pen from the coffee table. After they hung up, he called Wolf in Valdosta, but there was no answer. He inhaled deeply and let the air escape slowly as he dialed his father's number, but it was his Aunt Louise, not Ray, who answered on the first ring.

"Lord, Ronnie," She said. "It does me wonders to hear your voice. Where are you, honey? Will you be here soon?"

"I'm in St. Pete, Aunt Louise. Can Dad come to the phone?"

A pause on the other end. "Oh, honey," she said. "I don't know that right this minute's the best time. I'm working with him, but I don't know that he's ready to talk right this minute. Can it wait till you get here?"

"Yes," he said. "Yes, ma'am." He breathed easier, swallowed a hard nothing. His father was too drunk to talk, which was bad. And yet, he was relieved. "My truck's running hot," he told Aunt Louise. His voice came out hoarse, strained. "I'm letting my engine cool off. "I'll leave when it cools off a little."

"Okay, honey," she said. Then another pause. "So you've done already taken care of the . . . ." She didn't finish.

"Yes, ma'am," he said. "It's all taken care of, but it might take a day or two for them to release her. There's a few things that's got to be done. It's just how they do it." He left out the other parts, the things they had told him as he signed a blur of forms: The cause of death was pending. There would be a toxicology report, maybe even a psychological autopsy.

And Aunt Louise, her voice thickening from a new swell of grief, "Okay then, honey. Be careful now. Don't you speed or nothing." Her voice failed on the last word.

Coughing, the back of his throat burning, Ron went to the refrigerator, which was nearly empty except for a tray of desiccated strawberries and three bottles of beer. At the kitchen sink he cupped his hands under the running faucet and tried to drink but couldn't get his throat to swallow. Finally, he forced a gulp past. It hurt, the tight dry constriction. He splashed water on his face and went back to the refrigerator, took one of the beers and held it unsteadily against his face. He looked through the kitchen drawers for a bottle opener, but finding none braced the lip of the cap against the counter's edge. The bottle shook in his hand. He hit the top of the cap with his free palm. Nothing. He hit it again, hard this time. The cap gave way, and cold foam ran over his fingers and onto the kitchen floor. He took very small sips at first, letting the beer find its way through, until his throat opened and he could drink freely.

Lenore

It wasn't like a full-blown relapse, only a minor setback, understandable under the circumstances. With the cigarettes bought and tucked safely in her purse, Lenore pulled out of the Circle K. She would smoke just one before picking Megan up from the Y, and a few more in the afternoon, maybe. She could allow herself this today.

She lit the end of a cigarette and inhaled the old sensation. She tried to conjure up a specific emotion, understand what her own feelings were, but in truth she'd only met Claire Ramsey a few times. At the wedding ceremony, of course, and the two of them had acted the role of new sisters, made harmless jokes at Ron's expense, drunk lots of champagne, and danced together to "We Are Family," at first only across from each other, both moving to the beat, then Claire grabbing Lenore by the hands, pulling her close, and then whipping her into a soulful swing, the little sister-in-law leading, spinning her around skillfully, and Lenore had surrendered to it, enjoyed the giddy feeling of submission. Afterwards, all agreed that the moment was precious.

There was that.

And years later, Claire's visit, her showing up with only a few hours notice, looking tired and edgy, like she'd been running from something that was still hot on her trail. She brought Megan a stuffed animal, probably grabbed up at some convenience store, and Claire had a hideous piercing in her nose, like some sort of tribeswoman. Lenore had tried to feel happy to see her even though Claire kept looking nervously over her shoulder at whatever it was she'd left behind. Had they all been young and unattached it would be one thing, but there was Megan to think about and the effect of inappropriate influences. But Megan had adored her aunt, just as Ron did, and the three of them became their own little clique, Claire the leader and Lenore—the forgotten mother and wife—old news.

Days after Claire had left, Lenore caught Megan watching herself in the mirror with a hoop earring hanging from a nostril, and before Lenore realized what she was doing, she had jerked Megan down from the stool and smacked her hard on the backside, and the look of surprised fear in those eyes of a child who had scarcely ever been struck before could still bring Lenore close to tears.

She was smoking in earnest now, driving along back roads, through neighborhoods, past houses—nice ones—the long-absent sensation of cool tobacco mist moving into her lungs, out her mouth, her nose. On the phone, Ron sounded okay. Not totally okay. He was hoarse, and when she had asked what she could do, how she could help, he had paused. That was the worst part of it, when she had waited out the silence, knowing that the right thing was to let him know they were on their way to join him—of course they were—and yet she waited, and he only said that the funeral—oh the sound of his voice on that word—would be in a few days, and only then adding that he'd really like to see Megan if it were possible, talk to her soon at least, that Megan should know about this. Claire was her aunt.

She would call him back very soon, Lenore had promised. She needed some time to digest, juggle some things around, find out what was possible. She was so very sorry for him, for his family.

Lenore lowered all of the car windows and put a mint into her mouth as she pulled up to the YMCA. Megan was waiting outside the building with the other campers. She wore a pair of shorts over her bathing suit, her bag over her shoulder and something in her hand, some sort of craftwork. She seemed tall and mature, growing so quickly.

She broke the news to Megan on the car ride home, evoking the aunt of birthday and Christmas cards, a vague entity no doubt. This was Daddy's sister, honey. She visited you when you were probably four, but you may not remember. But Megan says she does remember, which is possible. Yes, the one who gave you the panda bear. Well, she went to be with Jesus yesterday, Lenore explains.

That look of surprise, such precocity, such an intelligence. Yes, that's right. She passed away. Yes, Megan, dead. She is with her mother now. Yes, the grandmother that you never knew.

Lenore searched Megan's face for further reaction, but she couldn't read her, which was bothersome. A mother should know. Wasn't there supposed to be some God-given intuition? Megan seemed to be thinking deliberately, absorbing this news. "Where is Daddy?" she said, finally.

You don't ever really move on, Lenore has decided, especially when there is a child involved. You may try and try, but you're connected forever. What God has joined, it was true. She pulled into the driveway and took up her purse. This notion of family, complicated by divorce, legality. She would marry Brandon Stockdale, and perhaps if they acted soon enough there would be another child, Megan's half-sibling, always half despite all attempts to mitigate the difference. And there would be Ron forever to contend with, which was not a fair way to think about him, she knew. It would be easier if he were one of those fathers who faltered with child support, who slipped into the background of irresponsibility. But he never would, she knew, and to him there would always be, even in the absence of love, obligations.

"Daddy's in Florida, sweetie," Lenore said. "He's with the rest of his family." That was an error in wording. She shouldn't have put it that way. They were his family too, Megan and her both. The next question would come: Are we going to Florida? And then: Why aren't we going to Florida? Or maybe, I *want* to go to Florida.

Megan only gathered her gear, unreadable, so much like her father in this way, and Lenore thought up reasons why it was impossible for them to make the trip right now. The price of plane fares. The condition of her car, not reliable enough, certainly not for a woman and a child alone. Megan was in the middle of camp. She had barely known Claire, really didn't know her at all.

When she tells Brandon about this, he'll probably offer his own car for the trip, even insist on driving down with them. But would that even be right, to introduce him into such a scene? Maybe it would be more insult to Ron than anything else. And the Ramseys themselves, would they welcome the evil ex-wife? They were fine people in their own way, just not what she was so used to.

As she unlocked the door, Lenore saw at her elbow the pull of Megan's lower lip, the dipping of her chin, and the tears forming in her eyes. Amazing, this daughter, such capacity to feel, even more than was healthy sometimes.

Megan clenched the piece of craftwork in her hand. It was a relief design, made with clumsily pasted pasta shells and doused with glitter. Why do they teach them such bad habits?

"Honey," Lenore said. "It's okay to feel sad about this." And no sooner than her words, an actual tear on Megan's cheek, which she wiped discreetly away.

The prices of plane fares. Her car not reliable. No way to get a sub for her summer classes. She had not always been such a terrible person, Lenore thought. There was a time when she thought herself very decent, not flawless or separate from the sinful masses, but decent nonetheless.

Ron

A turn of his truck's ignition produced an awful grinding sound, abrasive and dry, confirming his suspicions that, despite what appeared like constant fluid levels, something serious and irremediable had been done. As it stood, his truck would take him no further today, definitely not to Ridgedale, some seventy-five miles inland. Thermostat, he thought briefly. Water hose? But it didn't matter. He was stuck for the moment, and having just paid bills and child support, left with something like sixty dollars in his bank account. He got out of the truck and moved briskly back to the apartment as if he had forgotten something there, feeling pained that, even today, there would be problems of the real world, logistical complications. Physics still applied.

Inside the apartment, he opened another beer and switched the air conditioner back on, not unmindful of the wrongness of it, hanging about in her apartment, drinking her beer. He did not want to call Ridgedale for a ride or for money, although he knew he could. Tragedy made things more pronounced, his mediocrity at it all: brother, son, husband, father, teacher, coach. He called Wolf again, but there was still no answer. This time he left a message. This was serious, man. It was about his sister. Could he wire him some money?

Ron paced through the room, began touching the things he recognized: a music box that had belonged to Mom, a miniature Empire State Building, a *Price Is Right* coffee mug, and a ceramic cocker spaniel with a chipped ear that he, himself, had inflicted in a childhood transgression of throwing-the-ball-in-the-house, for which Mom had spanked him thoroughly on the back of the legs with a fly swatter. She had snatched up the Nerf football—a green one that smelled of mildew and that was split along the fake threading—and threw it in the trash. She glared at him, eyes glossy and big, and he understood without her saying a word that the ball was to be gone forever. And there was Claire watching the whole thing and smiling like, *"You're getting exactly what you deserve, little shit."*

The wall unit blew fiercely, the room darker and very cold now, and he heard the faintest little knocks at the door. Gina again. He just sat still on the couch and waited for her to go away, but the knob turned slowly, the door opening.

"Ronnie?" Her voice was a whisper.

He stood in the center of the room. He said, "Come in." She entered, a shadowy figure between him and the dim light outside. She stepped inside and did a set of calf raises. "I saw that your truck wouldn't start," she said. "Do you need a ride? A car?"

Even in silhouette she was obviously pretty. He had noticed this before, amid the pain and confusion, the embarrassment of vomiting in front of her. Amid all of this he had noticed that she was pretty. He cleared his throat. "It's just overheated," he said. "The engine needs to cool down." She was here again, Gina-a-friend. They had met before, a year ago, at the party after the play, but he didn't remember. She worked at a bookstore. And Claire was dead.

"I have a car," she said. "It's not in great shape, but I can get a better one for you. From a friend of ours. I just got off the phone with him."

Ron said nothing.

"He said it's no trouble at all," she said. "He wants you to use it for as long as you need it. I think it would make him feel good to help."

Was this it, what he was to take from her? Take this offer, a car. He could use it as long as he needed. She had just said so. Maybe he could do this, help himself and satisfy her, put away her searching face.

"Thanks," he said. "But I couldn't do that."

"Are you hungry?" she said. "Can I bring you something? A sandwich? I made a pasta salad this morning."

"No thank you."

"Coffee? Juice?" she said. She looked at the empty bottle on the desk. "A beer, maybe?"

"No, thank you," Ron said.

"Blake—he's the friend I mentioned—he's bringing the car over," she said. "He'll insist you take it."

"I wouldn't be able to bring it back right away," Ron said. "It might be a couple of days before I could bring it back."

"It's no problem at all. He doesn't need it. He lives a few blocks from his work. He could pick it up . . ." Gina looked down, raised herself onto her toes, and descended. "When we come for the service, the memorial."

Service. Memorial. She meant funeral. She would come to the funeral. He hadn't considered this before. "That will be in Ridgedale," Ron said.

"Right," Gina said. "Of course."

Of course. Sure. She could go to Ridgedale, to the funeral. There was nothing to stop her. They could all come, the whole cast of them. It wasn't some place with gates and locks. If they wanted to come, who was he to stop them?

Louise

She poured three capfuls of Jack Daniels into the glass of sweet tea and stirred it quickly with a spoon. She needed to hurry, get this to Ray before he took the notion to find the bottle himself. Things were bad enough already, and she wanted him sober for this. It was his own child after all, and he should have to feel this loss with the rest of them.

Not that she couldn't understand a little. There was times she wanted to crawl away and hide, times where, if she didn't know better, it seemed like God had forgot all about them, and she wanted to look up and scream at the sky, call out for an answer as to how—when he was supposed to love them—he could visit so much trouble on one family. She knew better, though. There weren't answers to something as bad as this, and lord knows if there was they wouldn't be at the bottom of some bottle. She had told this to Ray, the man who was her brother but who had seemed to forget this a long time ago, who treated her like some kind of aggravating burden he had no choice but to endure. It was good that their daddy didn't live long enough to see them this way.

She found Ray where she left him, in his chair in the family room, staring forward at the television and not so much as blinking as she approached. He looked small and helpless, an old man now. She sat the glass on the TV tray beside him, and still he didn't turn to her. Something inside her turned sour, and she wanted to slap him good, this old man, her brother. Or grab him and hold him tight, so tight he couldn't get free.

"Ray, you need to eat a little something before long. Here? Can I fix you a biscuit or something?"

Ray said nothing, and she went back into the kitchen and leaned against the counter. Lord knows she tried to hold things together as best she could and yet this is how it works out, Ray a drunkard who won't give her the time of day. Her only son in jail for two years while his wife and kids, her own grandchildren, live like trash, and Ronnie moved off and never coming home even for the holidays, depriving them of knowing his own little girl. God knows he was busy. She understood that, but to pull away so completely, it wasn't right. And Claire was now passed. That was the awful thing in front of them now, the truth of it hitting her fresh in her chest, Claire gone and with her mama, but taken from them and from the world, before her time dead and the rest of them scrambling around not knowing how to act, each living it in a private place when they should be holding each other up.

Ron

They were sitting on the bed together, and he was wrapped in the comforter, which smelled like Claire.

"It's okay," Gina said. She poured a bit more water into his cup. "Drink this."

Like a small child following directions, he drank.

"I can drive you there if you'd like," Gina said. She was looking at the mess he'd made, papers and books and clothing strewn across the floor.

"I was looking for, something," he said, trying to account for this, for the feelings that had sent him out of himself for a short time, and that were now already seeming distant to his mind. "I'm not sure," he said. "I don't know exactly."

"You don't have to explain anything to me, Ronnie," she said. "Not ever."

He was grateful for this small license and even that she called him Ronnie. When she said it, he didn't mind. It was dark, and he wanted her here now. He was glad he hadn't left, although he had meant to leave, had sat in Blake's car for a long time, the engine running. Outside, the sky had turned light charcoal.

And now the way the shadows fell on her face, something stirring in his memory, the shape of her chin and something about her eyebrows. He liked her eyebrows, the way she allowed them to grow thick and full.

"You were in the play," he said.

Her eyebrows were thick and full, and she lowered them at him. "What?"

"A year ago. The night I was here." He was sure of it now. Of course he had met her before. He remembered. "You played the oldest sister, the nearsighted one who was so into bugs."

"That's amazing," Gina said.

"She wanted to be an entomologist," Ron said. "But she gave up her dream to stay home and take care of her grandfather. I talked to you at the party afterwards."

"Yeah," Gina said. "You did."

"I'm sorry I didn't remember before. This whole thing, you know."

"Of course," she said. "It's crazy that you remember at all." She looked away from him now, seeming to focus on something in the corner of the room. "You're just like Claire," she said. "She has this way with details. We all laugh because she's never great at memorizing lines, but she can quote verbatim something someone said two years ago." A thing close to a smile played across Gina's face, just for an instant, and it was gone. "If you ever want to settle a question," she said. "If you want to clarify a timeline or remember the name of the bartender from the one night in Key West in 1998, you ask Claire."

She stopped talking, but Ron wanted more of this. This was Claire, her life here, and he wanted anything Gina could offer. But she had stopped talking. And she held herself with her arms across her front. She was cold. He shifted, drew slack from the comforter and offered half to her. She accepted.

"Thank you," she said. "You're the same way, aren't you?"

"With remembering stuff?" Ron said. Sophie crossed the room toward them. She leapt onto the bed and rubbed against Gina's thigh.

"I'm talking too much," Gina said. "I'm sorry."

"No," he said. "Keep talking." This was something, part of Claire that he didn't know, and he wanted more.

But she was quiet now. He could feel her heat with him under the blanket.

In Ridgedale they were expecting him, but he had not even left yet. He sat with Gina, their backs pressed against the wall, wrapped in the comforter that still smelled like Claire, and for now this was what he wanted, he and she closer now and occasionally the cautious grazing of bodies, that incidental touching that was not incidental really but two people feeling each other out, those cautious steps toward something else. Their thighs were flush together, no mistake, then shoulders pressing, harder, until both turned in and met lips together in a spilling over of warmth and hurt.

Wolf

Parked alongside the curb of the Ramsey house, Wolf watched Ron and his daddy get out of the limousine and step into the front yard. Ron must've taken after his mama, Wolf thought, because Mr. Ramsey was a good four inches taller than Ron, and thick shouldered. If the old man had played ball, he'd probably been a tight end or even an offensive tackle.

In the yard with them was the woman Ron had pointed out earlier as his Aunt Louise. She was tall too, for a woman, but also draped with rolls of fat, and next to her was a shorter man Wolf hadn't met yet.

He should wait a little while, though, until some more people showed up at least. He had never been good at this kind of stuff, never knew the right thing to say. What could you say but I'm sorry, and after that you're just standing around like a dumb ass. And it wasn't like this was a grandma or a great uncle, something that was naturally bound to happen. This was Claire, and Wolf had never been a part of anything like this before. What the hell could you say that didn't come off dumber than shit?

Mr. Ramsey stretched and moved slowly toward the front door. He looked uncomfortable in the suit and tie, like he'd made himself fit into something that would barely hold him in and at any minute the seams might give way.

Yeah, better that Wolf wait just a little while before he went in. This was family time. But then Ron paused at their front door and looked right at Wolf, like he was waiting for him to get out of the car. Ron began walking down the driveway, and Wolf rolled down his window when he approached.

"Come inside," Ron said when he reached the window. He wedged his finger underneath his collar and stretched it out as far as he could, frowning and craning his neck to the side.

"Thought maybe I should wait until some more folks got here," Wolf said. "Give ya'll some time to yourself. How you holding up, anyway?" And damn if that wasn't the dumbest thing he could have said.

Ron shook his head. "I don't know." Sweat bubbled up on his forehead, and he fiddled more with his collar, which, like the rest of his outfit, looked stiff and new.

"I've got your clothes right here," Wolf said. He pointed to the bag in the back seat. "Didn't know what to bring, so I just packed whatever I could find."

"Thanks for that," Ron said. Then, "Hey, unlock the door. Let me in for a minute."

Wolf cranked the engine and let the car idle. He tried to think of something else to say. Ron turned the AC vent toward his face. This was Ron, his best friend, the man who lived with him and coached with him, who had played beside him for four years and now was a normal part of damn near every day of his life, but now sitting here at Ron's daddy's house, them here because his sister was dead from a head-on crash with a telephone pole and surely the family wondering but not saying anything about it, and the talking that was so easy for him and Ron before felt now like the hardest thing in the world.

"There was a bunch of people at the church," Wolf said. "A whole lot."

"Yeah," Ron said. He looked up nodding, and Wolf felt like maybe saying this was the right thing.

"The ones that set in front of me," Wolf said. "Those were her friends from Tampa, I reckon."

"Right," Ron said. "Tampa and St. Pete, mostly. Why?"

Now Ron's look was different, so Wolf just squinted into his rear-view mirror, saw a pickup truck approach and move past them. It turned into the Ramsey driveway. Another car followed, a long station wagon with paneled sides.

"Let's go inside," Ron said. "Yeah?"

IN WHAT SEEMED like only a few minutes, the front room of the house was filled with people. The older ones sat on couches or the extra chairs that had been set up along the walls. Wolf stood at the edge of the room. He watched Ron, who stood beneath a mounted deer head, talking to a man and a woman. The couple was clean and neatly groomed, but there was something about them, the man's hair thick from home haircuts, and the woman's dress long and not with the times somehow. But more than that there was that way about their faces, the look that was hard to explain but that says hard work and lots of going without. Wolf knew that look.

There was a smell in the room, not stale exactly, but something like time and mothballs, but also the smell of good food. The house was smaller than he had imagined it would be. Ron's family had citrus money, but there was nothing special here.

Wolf made his way into the kitchen, and here he pretended to be interested in the cabinets. They were made of solid wood, old but well constructed. He traced his finger down the routed groove. On the kitchen counter were several covered dishes of food. The warm smells were good, and Wolf was very hungry. He hadn't had anything to eat since five in the morning when he set off for Florida. But no one else was eating right now, and he wasn't going to be the first.

He felt awkward, like he couldn't get any traction. It was like one of those football dreams where you are yourself today but also you're expected to suit up and play for the old team, either in high school or college, or sometimes some weird mix of both, but there's always something wrong. You can't find your helmet, or if you do find it, it is a motorcycle helmet or maybe you look down to realize you're bare-foot, and Coach yells at you to get your goddamned shoes on, so you're searching all over the sideline, but the only shoes you can find are penny loafers, so you put them on. Wolf hated those dreams.

Ron's Aunt Louise came into the kitchen. Her eyes lit up when she saw Wolf, and her arms were held out to him. He lowered himself into a hug with the woman, gave in to her softness, the spongy flesh of her arms and bosom.

"We're so glad you're here," she said, and released him, but her hands still held onto his forearms. "Wolf," she said. "Is that right?"

"Yes, ma'am," Wolf said. "Or Andy is fine, too."

"Well, I'm Ronnie's Aunt Louise. I know it means a whole lot to him that you're here," she said. She studied him a moment, still holding his forearms. "I've heard so much about you, I feel like you're family." Finally, she let go of him. "Are you hungry? Can I fix you a plate of something?" She gestured toward the dishes on the counter. They were still untouched.

"No ma'am. I'm fine, thank you."

"Are you sure? Can I get you something to drink? Some coffee or iced tea?" Her eyes were red from crying, but right now she wanted only to get him something. He knew this woman, he thought, like so many in his own family, and he felt like hugging her all over again. "Yes, ma'am," he said. "Some coffee would be real nice."

She took a mug from the cupboard and made a motion to someone in the living room before filling it with coffee.

A man entered the kitchen, the one who had gotten out of the lim-ousine with Aunt Louise. His skin was tan, and he had a thick auburn mustache.

"Paul-honey," Aunt Louise said. "I want you to meet Ronnie's friend." She paused a moment, considering, then said, "Wolf."

Paul offered his hand, and Wolf took it. It was a small hand, but the grip was firm, the skin rough and calloused.

"He drove down from Valdosta today," Aunt Louise said. "Wolf-honey, do you take cream and sugar?"

"Yes, ma'am," Wolf said. "Thank you." He released Paul's hand.

Paul said, "You're the one that's coaching football up there with Ronnie, huh?"

"Yes, sir," Wolf said. And he thought he should say something else. The pause was too long. But football didn't seem like the right topic. Aunt Louise handed him his coffee.

"Thank you," Wolf said.

Paul took a pack of cigarettes out of his shirt pocket. "Heard ya'll didn't do much good last year."

"No, sir," Wolf said. "We went one and nine. Not so good at all." He took a small sip of the coffee. "Next year we'll have some returning players," he said. "And we've got them on a weightlifting program, so things should get better." This was good. Football talk he could do. He could talk football all day and forever.

"Well, you'll come along then," Paul said. He took a cigarette from his pack. "Excuse me for a minute," he said and turned for the back door. Wolf wished that he were a smoker right now, that he could escape with Paul and smoke the hell out of a cigarette, suck down a whole pack even. But then he saw that Aunt Louise was putting plates and forks next to the food. One dish, lasagna, looked especially tempting, but Wolf was thinking of taking a square of the cornbread, something he could snag quickly and polish off in a few seconds.

It was wrong, though, to be thinking this way when you should be trying to find a way to help your best friend, whose very own sister was now dead, and whose wife and daughter were nowhere to be seen, all of this coming at Ron when he'd been doing so much better and it looked like he was starting to come out of his funk and act something like his old self again.

Ex-wife is what he'd meant. That's what Lenore was. Damn, but if she were a man he'd ring her neck good. She had called him yesterday, explaining, to *him,* why she couldn't make it down for the funeral. Megan didn't even know Ron's sister, she'd said, and did he, Wolf, think it would be okay if they didn't come. Megan would be down in Georgia for her visit in a few weeks anyway, she'd said.

And what the fuck was Wolf supposed to say to that? It was okay? He understood? Hell, Lenore. You need your people around you at a time like this. He had told her that much at least, and if she was pissed at him, that was just fine, because this was Ron's one-and-only sister, and for it to happen the way it did, all of these sweet people knowing but not talking about it, only the thing that the preacher said, something about the burden of those who feel the pulse of the world at the end of their fingertips, how we should understand that to despair, for some, was to be capable of envisioning a Christ-redeemed earth.

He had to do better than this. And he would, too. Gut-check time. Suck it up. Wolf took his coffee mug and moved in among the people. He would, by God, find someone to comfort, or at least offer a damn sympathetic ear. Hell, that's all people wanted half the time anyway, someone to just show some interest. He targeted an old couple sitting together on the couch, beside the piano, and they had might as well get ready for some first-rate condolence because he was on his way.

But before he could get to them, a jam of people paused at the door. They had seeped in but then stopped, butted up there against each other in the square section before the living room. Here were the Tampa friends, and Wolf didn't like the looks of things. The little pasty fella with the hair worked into tall spikes: he was a queer for sure and didn't worry about hiding it. He held a covered dish in front of him. And then the black woman with the fancy braids, who stood tall behind the rest. She was taller than Wolf was even, maybe six-five, but that was probably wrong, only that tall with heels on, but strong-looking too. She had muscles. She could play defensive end he bet, and still she was beautiful, a face strong and narrow like some kind of old-time queen. It wasn't that he was a racist or a homophobe even. Hell, he'd been around. He'd met all kinds of people. But here in this house, with these folks who reminded him so much of his own, it wasn't likely to be an easy thing.

Everyone was quiet all of a sudden. The bunch of them stood there at the edge of the room, waiting it seemed like, and everyone's eyes, Ron's too, falling on Mr. Ramsey, waiting to see what he did, but he was distracted and hadn't even seen the group until finally he caught on to something going on, and when he turned toward the door, he only paused an instant before he smiled and nodded. "Ya'll come in," he said, and he began walking toward them.

Ron

Ron let the door of the bar close behind him. He stood in the smoky half-light, allowing his eyes to adjust, his fists clenched and throat still warm from the whisky, his tongue still sweet with the taste.

Country music played from the jukebox.

This was the Checkered Flag, the bar you came to at times like Thanksgiving or Christmas break, when a lot of those who had gone off to college or moved away were visiting, and at times like those it took on a whole different atmosphere, packed with Ridgedaleans past and present, full of talk and memories.

Tonight was not one of these nights, but about a dozen people were here, youngish men mostly. They seemed to look at Ron, some of their faces vaguely familiar, liked age-progressed photos, or maybe younger siblings of his classmates, grown into adults in his absence. He spotted Cybil in the corner beside a pool table. She held a pool stick by her side, waiting as one of the others took his shot. This guy taking his shot was named David, and he had gone to college with Claire, and now he was teaching at the university. He seemed like a nice guy, a little nervous and edgy maybe, but otherwise normal and nice enough.

Wolf was sitting his big ass at a table beside the boy who had worn white-blonde spikes to the service and who now had mercifully put on a baseball cap for the occasion. His name was Mark, and he wasn't really a boy. He was a young man, but the hair made him seem frivolous, juvenile. Gina was not with them, which was a good thing, probably, but Ron felt disappointment nonetheless.

Wolf caught Ron's eye, seemed startled a moment, then rose quickly and met him halfway across the floor.

"What the fuck's going on?" Ron said. He said this loud. He wanted to be done with the whole bullshit of this thing, to break through to something selfish and real.

Wolf moved back at the words. Had it been any other situation, Ron knew Wolf would have come right back at him, but tonight Wolf just looked embarrassed. He took a sip of the beer in his hand. "It's settled down now," Wolf said. "You missed it. I hope you didn't come here because you was worried."

The anger warm in his ears, Ron said, "You *called* me." Across the room, two men in work clothes seemed to watch the kid in the baseball cap, and to watch Ron too. One said something that made the other laugh. "You said there was trouble," Ron said.

"I'm sorry about that, man," Wolf said. "At first I was just getting a vibe. Then some fella in a rebel flag hat started talking his shit."

"Who? What did he say?" Ron took the mug from Wolf's hand and drank the beer down quickly. If he had to do this, take on a goddamned stereotyped version of the world, he needed to get himself ready.

"It's okay now. We're all about to leave, go back to your lake house."

"Why did you bring them here, Wolf?"

"I didn't." Wolf turned his palms up and shrugged. "They were coming with or without me. It was their thing. I think for them a place like this is . . . ." He thought a moment. "What do you call it? Exotic, or something."

"You should've told them it wasn't a good idea." Ron wiped the foam from his lip.

"I did," Wolf said. "I did, sort of." He turned and looked toward Cybil, who bent gracefully down to the table to take her shot. "You know I ain't good at handling these kinds of situations. I didn't want to sound prejudiced or anything. I don't really know how things are here."

"You know," Ron said.

THE BARTENDER greeted Ron by name. They were close to the same age, but Ron didn't recognize him. They shook hands. "Matt Yarbrough," the bartender said. "Bill's brother."

Ron nodded. "Right," he said. "How you been?"

"Good," Matt Yarbrough said. He finished filling a pitcher and sat it on the bar along with a fresh mug, which Ron filled to the top. He took out his wallet, but Matt Yarbrough waved him off. "On the house," he said.

"Thanks," Ron said. "My friend tells me there was a fuss before."

Matt Yarbrough shook his head. "A couple of peckerheads said a couple things. Once they figured out who the folks were, they cooled down. Everyone's real sorry to hear about Claire."

"Good," Ron said. He took a deep pull from the mug. "That's goddamned good for them." He went back at the beer. He'd been without his pills for a few days now, and he liked the edge he felt surfacing. It felt good to drink and to be pissed off. Give him more beer. He'd drink until he forgot everything, just the way Ray did, and *oh,* the surprise on the old man's face when, after Wolf had called, Ron snatched up Ray's bottle of whisky and turned it up, putting a good eight or ten bubbles in it before sitting it back down on the table. That's right, Ron had wanted to say to his father, who had never seen him take a drink in his life. That's right, two can play at this. Maybe later we'll polish the bottle off together, old man, start another one and drink on until every single bit of human life in us is gone.

"Look, Ronnie," Matt Yarbrough said. "I got no problem with anyone. It don't make a bit of difference to me. They can stay here all night as far as I care, but you know how some folks are around here."

"Which folks?" Ron said. "You tell me which folks." He filled up Wolf's mug and clinked it against his own. He was ready to take on all comers, make a stand against racism and homophobia right here in the bastion of ignorance. He would defend the dingbats who were too clueless to know they were in the wrong place, or in Cybil's case, big and black and crazy, she was probably here *because* it was the wrong place.

Good enough. She could join in. The two of them and Wolf could stand back to back and take on all comers. Ron was ready.

"Now Ronnie," Matt Yarbrough said. "I don't want any trouble. Maybe if you was to get a couple of your old friends in here it might be better. This ain't the big city, you know."

And as if this was some goddamned movie, a hand gripped Ron's shoulder. He looked up and here was Freddy Clevenger. Big fat Freddy, who wasn't fat anymore and not thin exactly but still a big motherfucker who you'd be happy to have at your back.

"Speak of the fucking devil," Ron said. "What's up, Biggen?" He stood and embraced Freddy. They had spoken briefly after the funeral and Freddy had given his number, so when Wolf called with this new trouble it had seemed like the right thing to call Freddy too, and fuck yes here he was now. To Matt Yarbrough, Ron said, "Looks like they're already getting here."

Claire

She had decided against any letters. This was outside of rhetoric. Nothing was left to say. Wasn't that the whole problem?

There were, however, issues of propriety, basic considerations for those who come after. Any sex toys would have to go, of course, not that she owned much in that department. One ancient vibrator. That was all. A hard plastic number, narrow and inorganic, the most basic and utilitarian of designs, almost puritanical, she thought. Squeamish. She unscrewed the end and dropped the batteries into the trashcan, then tossed the hollow unit in after. It landed softly, benignly, and there was something vaguely sad about it.

She turned the stereo volume up so that Billie Holiday's voice rose loud in her studio apartment. Sophie, on the bed, started momentarily and stood to watch Claire a moment before settling back into a cozy ball. It was early still, not yet seven o'clock, but already warm. The sun shone through her window and against the sofa. A mist of dust, raised from her cleaning, floated in the white light. Billie sang, "*This is a fine ro-mance,*" but she meant it ironically, and Claire thought that this just about summed it up.

She searched her bookshelf for anything remotely scandalous but found only a collection of erotic art—nudes posed in minimalist interiors—men with women and women with women and men with men, but the scenes were only suggestive. No penetration, no erections even. She dropped the book into the trash.

In the bathroom she donned the rubber gloves. She had left the toilet bowl to soak with bleach overnight, and now she scrubbed carefully with the brush, watched as the ugly brown water line disappeared. She flushed and all was white and pristine again. She dropped the brush and its holder into a trash bag.

From the bathtub drain she removed the filter. It was long and rusted, its grooves caked with a gray sludge. And hair, a lot of hair, sprouting from the muck like part of some terrible tumor, the smell rich and soapy-sour. This was what we were, no? Boiled down and simplified. The detritus of the human animal. Claire gathered a handful of toilet tissue and began a tentative cleaning of the filter, dropping the used paper into the trash bag. But it was too gross. She filled the sink with water and Lime Away, set the filter in to soak.

In her desk drawers she found things: paper clips and markers (permanent, dry-erase, and highlighter). Thumbtacks, glue sticks. Scotch tape and rubber bands. Notepads, a bottle of expired vitamins, and a lump of Sticky-Tack coated in glitter and dirt. A small set of acrylic paints, the contents now dried and solidified. In the back corner of one drawer, hidden at first in pencil shavings and dust, she found a Susan B. Anthony dollar. This she held under the flow of the kitchenette sink, worked it between her fingers until it was clean, and set it on the counter.

She threw out all of her prescription medication, her lithium and her Xanax both. This felt the most final.

The key was not to set a strict timetable, to give oneself the permission to delay as long as needed. Let the impulse sneak up on oneself, then act. She was sweating now, and she pulled off her top, then her bra, and turned on the air conditioner, let her breasts take in the cool wind. The sweat turned cold and icy, and the sensation was lovely. Her nipples stood long and erect with something like hope. That's the way it always is, when you've finally given up; everything feels like untapped possibility. Seller's remorse. She had read once that of the twenty-six people who survived the jump from the Golden Gate Bridge, all described a wave of regret in the four seconds it took to plunge into the bay. They realized, the article explained, that every problem in their life was solvable, all except for the one they had just created.

Back in the kitchen, Claire scrubbed hard at a stain on the counter, but it wouldn't budge. She needed something stronger, something with super stain-fighting intensity. You wouldn't find it on the shelf at Target though. It would have to be something industrial, available only through certain channels. She would need an *in*, a contact. A hookup.

The article about the bridge jumpers had missed the whole point, she has decided. Of course the survivors felt that four-second regret. The others plunged guiltlessly into the bay, sank without remorse into the cool, forgiving depths. We celebrate survival. The mantras are all around us, ridiculous in their banality, how it's a permanent solution to a temporary problem, the easy way out, the coward's path. Bullshit. The truth is that nothing is more terrifying, nothing more against our natural impulse. Cowards shelter themselves into bubbles of social construction. Even those who denied transcendental truth (Sartre? Camus? Derrida?—all Frenchmen, strangely, perhaps something in the national consciousness?) had to make a holy enterprise out of the denial. Transcend through denunciation. Forge purpose out of refutation.

The air conditioner clicked off. Billie sang now about "*reaching for the moon,*" and Claire extended her hands, could feel the notes at the end of her fingertips. Why must everything be so goddamned, unrelentingly significant? Her mother—God rest her soul—used to say the Lord works in mysterious ways. It's not for us to try to understand. And, maybe. What about that, the possibility of eternal life, the chance of communion with souls of those passed, discrete and true interactions? Anything was possible. Even years of staunch skepticism can't erase some lingering ideas, quell all hope and fear. Once, at a cathedral in Manhattan, her friend Sally had asked Claire to pose for a picture inside a confessional, to get on her knees and take on a mock prayer stance, and Claire, who wasn't even Catholic, had refused. What had it been? Residual faith?

She slipped on a tee-shirt and began tying up the trash bag. Satisfied, she lifted it from the can, took the other bag from the corner, and headed with them toward the alley dumpster.

Ray

There had been four of them once, but now only two, and Ray was still alive. He drank straight coffee, the whisky sitting on the table untouched for over an hour now. He had weaned it out two full cups ago, and he could feel the fog lifting from him, the clear and bad feeling in his shoulders and chest.

It should've been him one of the times. That was straight truth. But he was alive, and tomorrow was another day he had to face. It didn't matter what happened to him. Later, he could fall all to hell if he wanted, but for now he had to do some things. There were duties. He sipped the coffee, warm, the taste a bitter that was coffee alone.

Mona's dying made something come between him and the kids. That was normal. Children loved their mamas, and he'd always gone through Mona to them, and then she died and they had seemed so far away. He should have remarried, maybe. But that time had passed, the idea never seeming right, another woman in his house, in his bed. And also he had thought that he would be dead too before long, that surely God wouldn't be so cruel as to have him live on after what he'd done.

How they'd even made it through that first year or so he wasn't sure. He couldn't remember much from that time. What had he done but gone to work, kept food on the table. He had done that. That had to count for something.

It was Claire to be sure, taking on the burden of the household, herself nothing more than a girl. And Ray had worked hard in the groves, bought and expanded. If only he could build up some savings, he'd thought, so they didn't have to worry about money, maybe it would make up for some of the other things he was no good at. So he'd worked hard and made more money than he'd ever imagined he could make, and the kids had gone off to good colleges, gotten educations, which he wanted for them because it was something that couldn't be taken away, but that had only set them further off from him. First Claire, then Ronnie, and there had been plenty of money left over, but then they'd stayed in other cities, away from home, and had hardly ever asked for anything. He drained the cup. He rose and went to the counter. He leaned his body against it for a moment and here almost gave into something, a thing that didn't have a name but that meant more whisky and giving up no matter what it was people expected of him. Instead, he filled his cup with only coffee again.

He couldn't reach them after that, once they'd settled off on their own. But even before that, hadn't he always been the one on the outside, even before Mona got sick. He could feel it when he walked into the room, the sudden quiet, like whatever was being said had to stop right then, and half the time it was like they hated him. And maybe he hated them too, sometimes, not hated but felt aggravated so that he'd do the only thing he could do which was to get mad and mean, and this worked, but less and less so, and then Mona died and later the kids left for college.

It was wrong, all of it, but how were you supposed to act when you were a stranger in your own home? And good God, after Mona was gone there was Louise, wailing and carrying on like it was one of her own who was lost, babying the kids so much that finally he had to send her away. They'd never get on with her always around. But if you were a man, how were you supposed to talk about it and make it right, in a way that made sense, when you couldn't just do it and make it so?

He wanted another drink, and the whisky sat right there in front of him, right there on the table, here in this same house, where they had moved on account of Mona's insistence. Because of the kids, she'd said. They needed better influences and they could get that in town. He watched the whisky closely. He could pour it down the sink, but there was still half a case in the garage. He could throw that out too, take a hammer to it, but he wouldn't do that, and he knew it.

If it had been up to him, they'd have never moved from the lake house. There were people out there right now, Claire's friends from St. Petersburg, who had come here for her, and Ray didn't like what he saw in them, it being so much about how far she had gone away from him, but they were the ones that came here for her, and so he had to do something. And so now they were staying out at the lake house and would be with the family tomorrow if they wanted to. This was a small thing that he could do for Claire because they were the ones who came for her, and whatever else about it he didn't understand could wait.

It was Mona who had him move here, and they'd hardly settled in when she started getting the headaches and dizzy spells. He counted the years, and it was sixteen years without Mona. That didn't seem possible, but time had gone on and he had lived, and maybe at some point, without even realizing it, he'd made this allowance for himself, to live on beyond his wife. And even though his daughter was gone, completely now and not just far off and unreachable, he knew that he would continue to live now, even though he didn't want to, even though he shouldn't. Because it's what you do. The other was the thing that God wouldn't forgive. He had been told that as a boy, but he couldn't believe that now, wouldn't allow himself to. And hadn't God left him a long time ago? And even if he did meet Mona in some kind of heaven, what would he say to her, she still a woman of forty-two years and he practically an old man now, who had failed her, failed her children.

They say, though, that the bodies we have in heaven will be different ones, not like those here on earth, and the way that you're together there is something different. That was not a comfort to him now. He wanted her body, the one she had before he'd destroyed it, drawing back from her when he felt the lump, hard and jagged like a chunk of gravel, and he pulling away in fright, and she turning over on her side, quiet in the darkness of their room. And what had he said, but nothing. For a whole year the two of them saying nothing, just carrying on like normal so that when she couldn't ignore it any more, it was too late.

And in this way he had killed her, and while he should be dead, he was still alive, and despite the wanting to be gone or to crawl into the whisky forever, there was also the thought that kept coming to him even now, the thing that made him want to try, to lift himself out of the dusty years and be a person again. The thought: He still had one of them left.

Gina

Stupid, she thought. She sat at the table in Claire's childhood home, across from Blake, who just stared at her. Stupid, stupid, stupid. She had made things ten times worse.

"Say something," she said. But Blake just stared dumbly. Then finally, "I don't know *what* to say, Gina. Seriously, I really can't comprehend what you're telling me."

He didn't even seem angry. That would have been easier, if he were the type to yell and curse and call her a slut. She had confessed everything, knowing that on some level he already knew. Men always know. He had asked pointed questions, coming closer and closer to the thing. He could read her, something she liked in better times, but now it was her downfall. Yes, it was true. She had slept with Ronnie Ramsey, yes slept with as in sex. It wasn't something she had planned. It happened, though. In Claire's own apartment. She'd really made a mess of things.

"You can't imagine how sorry I am," Gina said.

"You're sorry," Blake said, not asking but repeating.

"Yes. Very, very sorry. You have to understand, Blake. People react in bizarre ways at times like this. It's grief. It's unpredictable."

"It's unpredictable."

"Yes, that's what I'm saying."

Blake seemed to break from his trance. He shook his head as if to clear it. "So what does this mean, Gina?" He looked around the room and then back at her. He stood. "I'm trying to understand what this means. Was it just a fluke, or do you care about him? I mean, is this something you want to pursue?"

She had expected such a question, and she had an answer ready, which was the truth. The whole thing was probably most definitely a fluke, two people sad and confused, but also everyone was too hurt and out of their minds right now to even talk about that. But before she could tell Blake any of this, she heard a car pull into the front driveway.

And at the front door, Cybil and the big muscled guy, Wolf, Ronnie's roommate. They stepped into the room. Cybil led Wolf over to them. They were arm in arm, and they stood somewhat formally next to the table.

"I think the three of you have hardly met," Cybil said. "Allow me to introduce Andrew Wolfenbarger of Valdosta, Georgia. Formerly of Knoxville, Tennessee: physical education instructor and football coach." Now Cybil gestured toward them. "Wolf," she said, "Gina and Blake, both of St. Petersburg: actors and booksellers, in that order."

Gina could tell they'd both been drinking. They weren't smiling, but there was something festive beneath the surface, held in check, but a sort of giddiness threatening to break through. Wolf extended his hand, first to Blake, then to Gina. His hand was large and strong, but also surprisingly soft.

"Pleased to meet y'all both," Wolf said.

Gina wondered if Wolf knew about her too, if Ronnie had told him about her: the grief slut.

"Wolfenbarger," Blake said. "I thought 'Wolf' might've been short for Wolfgang."

"Nope," Wolf said, and laughed. "Not hardly."

But he *looked* like a wolf, didn't he? His hair had a thick shagginess about it, and Gina thought if she ran her hand across it, she would find sheddings in her palm. His face too, full in the cheeks, but his features sharp and pointed. Lupine.

"Ron is on his way." Cybil said. "He's coming with the others. They stopped by the store. You should have seen all the people who showed up at the bar. And they were all so nice."

Ron, Gina thought. He went by Ron, not Ronnie. She would need to remember. He was a grown man after all.

Now their giddiness was gone, and Cybil was biting her lower lip. She sniffed. "We were all sitting at a table together and talking, telling stories about her, and I just kept expecting her to walk through the door, spring in front of us and take a bow, you know?"

"I know, sweetie," Gina said. She started to rise for her, but Wolf pulled Cybil close to him. Cybil pressed her face to his shoulder for a moment, and when she reemerged she was composed.

"You said Ron's on his way?" Blake said. He twisted his torso, cracking his back the way he always did in preparation for leaving some place.

"They stopped by the Jiffy Store to pick up some beer," Wolf said. "But they're on their way out."

"I wish I could stay," Blake said. "Spend more time with everyone, but unfortunately I have to get back to St. Pete tonight. I have to open the store in the morning." He turned to Gina. He was calm, still very calm. "Do you want to come with me, or will you catch a ride back tomorrow?"

An ultimatum.

Cybil seemed to sense the tension and led Wolf deeper into the house. "I wish you both would stay," she said, but only halfheartedly. "We'll be in the living room. Let us know if either of you leave."

"We *are* sort of committed," Gina said.

Blake nodded slowly. "You're staying then," he said, like it was some casual observation.

"They're expecting us to," Gina said. "We told them we'd be here tomorrow. We can't just leave now." She wasn't worried that Blake would make a scene. He wouldn't, no matter what. Right now, she loved him for that.

"Well, I guess that settles it," he said. He took the keys from his pocket.

"I don't think it should settle anything, Blake. All I know is that Claire's father asked me to stay for lunch tomorrow. I said I would, and I'm going to be there. That's the least I can do."

"But you've done so much already," Blake said quietly. There was almost no irony in his tone.

"Blake," Gina said. "Please don't." She would like to explain to him how it really was, how it wasn't some perverse hookup but rather two injured human beings trying to help each other. In a way, it wasn't even sexual. She had only wanted to help Ronnie, to reach out in some way, and he had been so understandably inconsolable. She wanted to draw him to her, coddle him, take him into her own self, if only a small part of him, give him just an ounce of relief, if only for a moment.

BLAKE HADN'T BEEN GONE five minutes before she heard the other cars arrive. When the front door opened, Gina was sitting alone at the small table, Wolf and Cybil gone to some other place in the house. And despite the fact that she was allowed to be here, had been invited, she felt caught, like an intruder.

Mark and David walked in carrying boxes of beer. They put them in the refrigerator and stood in the kitchen.

"You should have come," Mark said to Gina. "It was nice."

"That's what I hear," she said. She was glad to see him okay. There was something Deep Southish about this town, and even with his baseball cap, she had been very leery of his plan to "act straight" as he'd put it.

Ron came through the front door and switched on a light that better lit the front room. He looked around but not at her. Another man was with him. He was probably Ron's age, but his cheeks were round and pink, fleshy, like a child's, Gina thought. Probably, she should introduce herself, but it was hard to know right now. Her instincts hadn't been good lately.

She stood, though, smiled to the boyish man, who smiled back. "I'm Gina," she said.

"Nice to meet you, Gina," the man said. He raised his hand, and his fingers seemed thick and foreshortened. "My name's Freddy."

"Me and Freddy go way back," Ron said. He looked at her now. Then, to Freddy, he said, "Excuse us for a second, big guy."

"You got it," Freddy said. He nodded to her. "Miss Gina." Then he went to join the others.

Gina couldn't help but smile. She almost laughed. These Southern gentlemen.

Ron hung his thumbs in his jeans pockets.

"Blake had to leave," she said. "He asked me to say goodbye. If he can do anything to call him."

Ron took his thumbs from his pockets. He nodded. "Can we go somewhere?" he said. "Can we like walk or something?"

He guided her out the back door, through a screen porch and onto the grass. At their presence, a set of floodlights came on automatically.

The back yard slanted at a sharp angle toward the lake. Below them, she could see a huge oak tree glowing in the light. Together, they made their way past it, moving further down the hill. Ron was quiet and she realized that she didn't know how to interpret this. She had no body of knowledge, no unspoken syntax for this man. Claire's brother. Ron.

"How are you feeling?" she said. A stupid question.

He was looking farther down the hill, squinting into the dim moonlight. He took her hand.

"Will you come with me?" he said.

She would. She would go wherever he needed to take her, because this is what he was asking, and she wanted to do what she was able. They continued down the hill and she could see the lake now, a black smooth surface opening in front of them. She could smell it too, she thought. It was fishy and rich with the smell of decaying vegetation. Claire had grown up here. This was the place she had talked about sometimes, the lake. The orange groves.

Ron led her to the bottom of the hill, to a wooden dock that extended about thirty feet into the water. They stepped out onto it. He stopped, looked down at the planks, stomped them twice with his foot.

"What is it?" she said.

"This is a new dock," he said. "Can't be more than year old."

They walked to the end of the dock where there was a light mounted on a metal pole. Ron flipped on the light, which lit up the dock but also triggered another light that shone directly down into the water. She could see small fish begin to gather in the light.

"Incredible," Ron said.

"Yeah," she said, not knowing to what he referred exactly, and yet, agreeing. It seemed incredible. All of it. That she was here, that Claire was dead and that she had called her a bitch and then slept with her brother and was now with him at the house where the two of them had grown up, looking down into the orb of white light where little fishes began to amass together.

Right now was not a problem, but what was next for them? Were they some sort of couple now? No, if there was any commitment that had passed between them that night, it was one of the particular moment. Two people agreeing to hold to each other while it felt like the world was spiraling away. Or maybe it was just some grief-born horniness. She didn't know.

"Ron," she said, trying to start, to begin something. "I don't know what to do."

He looked at her. Was he smiling? No, not smiling but just watching her with the careful way of his, a shyness, but what was behind it she didn't know.

She had to give him more to go on than this. "I'm so grateful," she said. "I mean, everything. Being here. Your family, the way you've made us feel like a part of it. It means a lot. To all of us." She swallowed. "But I don't know."

This didn't work, but maybe it didn't have to work now. It didn't all have to be said. They were alive, and that was something, and there would be time for whatever it was she was trying to say. Or not to say but to feel, to understand, how she came to be here on a wooden dock with this Ron, and Claire buried now in the ground.

"I know," he said. His voice had a thickness to it, and he turned away, placed his hands on the dock railing and leaned forward.

She liked to look at him. That was another thing. He was short, not her type usually, but she liked his frame, his muscles. Short arms that held you tight, strong hands that really gripped you. And his face: he was not handsome exactly. Or he was, but there was something else about it, a troubled dignity maybe, with lines in the forehead that shouldn't be there yet, suggesting perhaps a sort of gravity, a weight, like Claire in this way. And yet he was not tragic. There was, in him, a certain hope. This, she thought, was what she liked most about him so far. She watched him kneel down and bend over the edge of the dock.

Then there was a noise, loud and high-pitched, like a brief blast from a blender, and a circular spray of something into the water below. The fish went wild after it.

"What was that?" Gina said. "Is that food?"

"It's an automatic fish feeder," Ron said. "Ray's probably got it on a timer, but I just set off a round."

They both looked down into the light. The fish continued to feed crazily, more of them now, larger ones, perches. They swam upward toward the surface, turning at the last second and kissing the plane, their broad bodies parallel with the waterline, just an instant, then descending headfirst.

"That's sort of . . . beautiful," Gina said. "I've never seen anything like that."

"We used to do this with breadcrumbs and a big flashlight."

"You and Claire did?"

Did he wince at her name? Was she wrong to say it outright, as if it were something that could be approached head-on like that, as if this were the same world that it had been a week ago?

"Yeah," he said. "Me and her." And there was the thickness again. He inhaled deeply, breathed the air out slowly. "I'm sorry. I haven't been here in a long time."

It had been easier in Claire's apartment, near Gina's own turf. But now here at his family's house, and she was spending the night. The rational thing had seemed to be for them to thank Mr. Ramsey for his offer, then return home, but David Feldman had raised the question of decorum. Would it be an insult to refuse such an overture? Were they obliged to accept? Was it some sort of Southern hospitality thing where to refuse might be seen as an insult? In the end they had decided that maybe some of them should stay after all.

Ron was here at the lake house. Would he spend the night? And if so would he expect a repeat of their night together in Claire's bed? She didn't know how to feel about it yet, about that night and this thing between them now that—despite the terrible circumstances—still felt like possibility, like hope.

And Claire: Dear friend, troubled artist, gone for only four days. How would this be to her memory. An honor or insult.

"I hope I didn't cause any major problems," Ron said. He was still looking down into the water. "Between you and Blake, I mean."

So he knew. These men and their intuition. Was she that transparent? She said, "You're not a problem, Ronnie. Not in any conceivable way."

He grinned slightly. "I'm drunk," he said.

Gina wasn't sure if it was a confession or just a statement of fact.

"I have a daughter," he said.

"A daughter," Gina said. "I mean, yes, I know you do."

"She's not here. Her mother . . . ." He shook his head.

Gina pressed her hand between his shoulder blades, felt the muscles there tense and then relax.

"Maybe you could meet her some time," he said. "My daughter. Would that be okay?"

"I'd like that very much," she said, and this was true.

In the water, she saw it, not yet anything recognizable but only a dark shape intruding into light, so incongruous with the other circling fishes, so startling in its hugeness that at first she thought it couldn't be a fish at all, only some trick of the shadows, some obstruction interposing between light and surface to cause the effect. But as it moved further into the light it was clear that it was a fish, long and plump, creeping massively, like something from the ocean depths.

"Jesus," Ron said.

"What *is* that, Ronnie?"

"It's a largemouth bass," Ron said. "A very, very big one."

And then the fish moved in, not so fast, only moving further into the light, then a sudden gulp of luminescence, which was something about its tremendous jaws, a quality that was a sort of flashing when the great mouth opened and not so much bit but sucked in one of the smaller fish, bringing the prey into itself, inhaling like a vacuum, swallowing in the way that was like a flash of luminescence and then, satisfied, gone back into the darkness.

Ron

They had not made love in the night, only slept in the bed together, holding tightly in the dark quiet. Ron opened his eyes, and this took him away from the place he had been, where Claire was there and yet not there too.

Daylight shone through the window, and Gina was pressed snugly to his back. They were in the room that had been his once, but that was a very long time ago.

The room, which had not been his for over twenty years, was sparely furnished now. Other than the single bed, there was a small writing desk and file cabinet. In the corner, a wooden chair. The walls were bare, and he could smell the faint evidence of recent paint.

And yet he was here again. He closed his eyes, willed himself back to where he had been before, at the funeral again, and Claire was dead, but she was also there with him, not in spirit but in real body, yet shrouded somehow, a physical presence but adjacent and slightly behind so that he could never get a clear glance. But she could hear him. He could talk, and she could hear him tell her things.

You will love this funeral, overcast in the morning and a drizzle as the parking lot of the church fills up, inside extra chairs set up in the center aisle but still not enough for the people standing in the back. Ridgedale's finest, quite a draw, and here is Reverend Carlyle, the same who baptized us, giving the eulogy, here all the way from a retirement village in Destin—old and shrunken—remembering Claire, the feisty little girl and how one day, before church, a day around Thanksgiving, she ran up to him with a gift made in Sunday school, a paper turkey, the kind done by tracing the shape of your hand and cutting out the pattern in construction paper, and a beak and eye added to the thumb, and then he, Reverend Carlyle, quoting from II Corinthians: "God loveth a cheerful giver," because that was you and here was the biblical tie-in.

Gina shifted behind him. This was called spooning, and he had lain with Claire this way before, when they were too old to do this, but not in a way that was perverse, only because they were sad together, their mother newly dead, and the rest of the world not able to understand, only the two of them, they who held the shame of playing strip poker as their mother lay dying in the hospital, killing her by sinning when they should have been only praying and hoping.

He held his eyes closed now, although this wasn't sleep any longer. It could only be something close, intermediary.

Listen to Aunt Louise sobbing, with Uncle Paul rubbing her back, and Dad drunk but not so much so, and him handing over a handkerchief so one could cry discreetly, for a sister who once sat in these pews, restless and bored, and Mom passing peppermints or something to read or draw on while a much younger Reverend Carlyle talked about sin and hell and Jesus.

But it was fading. The spell, or dream, or whatever it was, was ending, and the room that had been his but wasn't his any more began to assert itself, the sun shining through the window, bright and real against his eyelids.

Lonnie Steward is here, Claire, and all of the Taylors, Emmit with his pregnant wife, Mary, who gave me a hug outside. Lots of nearly forgotten kin, who one remembers as perpetual children but grown now into grotesque versions of themselves and with children of their own, and here is Mr. Mann from the elementary school days, also your what's-his-name piano teacher and others too, but the St Pete friends stealing the show—maybe twelve in all—and deserving a good bit of credit because here they are after all, bowing their heads right along with the rest, and Cybil especially, a head above the rest and the only black person we'll probably ever see in this church, sitting next to Jimmy Gulbreth, which makes you just laugh, I bet, and Dad's thick and steady breathing smelling of whisky but not so much so.

But it was over. There was more to tell, to explain, the reasons why Megan wasn't here, but no; that hurt was his only. He lifted Gina's arm and slid to the edge of the bed, made it to his feet. Across the hall, in his parents' old room, were Wolf and Cybil. He could hear Wolf's distinct and rhythmic snore. In the night there had been other sounds from that room.

On the bathroom counter was a new bar of soap, and he unwrapped it, removed his clothes, and turned on the shower as hot as he could stand it. He wanted to feel the burn on his skin. The water smelled slightly of sulfur, water that had always made visiting city friends hold their noses as they drank it. After his shower, he stepped onto the bathroom mat and dried off. He took a razor from the bag that Wolf had brought for them and lathered his face with shaving cream. He shaved slowly, and it was good to do this normal thing, which was what people did, he guessed. Stubble grew on your face, indifferent to circumstance, and you scraped it off. He had done this after the divorce, he must have, but he didn't remember much about then, only lack, like now.

By the time he returned to the bedroom, the bed was made and Gina was not there. He put on his jeans from the night before and moved into the house. He found her on the back porch, drinking coffee with Ray, who was talking in a deep steady murmur. Ray looked up at his approach, and Ron was suddenly self-conscious that he was shirtless, no doubt a rudeness in Ray's eyes here in front of a guest.

From the porch, Ron could see the lake in full daylight, the yard seeming stripped clean with no garden or animal pens, a clear lane to the lake, and the water opened itself now like a giant lens. His father and Gina were here on the same porch, him too, all brought together by Claire. And here was that feeling again, the realizing it new and as for the first time.

"Excuse me a moment, Mr. Ramsey," Gina said. She said, "Good morning Ronnie," and walked passed him and into the house.

"I'm sorry," Ron said when she was gone. "I should have called to let you know I was staying out here."

"There ain't a line out here," Ray said. "I had to drive out last night and check to see if the Ford was here."

"You . . . ," Ron said. "Last night, you drove out here?"

"The way you left, I figured I should."

Ron cringed at the memory, could almost taste the Jack Daniels in his throat again. "Well, I'm sorry if you were worried."

"Your . . . ," Ray began. He paused, seemed to think a moment. "Megan's mama called the house this morning," he said. "She said they was about a hundred miles north of Gainesville. I told them they could come straight out here."

"Lenore," Ron said. "She called?"

"Said they was on their way down."

"With Megan. She's on her way with Megan," Ron said. He needed to rehearse this, because what was real lately wasn't always clear.

"Yeah," Ray said. "I talked to Megan a little bit, told her she'd near about grown up on me from the pictures I seen."

Ray took his cell phone from his belt and handed it over to Ron. "Here," Ray said. "I gave her my car phone number in case they need help remembering how to get out here."

"Good," Ron said. "Good, good." Megan was coming. Lenore was bringing her to him, and this was good. They had missed the funeral, but that was done and they were on their way now, and he would see Megan. It would be strange, but he would handle it. It would be good. Just to hold her now would be something that would help.

"There's fresh coffee and donuts in the kitchen," Ray said. "Is there anything ya'll need? Towels or anything?"

"No, everyone's fine. There's only four of them left. Two of the fellas and Gina and Cybil."

"I can come back later," Ray said. "Folks won't start getting here for a while."

"No," Ron said. "Just let me get dressed." Ron stood with his arms folded across his chest, not sure why he was telling Ray to stay, what it was they would do with the time before the others began to arrive. They had made it through the hardest part. That's what he had thought yesterday, after the funeral. He would need to stay a while longer, but soon he could go back to Valdosta. But for now Lenore was bringing Megan to Ridgedale and to him.

"Put on your shirt and I'll show you the new dock," Ray said. "We built it last summer."

"I went down there last night," Ron said. Then, not wanting to discourage something for them to do and talk about, said, "It was dark, though. I couldn't see it that well."

Ray took out a pouch of Levi Garret and extracted a thick pinch of the dark leaf, slid it into the side of his cheek. Here was Ray, who had driven out here last night, to check on him, who was here now with coffee and donuts. There was something different about him, Ron thought, something more than sobriety

"I'll show you my fish feeder," Ray said, the tobacco a lump in his cheek now. "Put on your shirt and meet me down there."

Ron dressed and walked barefoot down the hill, across the damp grass. In the daylight, the yard was green and alive. When they were both on the dock, Ray tripped the feeder and the fished gathered immediately.

"Did you see this last night?" Ray said.

"I did," Ron said. "Saw a big bass, too. Must have been fifteen pounds."

"There's a few of 'em near about that big," Ray said.

They were talking about fish, which was stupid or wrong or just what it always was with them, which was hard, and that was even in the normal times, but now just the two of them were left and this was the most terrible of times, and they were talking about fish.

"Do you ever fish for them?" Ron said.

"Me?" Ray said, as if such a possibility had never occurred to him. "No. The Yankee fella catches shellcracker sometimes. He tries for the bass, but he uses a cane pole and nightcrawlers. Course, they're way too smart for that."

"Claire used to do the same thing," Ron said. "She'd sit and cuss them. 'Don't just stand there looking at it,' she'd say."

Ray stood looking out across the lake. Ron tried to follow the path of his eyes. There were several new houses on the other side where the land had once been only horse pasture.

"Both of you used to do that," Ray said. "You called them Bass-tards."

"Yes we did," Ron said, surprised that Ray would recall something so small and particular. "I can't believe you remember that." But it was true, this small thing that Ray had pulled out of the past. Ron remembered it too. "Sometimes we called them dum-basses," he said.

Ray exhaled a brief chuckle. He lowered himself onto a twenty-gal-lon bucket that rested upside down. He ran his fingers through his hair. It was almost all gray now. When did he get so old? "That sounds like something your mama would've made up," Ray said.

"Yeah," Ron said. "That sounds like Mom." These were the right things to talk about, about Claire and his mother, but with Ray it felt like too much. There were too many years of tension and sidestepping between them.

"It'll be sixteen years come November," Ray said. He sat with his hands resting on his knees, still looking out over the lake.

It was too much for them, Ron thought. Or at least too much for him. This wasn't some TV special. There just wasn't any foundation, and anything Ray might be working toward, anything that they may forge out together, it would be grafted on, an awkward appendage with no lifeblood to it. But Ron began counting up the years, checking Ray's math. Had it really been only sixteen?

"That's right," Ron said, once he confirmed. "Sixteen." He wished it had been more. It was better to think about his mother as someone from another life and place, rather than in any way connected to the way things were now.

"There's nobody renting the house until September," Ray said. "You're more than welcome to stay out here the rest of the summer, and on past that if you want."

Ron turned to look up the hill. He could see the figures of Cybil and Wolf, and the two other guys sitting on the back porch. Gina must have been somewhere inside. He would have to talk to her, once he figured out what he wanted to say.

"Yeah?" Ron said. "I'll think about it."

"I FIXED YOU A PLATE," Gina said. She smiled tentatively, shyly, a paper plate held in front of her with samples from a selection of dishes. The others were seated beneath the oak tree, eating and talking quietly.

"You *fixed* me a plate?" Ron said. He couldn't help smiling at this.

Gina nodded hopefully. "I hope I didn't overstep," she said. "Your Aunt said that, maybe if I did, you might eat a little something."

"Eat a little something?" he said. He knew she wasn't making fun, only trying to help and he had the urge to pull her close to him.

She nodded again. "I wasn't sure what you liked."

"Thank you, Gina," Ron said. "It all looks good." He sat down beside her at one of the tables, across from Emmit Taylor. Emmit was one of Uncle Paul's nephews, and outside of the funeral Ron couldn't remember the last time he'd seen him. At a nearby table, actually a giant wooden spool, Cybil and Mark sat with Jack, one of Emmit's brothers. Mark's white hair was combed straight back this afternoon. He looked almost normal. A few of the children had gathered around their table, no doubt fascinated by these exotic newcomers. Wolf was at a table with Ray and some others, including David, the professor. Emmit's wife took a seat across from Ron, and he smiled to her. Behind her the hill rose steeply up to the house.

Ron took a bite of potato salad. It tasted good and the potatoes just freshly boiled too, because it was still slightly warm. And this was not a betrayal to Claire, to eat and enjoy, even though it felt this way. He would eat many more meals, he knew, and this one was so hard only because it was the beginning. He smiled to Gina and took another bite.

He was about to bring up the subject of water levels with his cousin Emmit, a topic he'd thought of earlier. He would ask whether all of the lakes were as low as this one was, and had they gotten much rain this summer, but before he could ask any of this he saw two figures exit out of the back porch and begin their way down the hill. Ron stood and stepped away from the table. He raised his hand. Megan saw him first, and she broke into a run toward him. His daughter was running toward him, taller than she had been only two months ago, growing.

She jumped up to him, and he caught her under the armpits, brought her in close. She was heavier than before, too. He latched on to this new heft. He could stay like this forever, he thought. Right here. Tears came now, and he did not fight them. He kissed Megan behind the ear. "Hey sweetheart," he said, his words thick with loss and fear and joy. "I missed you so much."

Lenore approached, but Ron put up an index finger to her. She nodded. Stopped. Turned. She moved toward Ray, who had risen and was walking over to greet her. Ron held Megan. He held her tight.

AUNT LOUISE WAS TALKING to Megan, stroking her hair and fawning. Some of the other children had gathered around, peevishly inspecting the new addition to their number.

"Goodness, but you've grown," Aunt Louise said. "You were just a teeny little thing the last time I saw you."

Megan smiled shyly. She was watching the other children watch her. And Aunt Louise, seeing this, called them over. "Here's some of your cousins," she said.

And they were, Ron thought, flesh and true kin, who she might never have met and who, unless he did something about it, she may never see again.

He dried his eyes before going to Lenore. They embraced tentatively, and she kissed his cheek. She looked very good, younger, like being unburdened of him for a year had recharged her anew.

"Thank you," he said. "Thank you for bringing her here."

"Ron," she said. "I'm sorry. We should have come sooner. She should have been here for the funeral. We both should have."

"You're here now," he said. "Is Brandon with you? He can come down. It's okay."

"He's at the hotel," Lenore said. "He sends his sympathy."

Was she blushing? Looking away in shame? Why now?

Under the tree, Ray moved among people, acting so much like a father, as if it had taken a blow like this to bring him back to himself, the way a second crack to the head could restore memory in television comedies. Gina was helping some of the other women clean up and cover the dishes. But also, out of the corner of her eye, she was watching him and Lenore. Ron could see it clearly.

Could you ever really leave a place, once it has become part of you? He'd thought so. And maybe you could become someone new and without a past. Maybe to a point, but to do it, to deprive your people of your physical presence in that way, and you of theirs: It seemed like a sin to him now.

He waved for Gina's attention and motioned her over to them. There was plenty of time for this, but he wanted her to meet Lenore, right now while he loved them both, while he loved everyone here. This and so many other things that were new upon him. He wiped away the fresh tears.

The two women, seeing his trouble, introduced themselves, and he was grateful to them because there were many things in his mind right now, and it was hard to focus in on just one. He turned to look at Megan

again, but she wasn't under the tree anymore, no longer with Aunt Louise. He could spend the rest of the summer here if he wanted, right in
the old house. Ray had offered. And this seemed like a possibility to him
now. Megan, maybe she could spend her three weeks with him here, get
to know some of her family. He had the summer off, and there was no
reason why not. He scanned the yard for her, not worried, only wanting
to keep her in his sight. Finally, he spotted her at the bottom of the hill,
near the lake. The glare off the water was bright, and he watched her
move in the sunlight, running along the shore with some of the other
children—her cousins—playing the way kids do.

THE OHIO STATE UNIVERSITY PRIZE IN SHORT FICTION